The first troll emerged fully fr_____ _____, molten rock oozing from its body. It glared at Tyr with its dark eyes. Standing twice as tall as the Aesir, it made for a formidable display.

The stoneskinned beast charged, poised to rend him limb from limb. As the troll's momentum took it past him, he swung about and brought his sword chopping down. The stroke caught the brute's arm at the shoulder and sheared it away. Molten, fiery liquid bubbled from the wound. The injured troll bellowed its fury, but a second sweep of the sword sent it crashing to the ground.

"Who's next?" Tyr shouted as he turned to face the other sentries. His confidence faltered when he saw that at least a score of the monsters had already climbed from the pools, with still more trying to rise. It looked as though their numbers might be limitless.

BY THE SAME AUTHOR

MARVEL LEGENDS OF ASGARD

The SWORD of SURTUR

C L WERNER

ACONYTE®

FOR MARVEL PUBLISHING

VP Production & Special Projects: Jeff Youngquist
Assistant Editor, Special Projects: Caitlin O'Connell
Manager, Licensed Publishing: Jeremy West
VP, Licensed Publishing: Sven Larsen
SVP Print, Sales & Marketing: David Gabriel
Editor in Chief: C B Cebulski

Special Thanks to Wil Moss

MARVEL

First published by Aconyte Books in 2021
ISBN 978 1 83908 037 1
Ebook ISBN 978 1 83908 038 8

Cover art by Grant Griffin

Distributed in North America by Simon & Schuster Inc, New York, USA
Printed in the United States of America
9 8 7 6 5 4 3 2 1

ACONYTE BOOKS

An imprint of Asmodee Entertainment Ltd

Mercury House, Shipstones Business Centre

North Gate, Nottingham NG7 7FN, UK

aconytebooks.com // twitter.com/aconytebooks

*To Gary and all his cohorts at Lone
Warrior Comics for the patience and
forbearance to suffer the patronage
of a bull-headed kid every time the
new issue of G I Joe came out.*

·ONE

The light of a thousand torches made the golden walls of Odin's hall shine like the sun, defying the onset of night across the realm of Asgard. Laughter and howls of jubilation echoed off the vaulted ceiling a hundred feet above the celebratory throng. The rich smell of roast boar, the flesh of the ever-regenerating Saehrimnir, wafted through the room as platters of the succulent meat were paraded out from the kitchens. Barrels, casks, and tuns were borne up from the cellars to provide a disparate variety of ales, mead, and beers for the revelers.

Hundreds of Asgardians were gathered about the dozens of long tables arrayed across the hall. Not merely those who dwelled within the great city itself, but stalwarts from the farthest regions of the land were gathered for the celebration. The desert-kissed Skornheimers and the dour Gymirsgardians were mixed among hunters from the Gundersheim and mystics from Ringsfjord. A rugged warrior from the Kingdom of Harokin traded stories with a white-bearded sea captain from dragon-haunted Nastrond. To every corner of the realm had Odin's decree been sent and from every corner of the realm had come those to pay tribute to Asgard's mightiest hero.

Tyr's blue eyes were as hard as ice as he looked across the celebrants. Each laugh, every smile only made him feel more out of place. He had no stomach for this frivolity, much less the reason for it. Had his father Odin not summoned him here, he'd have stayed as far from the celebration as he could manage. But one didn't ignore the All-Father, not even when you were the God of War.

Upon a raised platform at the top of the hall stood Odin's table. Tyr's father retained the physique of his prime despite the snowy beard that fell almost to his waist. His remaining eye sparkled with the vigor of a much younger Asgardian, hale with mirth and merriment. The other, sacrificed to gain wisdom greater than any other Aesir, was covered by a patch of gold that gleamed like a fiery ember. As much as anything, Tyr thought it was his father's surrender of his own eye, sacrificed so that he might better guide the people of Asgard and defend them from harm, that made him worthy of his rule. Though there were times – such as now – when Tyr bristled under Odin's commands, he had too much respect for his father to defy his authority. Such capriciousness was the province of his half-brother, Loki.

Perched on the ornately carved back of Odin's chair were his messengers, the ravens Hugin and Munin. Their studious eyes surveyed the celebration, catching even the least detail to whisper to the All-Father after the revelers departed. At intervals, Odin would proffer one of the birds a morsel of flesh, disrupting its vigilance while it gobbled the meat, but never would both be distracted at the same time. Tyr often felt the discerning stare of the ravens fix on him and could imagine what story they'd tell his father later.

Crouched under the table were two animals Tyr resented far more than the spying ravens. The wolves Freki and Geri gnawed on boar bones and lapped blood from silver bowls while they sat at their master's feet. Massive in their proportions, ferocious and proud in their bearing, they were the most loyal of Odin's protectors, ranging with him on his travels through the Nine Worlds. In the prophecy of Ragnarok, it was foretold that Freki and Geri would die defending Odin from the Great Wolf Fenris.

Thoughts of Fenris caused Tyr to set the horn of mead he'd been drinking from into the gilded stand on the table crafted for just this purpose. He clutched his left hand. Or at least the metal cup where his hand had been. He looked again at the celebrants around him, their joy and laughter bitter to his ears. Once they'd feted the God of War for saving Asgard from the menace that threatened to devour them all. The Great Wolf, that monstrous whelp of Loki, had grown so mighty and fierce that no god could prevail against it. In its savagery, Fenris could have laid waste to the entire realm, had its ravenous hunger provoked it to do so. Every manner of chain had been employed to try and bind it, but even those forged from Uru, the enchanted metal of Asgard, failed to hold the beast. It became a game to the Great Wolf to let the gods try to chain it, a display of its growing power that it knew would make them fear it.

Finally, Odin had the dwarves forge a magic cord, Gleipnir, which would be unbreakable. The cunning Fenris scented trickery when it saw the seeming fragility of the leash and only agreed to be tied with it if the gods vowed to release it if it failed to free itself. To ensure the gods would hold to their vow, the Great Wolf demanded one of them place their hand in its mouth.

Perhaps he'd been inspired by the example of his father, Tyr didn't know, but in that moment when the courage of the gods faltered, he stepped forward and accepted the Great Wolf's challenge. Gleipnir held the beast fast and when it couldn't break free, the jaws of Fenris snapped tight. In an instant Tyr's hand was gone, swallowed by the deceived beast. But Asgard was saved from the monster's menace. At least until the time of Ragnarok, when even the magic of Gleipnir could no longer restrain the Great Wolf.

Tyr lifted his gaze back to the platform and Odin's table. To the All-Father's left sat his queen, the Vanir Frigga. While Odin joined in the revelry, laughing and boasting, Tyr's mother maintained a pose of regal aloofness and composure. In her fashion she was much like the ravens, observing everything without joining the frivolity. Those around her might feast, but she displayed a more judicious appetite and a more cautious attitude to the mead that was flowing so freely at other tables. Her attention would always be drawn back to the bright-faced Balder, the favorite of her sons and the one who was ever the focus of her maternal concern. Tyr well understood his mother's worry for Balder, for his death too had been foretold, and that was a heavy weight upon Frigga's heart.

Seated to Odin's right was the hero in whose honor this feast was being held. Tyr frowned as he stared up at Asgard's celebrated champion, his younger half-brother, Thor. The God of Thunder had taken after his mother more than his father, for there was little about his features that he had in common with Tyr. Tyr's hair was black while Thor's was a golden blond. Tyr's face was hard and severe in contrast to the boisterous exuberance of Thor. Only in their eyes was their kinship unquestionable, for both had the same piercing blue color.

The mighty hammer Mjolnir rested on the table beside Thor's platter, and beside the weapon was a trophy that marked the cause of the celebration. A great slab of hoary ice that refused to melt even in the warmth of Odin's hall. As he looked up at the fantastic object, Tyr heard his father's voice boom out across the feast, ringing down on the revelry.

"Asgardians! Aesir and Vanir and friends from afar!" Odin stood and toasted the throng. He turned and laid his hand upon Thor's shoulder. "Look on this, my son of whom I am so very proud. By himself he has penetrated the frozen vastness of Niffleheim to beard the King of the Ice Giants in his own palace!" He gestured to the white slab sitting on the table. "Behold a tuft from the very beard of Ymir!"

Raucous cheers rolled through the hall, rumbling like Thor's thunderbolts. Warriors stood and clashed weapons against their shields. Many stamped their feet until the walls began to shake from the vibrations. Over and again was one name shouted: "Thor! Thor! Thor!"

Odin drew Thor to his feet. "Today we celebrate the

defeat of Ymir. Tomorrow perhaps you will bring Surtur's sword to rest beside the ice giant's beard!" Thor clapped his father on the back as the two gods resumed their seats.

Tyr picked up his drinking horn and rendered a salute to his younger brother, but nothing more. The boisterousness of the throng was excessive enough without his participation. Certainly, Thor had accomplished a mighty feat, but to what purpose and with what intention? Had he risked himself to protect Asgard or had it been merely to indulge in the adulation he was now receiving? Thor's exploits were indeed heroic, but they often struck Tyr as reckless and ill-conceived. Tyr understood that the triumph of today could breed the defeat of tomorrow, but he wondered if his brother took the same caution into consideration when he embarked on these ventures against the giants.

"You look ill at ease." The voice that spoke the words was barely a whisper, yet Tyr could hear them distinctly even through the tumult in the hall. He knew they were laced with magic to be so clear in his ears. Moreover, he recognized the speaker even before he turned his head.

"Loki," Tyr addressed the man who now sat beside him. He couldn't see what had happened to the the flame-haired valkyrie who'd been there before, but now there was the lean figure of his dark-haired brother arrayed in green tunic and a golden cloak. Perhaps she'd merely been one of Loki's disguises, for the mischievous god was ever fond of shifting his shape. Tyr often wondered if that magic contaminated his offspring and caused him to father monsters like Fenris and the world serpent Jormungand. "You're bold to be sitting in your father's hall after the trouble you started with the stone trolls."

Loki's sharp features drew back in an impish smile and his green eyes glittered with amusement. Tyr was always struck by the almost reptilian aspect of those eyes. Maybe it wasn't so strange he'd fathered Jormungand. "There's always trouble with the stone trolls. All I did was to give their malice some direction and put them where Brunnhilde and the Warriors Three might intervene. The trolls will be quiet for a while now, and no harm has been done. Odin will see that soon enough." He sighed and shrugged his shoulders. "Until then, I fear I'm here only under sufferance." He pointed to Odin's table and the icy tuft from Ymir's beard. "Our brother's mighty deeds are such that even my current disfavor isn't enough to keep me away. Can you imagine the bravery it must have taken to do such a thing?"

Mead rushed down Tyr's throat as he took a long pull from the horn. He wiped the residue from his lips with his left arm. "It *was* a brave deed," he told Loki. He might not like Thor's recklessness, but he'd not have a sly tongue disparaging his courage. Any conversation with Loki was riddled with insinuations as barbed as a thorn bush. Some Asgardians found his tricky manners amusing, but Tyr wasn't one of them.

"To be certain," Loki hurried to say, his tone conciliatory. "I admire what our brother has done. No coward ventures into Niffleheim." This remark had more than a suggestion of pride wound within it, for Loki had often journeyed into the land of the ice giants in different guises. "Truly, it is no mean thing to challenge Ymir."

That reptilian gleam was in Loki's eyes when he paused and stared at Tyr for a moment. "Yet I say again that *you* don't appear in a celebratory mood. I have to ask myself why this might be so." He tapped his fingers against his chest. "I admit there are times when I've been at strife with our brother, but I can still be happy for him when he has a great victory. All Asgard can rest easier now that the King of the Ice Giants has fallen and must regather his strength."

"It is a great victory," Tyr said, but despite his caution he knew Loki had picked up on the bitterness in his tone.

"Asgard will remember this day." Loki nodded. "Yes, Asgard doesn't forget its heroes."

"Nor its villains," Tyr snapped. The verbal barb from Loki had pierced him like a spear, striking at the core of his dark mood. Jealousy. Petty and unseemly as the emotion was, Tyr was filled with it just the same. It had taken Loki's nettling words to make him realize it, but he was envious of Thor's acclaim. He felt eclipsed by this adulation of his brother.

"I was merely trying to be understanding," Loki protested as he rose from the table and strolled off into the crowd. The smirk on his face put a different meaning to his words. Tyr was certain that Loki appreciated the effect of his goading. The problem was, even knowing how his subconscious resentment had been stirred up by him didn't lessen its hold.

Tyr raised his eyes back to Odin's table. A line of Asgardians was filing past, taking a closer look at the slab of ice and offering their gratitude to Thor for his victory over

Ymir. The longer he watched the procession, the more his resentment grew. Finally, his temper moved him to march up onto the platform, pushing his way through the other Asgardians. He looked down at the tuft from Ymir's beard, feeling its eerie chill drive back the warmth of the hall. Even this small piece of the giant exuded a baleful power. It made the magnitude of Thor's victory undeniable and Tyr's jealousy only worse.

"A fine trophy, is it not, brother?" Thor bragged, his face jubilant.

Tyr met his brother's toast with a scowl. "It strikes me as hubris to go all the way to Niffleheim simply to play barber."

The caustic retort stunned those on the platform. From there, a tide of silence swept through the hall. Laughter dropped away as tension filled the air. Every ear was sharp to listen to this exchange between Odin's sons.

Thor tried to brush off Tyr's remark as a jest, but he could see the sting in his eyes. "A hammer serves better than shears when the beard is made of ice," he boasted, slapping Mjolnir with his hand.

The effort at joviality was wasted on Tyr in his current mood. "A weapon is never a toy," he scolded. For an instant there was a pained look on Thor's face, then the God of Thunder's visage turned dark with anger.

"Because we are brothers, I'll forgive your speech," Thor warned.

"Because we are brothers, I'll speak to you as you deserve," Tyr countered, matching Thor's glowering gaze with his own.

"Enough of this!" Odin roared, his fury such that the

wolves scurried out from under the table and the ravens took wing. He looked over both of his sons, but it was on Tyr that his angry eye settled. "You will apologize for your rudeness," he declared.

Defiance welled up inside Tyr's heart. He didn't balk before his father's ire. "Someone needs to remind my brother of his responsibilities." He glanced over the crowd and raised his voice. "His obligations to Asgard. Reckless adventuring puts those he is sworn to protect at risk." He pointed at Mjolnir. "What if Ymir had prevailed and your hammer was taken?"

"Only the worthy may wield Mjolnir," Thor retorted, pride in his voice.

"Such is my point," Tyr persisted. "If you had fallen to the ice giants, a powerful weapon in Asgard's arsenal would have been lost. The realm's defenses would be weakened."

"Niffleheim has long plotted to invade Asgard," Odin reminded Tyr. "It will take Ymir a long time to recover from this defeat."

Tyr shook his head. "Niffleheim's plans are only delayed. Had we fought the ice giants in battle, united against their threat, we should have made them abandon their designs. Shown them the folly of striving against us." He turned to Thor. "Instead Ymir has been dealt another hurt to brood upon and plot his revenge."

"You dare question the merits of what your brother has accomplished?" Odin's voice dropped to an angry growl.

Tyr brought the metal cup that covered the stump of his missing hand crashing down on the slab of ice. The Uru cup sent fragments of Ymir's beard flying in every direction.

"An accomplishment without sacrifice leads to arrogance." He held up his left arm so that everyone in the hall could see it. "The Great Wolf is yet chained in Varinheim, and its shadow no longer hangs over Asgard."

"But it hangs over you," Thor snapped. "You hold fast to the glories of yesterday and cannot stir yourself to new ones. That is why you resent my feats, because you've lost the valor to claim new victories of your own!"

Tyr clenched his fist, ready to plunge across the table and make his brother eat those words. Thor, for his part, was ready to meet his challenge, but Odin's arm came down between them and pushed the younger away from the elder.

"Must you meet Tyr's unjust words with your own?" Odin told Thor. "His sacrifice let us subdue Fenris…"

"And what has he done for Asgard lately?" Thor snapped. Almost instantly a look of contrition came upon his face. Tyr knew his brother would have taken back the angry words if he could. But it was too late. Repentant or not, the thrust had been made and it had pierced him to the heart.

"I'll remind all Asgard of my valor," Tyr said. He turned his back on his father and brother and stalked away from the platform. One of the wolves stepped into his path, but for once it knew better than to bare its fangs at him. A single glance had it draw back with its tail between its legs.

The Asgardians gave ground to Tyr's anger as quickly as the wolf had. A path was cleared for him as he withdrew from Odin's hall. Only one voice called after him, that of Bjorn Wolfsbane, a young huntsman from Varinheim. Tyr rebuffed Bjorn's effort to draw him back to the feast and kept walking.

In his heart a new determination smoldered. Thor might have surpassed Tyr's status as Asgard's greatest hero, but he would remind his younger brother of his mettle. He would show Odin that the God of War was still capable of mighty deeds.

Two

The great city was miles behind Tyr when he reached the Greenfirm, the quiet forest on the Plain of Ida. Many were the times when he sought repose in its tranquility, but such were his brooding thoughts that every sight and sound only seemed to vex him. There was no satisfaction to be had in the crisp smell of the pines, no joy to be found in the vibrant songs of the birds. Everything felt like an intrusion on his problems rather than a refuge from them.

He looked at the arboreal splendor of the land. His eyes caught a deer watching him from behind a stand of bushes, ready to bolt at the least hint of aggression. He saw a badger pushing earth out from its burrow, its dirty nose twitching as it sniffed the air and caught his scent. A flash of color and he caught the crimson brush of a fox vanishing into a hollowed log. This, Tyr mused, was why it was so easy for him to resent his brother's ever-rising fame. Thor was brave and valiant, but he gave too little thought to what he was charged with protecting when he struck out on his bold adventures. Asgard wasn't just the people, but the forests and rivers, the mountains and meadows, the trees and animals. All of it was Odin's domain and therefore it was their duty to defend it. Tyr worried Thor focused too much on what was to be gained by his forays across the Nine Worlds and not enough on what could be lost.

The sound of running feet stirred Tyr from his somber pondering. He turned about and saw a man hurrying toward him through the forest. A head shorter than the god's imposing stature, the man was more stoutly built with broad shoulders and a bull-like neck. His limbs were thickly muscled, his leather leggings and jerkin stretched taut when they flexed. His pale blond hair was tied into a long braid and the beard that fell from his chin was likewise twined into plaits and beaded with the sharp fangs of dire wolves from Varinheim's remote woodlands. The black pelt of one of these massive predators had been shaped into the cloak he wore, the preserved head of the animal serving him as both hood and helm. From the loops of his belt, a set of throwing axes hung, and a large, double-headed war axe was slung across his back.

"I've been following your trail for hours," the man said, stopping his run to draw breath into his panting lungs.

Tyr smiled and shook his head. "Surely my path wasn't so difficult to find that it taxed the endurance of Bjorn Wolfsbane?" He wagged a reproving finger at the huntsman. "You indulged too freely in Odin's hall and drowned your stamina in ale and mead."

Bjorn returned the smile with a laugh. "If that's true, then it means I'm getting old. No longer do I want to hear you call me a young pup."

"That is just the sort of thing a young pup would say," Tyr observed. He looked over the huntsman for a moment. "Your beard's grown longer, but I still see too much of the boy who came to the City of Asgard and begged to enter my service. The one who vowed to bind the grip of his axe with hairs from the Great Wolf's tail."

"And you said one day you would take me back to Varinheim and show me where the beast is bound," Bjorn reminded him. "It needs someone who knows the way to find the valley where Fenris is chained."

The rejoinder killed the smile that had so briefly worked its way onto Tyr's countenance. "Don't be overeager to seek out monsters. They tend to find their way to you in their own time."

Bjorn was quiet for a moment. When he spoke again, it was on the topic that had sent him hurrying after Tyr. "Your abrupt departure from the feast has upset Odin and Frey. They say it was a grave insult you did your brother and one that won't quickly be forgotten. Frigga spoke on your behalf, reminding the All-Father that though your words may have been ill-chosen, the sentiment behind them was sincere."

Tyr had expected as much. Odin was wise, but he also had a quick temper that often slipped past his wisdom. To have remained would only have made the situation worse, driving still more anger into an argument already charged with emotion. He might have expected his mother to take his defense, just as the Vanir Frey and many of the other gods would side with Odin. Curiosity put a question to his tongue. "Did anyone else speak for me?"

Bjorn nodded. "Yes. Your brother."

"Which one?" Tyr asked. "Balder? Hermod? Vidar?" He didn't like to think it would be Loki, for the more he considered the god's slippery ways, the more he came to realize that it was he who had provoked Tyr into what had happened at Odin's table. If Loki was pushing further into the matter it could only be to advance some deeper scheme.

"No. It was Thor who tried to lessen your father's ire," Bjorn said. The surprise Tyr felt must have shown on his face, for the huntsman hurried to continue. "He reminded Odin of what you'd done for Asgard and that you'd earned the right to speak as you did."

Tyr frowned and turned away. Such fairness from Thor after their heated exchange only made him feel worse than he already did. Not merely for casting a pall on his brother's victory, but because for the first time he began to wonder if, after all, it wasn't right that the God of Thunder should eclipse the God of War as Asgard's greatest hero. Yet another reason for him to envy Thor's defeat of Ymir. It was an untarnished victory.

"It is right that I leave the city," Tyr said. "I am no longer the champion our people need."

Bjorn looked at him with shock in his eyes. The wolfhunter from Varinheim venerated Tyr and had often told him that he was all an Asgardian should aspire towards. He did so now, trying to reassure him of his greatness. "Asgard will always need you. Who among the gods is as devoted to the defense of the realm as you are? Who trained our warriors to fight as an army, not as a disorganized horde?

Who argued to raise new walls about the city after the war with the Vanir and then planned their defense against the giants of Jotunheim?" He clenched his fist and cracked his knuckles to emphasize what he felt was the greatest accomplishment of all and the one that had caused him to worship Tyr. "It was your hand that rested in the mouth of Fenris when all the other gods trembled before its threat. You knew what it meant, what it would cost you, but you didn't balk from the sacrifice."

Tyr gave Bjorn a grave look. "It is that deed, more than any other, by which I am diminished," he said. They were words he'd never spoken to Bjorn before. When the huntsman looked at the metal cup covering his stump, he knew that his meaning was mistaken. "I do not mean the loss of my hand. Though I may no longer be the fiercest archer in all Asgard, I've honed my sword until I'm as matchless with it as I ever was with the bow." He dropped his hand to the gold-hilted sword that hung from his belt.

"A different blight taints the greatest deed of my life," Tyr continued. He had come this far, he intended to explain all to Bjorn. "The bravest thing that any god in Asgard has done, save my father when he hung upon the World Tree. There is none who can take the courage of my act from me." Tyr scowled, and his hand plucked at the bindings around his sword's grip. "No, there was great courage in that moment. But there was also terrible shame. A shame that cannot be undone, for it would mean the ruin of Asgard."

Bjorn shook his head. "I don't understand," he confessed. "How can a deed be both brave and shameful?"

"The binding of the Great Wolf," Tyr explained, "was built upon treachery."

The God of War closed his eyes, recalling the moment that was forever etched upon his soul.

THREE

The Great Wolf towered above the gods, its eyes gleaming with sardonic humor. The beast exuded an arrogant confidence, a ferocious disdain for the world and everything within it. Such was its might that nothing could oppose its strength. It was whispered among the seers that one day Fenris would stretch its jaws and swallow both sun and moon, so enormous would its power have become.

The wolf made its lair in a narrow valley in the snowy mountains of Varinheim. Odin had made that decree years ago, when Fenris grew too enormous to dwell with the gods in the city of Asgard. Though the beast could change its size and even alter its shape somewhat, it preferred a gigantic aspect to better show off its ever-increasing power. After it attacked the goddess Idunn, the All-Father decided the wolf was becoming too dangerous to allow to roam the city. Haakun the Hunter, who'd intervened and saved Idunn from the wolf's attack, had been charged with removing the beast to Varinheim, at the very edge of Asgard. Time had only made the beast more powerful, however, and it was widely believed it accepted its exile more from choice than any deference to Odin's authority. One day it would defy Odin's rule and ravage the whole of Asgard.

Tyr felt a shiver run through him when he looked up at the Great Wolf. Fenris had grown even larger than the last time he'd laid eyes on the beast. The wolf now stood a hundred feet at the shoulder, ten times as big as when it left the city of Asgard. Then it had been strong enough to snap a giant in half with its jaws and to dig up the roots of a mountain with its paws. He'd seen it devour an entire herd of cattle at a single meal and lap a pond into a mere puddle to quench its thirst. Once it had taken all of Odin's sons to wrestle the wolf to the ground when they were playing with the beast, and even their combined strength had barely been able to hold Fenris. How much greater had its power become in the years since?

The wolf's valley was littered with evidence. Poking up from the snow were the splintered fragments of hundreds of chains. Fetters of iron, steel, and Uru, even a great cord that had been sculpted from molten granite and a cable of forged obsidian lay shattered and forgotten about the wolf's lair. All had been crafted for the express purpose of binding Fenris, but none had been equal to the beast's strength. Others of Loki's monstrous brood had been bound by the gods. The great serpent Jormungand was chained in the seas of Midgard, and the sinister Hela was sent to govern the spirits of the dead in Hel, but the Great Wolf resisted all efforts to restrain it.

The wolf exulted in the failures of the gods to bind it. Like badges of honor it wore the broken chains, their links just visible amid the thick gray fur that clothed its massive frame. They were a visible reminder to all who gazed on Fenris of the beast's might and that its strength was such that it could brazenly defy the will of Odin. Indeed, since being exiled to Varinheim, the wolf had become more savage than it had ever been before. Now it didn't simply devour the herds and flocks, but ate those who tended the animals as well. Entire villages had been massacred by the marauding beast, fairly daring the gods to try to stop it.

"To think we once made sport of that thing." The remark was spoken by Balder, but the quivering tone to his voice was alien to his usual boisterous nature. Tyr looked over at his brother and saw that a shadow had fallen across his bright features.

"Now the beast makes sport of us," Thor agreed, one hand clamped about Mjolnir's head. He too was shaken by how mighty Fenris had grown. He looked at his hammer, a weapon that had slain more giants than any other in Asgard's arsenal, with a troubled cast in his eyes. Tyr could well guess his brother's worry. Would even his famed hammer have the power to hurt the Great Wolf if it came to a fight? Such combat had been forbidden by Odin, so it was clear their father's wisdom led him to believe who would prevail in such a fray.

Tyr shook his head. Odin had done more than merely forbid Thor to fight Fenris, he'd commanded that no god, be they Aesir or Vanir, should battle the Great Wolf. Doing so, it was argued, would only provoke the beast. While it was content to remain in Varinheim, at least the rest of Asgard was spared its rampages.

"At least Fenris is still amused by us," Tyr commented. He gave his brothers a grim nod. "I think it knows how powerful it has become. It stays here because a whim makes it do so." He frowned and slammed his fist into his palm. "Or else it is biding its time. Waiting until its strength has grown to such a degree that there's not the least chance we could defeat it in battle." Tyr noticed one of the wolf's ears twitch and it seemed to him that a sneer curled the corner of its mouth.

"You should be mindful of what you say. The Great Wolf has sharp ears." The admonishment came from one who should know, the monster's own father. Loki sighed and waved his hand at the giant beast. "Underestimating an adversary is always reckless."

Two dozen of Asgard's gods had made the journey to Varinheim, the same as always came for the yearly contest with Fenris. Odin said any more than that would leave the realm exposed to dangers from the giants and other invaders, but any fewer would be too few to intimidate the wolf and make it show even a modicum of deference to them. Still, except for the All-Father himself, who came and who stayed was always changing. This, however, was only the second time the capricious Loki had been selected to make the trip.

Tyr looked to where Odin sat astride Sleipnir, conversing with Fenris, his golden armor glittering in the wintry sun. The King of Asgard was the only Aesir that the wolf still deferred to and his was the only voice that retained any authority at all over the beast. Knowing this, Tyr wondered why their father had asked Loki to join them this time.

Though he'd sired Fenris, the days when the wolf felt any sort of obligation to its parent were long past. Why then had Odin made it a point to bring Loki along? Truly, the wisdom he'd gained from sacrificing his eye at the roots of Yggdrasil led to strange choices.

"Are your words for us or for your spawn?" Thor put the question to Loki.

"I've as little to gain as anyone else if Fenris takes it in mind to extend its territory beyond Varinheim," Loki countered. "It is a willful beast and attends my speech as little as it does your own." He nodded towards Odin. "That our father can still command even a small measure of obedience is a testament to his power."

"Perhaps it is because your father treats Fenris with respect." There was a note of sadness in Frigga's tone when she spoke. There was no reproach on her face when she looked at Loki, only an expression of pained regret. "A child nurtured on love may grow into greatness. A child weaned on hate is shackled with a chain stronger than any that we've tried to bind the wolf with."

Tyr hated to disagree with his mother, but he felt that on this point she let herself be blinded by idealism. He thought of how greatly she'd indulged Loki and how malicious he was despite – or perhaps because of – that affection. There were some who simply had a darkness within them, a darkness that wasn't banished by compassion but simply found in the love of others a thing to be exploited. In that respect, Fenris wasn't so different from its father.

"Mother, your sympathy for Fenris is misplaced," Tyr said. "Even if there was a time when it could have responded to compassion, that time is long past. When it attacked Idunn and tried to steal the golden apples for her, the wolf showed its true nature. It was testing to see if we had the strength to stop it. It responds only to strength. Odin knows this, just as he knows the Great Wolf will one day be stronger than all of us." Tyr's hand closed about the hilt of his sword as he stared again at the colossal beast. "If it isn't already stronger than us."

"I thought only to protect Asgard," Loki said. Whether feigned or genuine, his voice echoed Frigga's regretful tone. "I tried to make Fenris a weapon against the giants, to protect us all from the threat of Jotunheim. My failing was to be too single-minded in that purpose. I taught the wolf how to be strong and to fight, but not why it should fight. Too late did I see that error." His eyes swept across the faces of the other gods as he made his apology. "I did bring the wolf to Asgard, tried to teach it to love our city as we do, but by then its heart was too filled with savagery to have a place for such sentiments."

Tyr wondered how much of Loki's remorse had to do with his inability to make use of Fenris for his own schemes, if he would have any regret at all if the beast remained obedient to him. Still, perhaps there was a germ of truth in what his brother had tried to do. The pups sired by Fenris were growing into loyal and devoted creatures, strong and noble in their lupine way. Odin and Frigga were raising them, careful to avoid the mistakes that made the Great Wolf so ferocious.

"So now it comes to this," Frigga said. She gripped the enchanted cord crafted by the dwarves of Nidavellir.

Gleipnir it had been named, and according to the dwarves it had been forged from such arcane materials as the roots of a mountain, the beard of a woman, and the breath of a fish. Tyr well knew the secret ways of dwarves and that whatever process they'd used, they wouldn't reveal it to anyone, even the All-Father.

"Don't be glum, mother," Balder advised. "If the thought of shackling Fenris upsets you, remember the wolf has broken mightier chains than this." He was smiling when he spoke, but Tyr could see the emptiness in his expression. Like all of them, he was frightened by the prospect that they might never find a way to bind the beast.

"The dwarves must be desperate to render such a fetter up to Odin," Thor said. "Gleipnir looks too delicate to hold a lamb, much less the Wolf of Wolves."

Tyr shook his head. "It has become a question of obligation for them," he told Thor. "Our father tasked them with crafting a chain to hold Fenris. Until they can do so, their many failures are a blot upon the honor of their people. They will strain the very limits of their knowledge to fulfill their oath." He laid his hand on Gleipnir, feeling the silky smoothness of its coils. "Frail it might seem, but the dwarves are confident in its strength, and so too is Odin."

"If it holds, then it will remain a cruel trick," Frigga sighed. "Shouldn't exile be enough?"

"The wolf won't remain content to stay in Varinheim forever," Tyr cautioned. "Even if it were, that would mean abandoning the people of this land to its hunger. To force it from Asgard to Niffleheim or Muspelheim would be pointless as well, even if we could do it. Without a means to hold the wolf it could come back whenever it chose to do so." Tyr returned his gaze to the monster in the valley. "No, it is here the reckoning between us must happen."

Fenris threw its head back, and a long howl rumbled through the valley. Odin turned from the beast and spurred Sleipnir back toward the other gods. The All-Father's visage was grim when he drew up before them. There was a note of foreboding in his eye.

"That took longer than usual, my king," Frigga said, worry in her voice.

"The Great Wolf wants concessions this time," Odin replied. He doffed his helm and set it beneath his arm. "Fenris, it seems, grows weary of Varinheim. It wants to expand its territory. Now it will roam Nornheim, Nastrond, and Gundersheim as well."

Tyr gazed at his father in shock. "That will subject a quarter of Asgard to the wolf's marauding! Fenris has snapped every chain that we've used on it. Are you so certain Gleipnir will hold that you would enter such an agreement with the wolf?"

Anger flashed across Odin's face and he tossed his helm into the snow in a pique of ire. "There was no agreement," he stated, each word hissing from between his teeth. "Fenris issued demands. It wanted half of Asgard to rove across, everything south of Alfheim and east of Nidavellir. I had to argue with the beast to make it settle for less." He glanced back at the hulking brute, its lupine eyes fixed on him as it watched him talking with the other gods. "The wolf makes sport of me... me, the All-Father and King of Asgard! It didn't try to hide from me that it was mocking my efforts to constrain its demands. Each concession I drew from it was like a toy tossed to a child. And, like a toy, what I've wrested from Fenris is something it thinks to easily take back when it has the mind to."

"If we let Loki's cur claim these lands as its territory, what is to keep it from demanding all of Asgard?" Thor asked.

"How would you stop it?" Loki snapped. "Will you swat the Great Wolf with your hammer? You've vanquished many giants with that weapon, brother, but don't think you can overcome all enemies with it. Mighty as it is, it has its limitations."

Thor bristled under the chastisement, but Tyr could see that there was a flicker of doubt on his face.

"Never force a fight you are uncertain you can win," Odin said. "Fenris has grown much more powerful since it was driven to Varinheim by Haakun." He nodded to the armored hunter, respectfully acknowledging the historic deed. "If we force the wolf into battle, it is a contest we must win. Because to lose would give Fenris license to rampage across Asgard with no fear that anyone could stop it."

Tyr heard the strain in his father's voice. It was a terrible burden to bear – the responsibility of trying to protect Asgard from the monster, even if doing so meant abandoning parts of it to Fenris. Varinheim had long suffered the wolf's hunger so that other lands could be free of its menace. The decision to leave other regions to the beast's doubtful mercy was something Odin would only do when there was no other choice. Tyr appreciated that no good general ever forced a fight he wasn't certain of winning in some way.

There was another reason as well. The prophecy of Ragnarok, that final war when the forces of good and evil would determine the fate of the Nine Worlds, was known to the gods. Most claimed that in that conflict, Odin was doomed to fall upon Twilight, the blazing blade of the fire giant Surtur, but there were a few who spoke of a different end for the All-Father. That the King of Asgard would be devoured by a colossal wolf, an omen that wasn't understood until Loki sired Fenris and the beast became savage. Then that aspect of the prophecy became clear: the Great Wolf was the monster of which the seers had foretold. Tyr wondered if that prediction weighed upon his father and caused his hesitance to force the beast into battle. Prophecy was a difficult thing to gauge. If accurate, did it mean Odin was invulnerable to Fenris until Ragnarok, or did it foretell that if he fought the wolf then he would die, regardless of when that combat occurred? And by avoiding that conflict, could he then avoid the prophecy? Tyr didn't know, but with his great wisdom, he thought that his father did. Another weight set upon Odin's shoulders, for it was more than just his own life but the leadership of Asgard that would be lost if the wolf defeated him.

Another howl rolled through the valley. Fenris took a few steps towards the assembled gods. Its lips drew back, displaying its fangs in a lupine grin. A strain of grumbling utterances rumbled up from its throat, bestial intonations in the language of wolves. The Allspeak, by which the Asgardians could understand the speech of dwarves, elves, trolls, and giants made the sounds intelligible to Tyr. *Hurry along and bind me with your chain*, Fenris was goading them. *I'm eager to prowl my new domains.*

"Bring forth Gleipnir," Odin declared, scowling at the wolf's impertinence.

Balder took the cord from Frigga. Of all the Aesir, Balder was the most beloved, and even Fenris had sworn an oath not to harm him. Alone among them, he could approach the beast without fear of its jaws. Yet, as his brother approached the wolf, Tyr saw the monster's eyes shift from the heavy collar slung over Balder's shoulder to the thin cord held in his hands. At once, a gleam of suspicion crept into the wolf's eyes. It backed away a pace and snarled.

What trickery is this? Fenris swung its head around and stared at Odin. *What manner of chain is this that you think it can bind me?*

"The strongest chains in Asgard are unequal to your strength," Odin told the wolf. "So now we will start again with the weakest."

Fenris took another step back. It bared its fangs at Balder. *Stay there. I've sworn to bring no harm to you, but do not test my oath too far.* When Balder stopped, the Great Wolf lurched forwards. Tyr thought his brother had truly earned the title "the Brave," for he did not flinch when the monster's snout was pressed close and its nose snuffled at Gleipnir. A snap of those jaws and he would have vanished into the beast's gullet.

This stinks of magic. The wolf reared away and fixed its glowering eyes on Odin again. *Is this why you accepted my terms?*

Tyr saw something in that moment that gave him hope. Always before when they'd tried to bind Fenris, the wolf had been brazenly confident. Now it was anxious. It sensed a threat in Gleipnir. "Surely the Great Wolf isn't afraid to continue our game?" Tyr called to the beast. He recalled all the times the monster had laughingly snapped its fetters. "Where is your confidence now, Wolf of Wolves?"

The taunt brought smiles to many of the gods, but Odin shot Tyr a look of such gravity that any amusement he felt at the wolf's uneasiness was instantly gone. There was a peril here that Odin had foreseen that the others hadn't. Tyr soon learned what that threat was.

There is trickery here, Fenris growled. It raised one of its feet and pawed the air. *A thin cord and a heavy collar. I learned enough of my father's lying ways to know better than to trust such things.* The wolf looked across the assembled gods, then fixed its gaze back on Odin. *I will play your game again, but I add another condition. You must promise to set me free if I cannot break the cord.*

Odin bowed his head. "The promise is given," he said. The All-Father's voice was so grim that he might have been pronouncing his own doom.

Fenris pawed the air again. *To ensure your promise, one of you will put their hand in my mouth. I give my promise as well, not to bite so long as the bargain is upheld. Should your trickery prevail and I can't break this cord, you must set me free. Otherwise, I snap my jaws and take the hand.* The wolf nodded to Balder. *I've sworn not to harm you, so it must be another who accepts my challenge.*

Odin turned to the other gods. "You need no more proof that Gleipnir will work than the wolf's fear of it," he said. "Consider that fact well before you make a decision. Remember *what* is at stake."

Tyr knew the meaning of his father's words, nor was it lost upon the gods around him. If they could truly bind Fenris, then the lands threatened by the wolf would be saved. At the same time, whoever answered the beast's challenge was certain to lose their hand. The recuperative powers of the Asgardians were great, but the arcane laws of sacrifice were greater. Odin had surrendered his eye for wisdom and so its loss remained. Whoever gave their hand to bind Fenris, it would likewise be lost forever.

Uneasy silence held the gods as they pondered the wolf's demand. Fenris grinned at their indecision, openly mocking their lack of courage and this proof that they meant to trick the beast. Even the usually bold Thor wasn't able to accept the beast's challenge. As minutes passed, Tyr saw Odin stir in his saddle. A hideous thought came to him. If no one else rose to the challenge, then the All-Father would take it on himself to do so. Perhaps bearing out the seers who claimed he was fated to perish in the wolf's jaws.

"I will accept your challenge," Tyr called out. He started to step forwards, but Loki grabbed him by the shoulder and held him back.

Who said that? Fenris growled. *Which of you will keep faith with me?*

"Quick, before it sees you," Loki hissed at Tyr. Before he knew what was happening, the trickster god was standing in front of him, his cloak spread to conceal Tyr.

Speak up, Fenris barked. *Who is it that has the stomach to reach between my fangs?*

"Let me go to the wolf," Tyr ordered. "I'll endure no more of its baiting."

"Fenris is my child," Loki said. "Don't underestimate its cunning. Before you go to it, turn your swordbelt around and shift your shield to the other hand." Loki gave him a sharp look when Tyr hesitated. "Do it, or your loss will be even worse," he snapped.

Tyr hastily complied while Fenris continued to mock the gods for their timidity. He thought Thor was about to respond to the wolf's goading, but before he succumbed to the beast's lure, Tyr came forward. "I am here, wolf. You can stop your yapping." Tyr saw the look of relief that was on the faces of the other gods. All of them knew this sacrifice was essential, but none of them wanted to be the one to render it. Frigga's expression was anguished; Odin's visage was riddled with regret. Tyr wondered if his father's wisdom had enabled him to foresee this moment, the demand of the wolf and the sacrifice that would be rendered. He wondered if Odin knew who would be the one to make that sacrifice.

With each step he took towards Fenris, Tyr felt dread boiling in the pit of his stomach. His shield felt strange in his right hand, and the sword felt odd resting on his right hip. At least there was the satisfaction of seeing the Great Wolf quail at his approach. It had been so certain none of the gods would risk losing their hand.

"Let's see if you can break Gleipnir," Tyr called to Fenris. He motioned to Balder and his brother stepped beside him and held out the heavy collar.

"You'll have to wear this," Balder told the Great Wolf.

The beast's eyes had a touch of fright in them now. It looked from side to side, as though seeking some route of escape. But it was caught by its own pride. Fenris had challenged the gods. It wouldn't let itself flee from that challenge. Slowly, the brute's colossal figure began to diminish, reducing itself until it stood only fifteen feet at the shoulder. Then it lowered itself to the ground, resting on its belly while Balder fastened the collar to its neck. It growled at him when he lifted Gleipnir.

Before you fasten the cord, I'll have my assurance to be set free. Fenris bared its fangs at Tyr. *Your hand, hero, unless you've reconsidered your choice.*

"I haven't," Tyr said. "My courage is no less than your own." He started forward to set his hand in the wolf's mouth. Fenris jerked its head back and glared at him.

No, not that one. There was a sneering quality to the wolf's expression as it glowered at Tyr. *Your swordhand, hero. That is what you'll lose if you break faith with me.*

Tyr had automatically reached forward with his right hand. The craftiness in Loki's plotting was borne out. The shifted belt and shield had deceived Fenris into thinking Tyr was left-handed. By the wolf's own demand, it was the left hand he held out as he stepped to the monster. The hot, reeking breath of the wolf washed over him as it opened its mouth. Tyr could feel the blood turn cold inside him as he set his hand into the dampness of the beast's maw. The keen fangs pressed down on his skin and he could feel the strength of the wolf's jaws. The least exertion and he knew Fenris could snap off his hand in an instant.

Satisfied with Tyr's hand in its mouth, Fenris let Balder wind the cord through the collar and fasten its other end to the Uru staple fixed to the valley floor. The Great Wolf rose to its feet again, forcing Tyr to stretch his arm to keep his hand from being cut by the beast's fangs. Fenris glared at him, but kept its head lowered so that he wasn't pulled off the ground. More than before, there was an air of panic in the wolf's eyes.

Tyr went stumbling from side to side as Fenris strained to snap Gleipnir. Incredible as it seemed, the cord held where mighty chains had failed. A low whine rumbled through the Great Wolf, pulsating down Tyr's arm until every bone in his body was vibrating from the beast's mounting panic. There was an almost desperate appeal in its eyes now. It was imploring Tyr to call out to the other gods to free it. That was why Fenris was reluctant to champ down on his hand. Tyr's peril was the only thing it had left to bargain with.

They had the Great Wolf! Gleipnir would hold! No longer would the lands of Asgard fear the beast's ferocity. More, Tyr thought of Odin and the prophecies about him and Fenris. That doom would be averted now, for the wolf would be safely shackled.

Tyr glanced back at the watching gods. He'd expected to see relief on their faces, even celebration. Instead he saw a mounting horror. They were waiting for Fenris to bite and the longer it hesitated, the more their resolve would falter. All it would need would be for one of them, any one of them, to untie the cord and everything would be undone. Any one of them. His brothers, his father, even his mother. Frigga was unable to look on the scene – how long could she endure before her position as Queen of Asgard no longer repressed a mother's fear for her son?

Tyr looked into the wolf's eyes. The appeal there was

piteous, but he reminded himself that Fenris was only so because it was desperate. Set free again, it would be twice the monster it was before, bitter at how it had been tricked. Never again would it make sport with the gods and give them another chance to trap it.

"No," Tyr told the Great Wolf. "You're caught, and you'll stay caught!" He smiled and raised his right hand. "By the way, this is the one I swing a sword with."

Savage in its temper even when it had been in the city of Asgard, Tyr's jeering and the revelation that Fenris had been cheated incensed the beast. Its jaws came snapping down, the fangs shearing through Tyr's hand. He was thrown back, blood spurting from the jagged stump. Balder hurried to his side and dragged him away.

Fenris threw its head back and swallowed Tyr's hand, then sprang forward in an attempt to claim the rest of his flesh. Gleipnir held it fast, however, and it could only gnash its teeth in futile protest as Balder helped Tyr back to where the other gods stood. Frigga hurried to him, winding her cape about his arm and trying to staunch the flow of blood. Odin leaped down from Sleipnir's back and dashed over to Tyr.

From his belt, the All-Father removed a small pouch. Odin reached in and produced a small vial and a poultice. "Something to dull the pain," Odin said, pressing the vial to Tyr's lips. He handed the poultice to Frigga. "Something to stop the bleeding," he told her.

Tyr had felt a stinging cold inside him, but when he drank the contents of the vial it was banished as warmth rushed through him again. He stared into his father's face.

There was guilt in Odin's eye. Tyr was right, his father had foreseen this. That was why he had the instruments ready to ease his son's wounds. "It was my choice," Tyr reassured him. "I knew what it would cost me, but I chose to do it anyway." The gratitude on Odin's face when he said these words was even more enervating than the potion he'd been given.

Oathbreakers! Fenris howled. *You swore to release me!*

Odin turned from Tyr and faced the Great Wolf. The monster raged against its bindings. It tried to swell its size to snap the collar, but its efforts only threatened to choke it. Trying to make itself smaller, it was frustrated to find that its bindings shrank to match its attempts to slip free. Try as it might, the wolf couldn't break the cord.

"One day one of us *will* free you," Odin told Fenris. "But it will not be today, nor many days to come. We made our bargain, beast, but you neglected to say how long Gleipnir would bind you." The All-Father clenched his fist and shook it at the monster. "Be thankful I have no taste for slaughter, wolf, or I would kill you while you're shackled for the hurt you've done my son!"

You've tricked me, Odin, and your son has cheated me! When I slip free…

"When you slip free," Odin snarled at Fenris, his voice more ferocious than the wolf's growls, "I will be waiting for you, and on that day, you'll not find me in a merciful mood."

FOUR

Tyr tapped the metal cup against his chest. "We cheated Fenris."

Bjorn stared in amazement at the god's contrition. "But you did what was necessary to preserve Asgard. Had Fenris remained loose it would eventually have wrought havoc throughout the realm."

"What I did was a necessary evil," Tyr corrected him. "There was bravery in my deed, but there was no honor. We all of us tricked Fenris, mocked its trust in us. I most of all."

"The Great Wolf had to be chained," Bjorn insisted. "Even today, Varinheim is scarred from its ancient depredations and infested with the descendants of its brood."

"Necessity isn't nobility," Tyr said. He sighed as he considered another point. "I wonder if Thor would have agreed to that final deception. To cheat the Great Wolf to the very last."

Bjorn grimaced at the remark. "He wouldn't because he didn't offer his hand to Fenris. You had the right of it when you called your brother reckless and vainglorious. He seeks mighty deeds for his own benefit, not that of Asgard."

Tyr's eyes flashed with anger. "I was unjust when I said that, and they are words it is unworthy of you to repeat." Before he could gauge the reprimand's effect on Bjorn, a sound from back among the pines caused him to spin around. In a flash his sword was in his hand, its white blade glimmering in the daylight.

"Show yourself," Tyr commanded.

From behind the pines a figure emerged. Tyr was struck at once by the long red hair that fell across the narrow shoulders, bright even in the shadow of the trees. The shape belonged to a woman, tall and lissome, arrayed in leather garb much like Bjorn. She had a bow and quiver on her back and a broadaxe on her belt. In her hands she carried a boarspear, its sharp head nearly a foot long and barbed along its edges.

"Forgive me," the huntress said, "I didn't mean to intrude." She shrugged her shoulders. "I was tracking an old grayback with doubled tusks when I chanced to come upon you. I was waiting for the opportunity to leave as unobtrusively as I came. I didn't intend to eavesdrop."

The woman's face was an image of loveliness, more beautiful than most in Asgard, yet there was a troubling familiarity about her that made Tyr suspicious. "What did you hear?" he asked.

The huntress shook her head and smiled in apology. "Something about the chaining of the Great Wolf. Something more about Thor and heroic deeds. I confess I didn't understand much of it."

The more she spoke, the more certain Tyr was that he knew this woman. Not well, but if he concentrated, he was certain he could put a name to…

"Lorelei," he grumbled when he realized who she was. He'd only ever seen her in elegant gowns and embroidered dresses, so rough hunter's garb had thrown him off.

"You needn't say it like that," Lorelei grumbled back. "You sound like you just found a viper hiding under a rock."

"Haven't I?" Tyr prodded her.

"That is a horrible thing to say to a lady," Bjorn said, rising to defend the huntress.

Tyr turned a warning look on his companion. "This is Lorelei, the younger sister of Amora the Enchantress." He could see that the information startled Bjorn, but not enough to dull the admiration in his eyes. The ability of Amora to fascinate men with a mere glance was notorious throughout Asgard, not that such knowledge was any protection against her wiles. Lorelei appeared to share her sister's art.

"It is a hurtful thing to always be in the shadow of your sibling," Lorelei quipped. She fixed Tyr with her gaze. "Wouldn't you agree? For better or worse, we are compared to their reputations."

"I am reminded of the time you tried to woo my brother with a love philter," Tyr commented. By an effort of will he managed to break contact and look away from her eyes.

"Thor prefers Sif," Lorelei stated, indifference in her tone. She smiled and laughed. "His loss, don't you think?"

"We were just discussing how injudicious Thor can be," Bjorn agreed.

Lorelei sighed. "Yet he's the one whom all Asgard celebrates." She stamped the butt of her spear against the ground. "It's unfair that Thor should be feted while the accomplishments of greater heroes are forgotten."

"So, you heard more than a little of our conversation," Tyr accused. He didn't like the way she was verbally poking at him. It reminded him too much of Loki.

"No," Lorelei insisted, "but I was in Odin's hall when you traded sharp words with Thor. I was impressed. It was high time someone tried to curb that ego of his."

"Small chance of that when he's constantly running off to fight giants and slay dragons," Bjorn said. "Every adventure only inflates his pride further." He saw the disturbed look on Tyr's face. "You said as much at the feast," he reminded him.

"Whatever I said, Thor *has* done great deeds," Tyr answered. "That cannot be taken from him."

"They can't be taken from him," Lorelei said, staring at Tyr's gleaming sword. "But have you thought that they might be surpassed?"

Tyr started at the remark. Despite his hesitance, he looked into her eyes. "What do you mean?"

An indulgent laugh rolled from Lorelei's lips. "I mean instead of being jealous of Thor's deeds, strike out on adventures of your own." She stepped closer and laid her hand on his shoulder. "After all, you are Odin's eldest son."

"Thor knocked away Ymir's beard," Bjorn stated. There was an edge to his voice, and Tyr noticed that his eyes kept darting to Lorelei's hand on his shoulder. "What can compare to that?"

Lorelei turned from Tyr and regarded Bjorn. "I saw you at the feast," she said, "so I know you also heard Odin's speech. Even as he praised Thor, the All-Father spoke of a still greater feat." Her voice dropped to a dusky whisper. "Surely to a brave and noble heart such as yours, a deed of such magnitude would be worthy of your attention."

Tyr stared at her in shock. He well remembered what Odin had spoken of, but he was stunned anyone could have taken his words seriously. "To steal the sword of Surtur and bring it back to Asgard," Tyr said, shaking his head. "My father spoke in jest. That is not a greater feat, but an impossible one."

"Thor wouldn't think so," Lorelei stated. "To him, the impossible is a challenge, not an obstacle."

Tyr looked over at Bjorn and waved his hand. "You see, young pup? She protests otherwise, but she still loves my brother." He was pleased to see some of Bjorn's ardor leave his eyes after hearing him state what should have been obvious.

"Yes," Lorelei conceded. "That's why I would like to see him humbled. His rejection hurt me, that is why I tried to ply him with a love potion." Again she cracked the end of her spear against the ground. "If Thor's pose as Asgard's greatest champion were challenged, it might cause him to amend his proud ways and not be so dismissive of me."

"So that's what you're after," Tyr said. "You want to humble my brother."

"And you want to make everyone remember that you are also a hero," Lorelei replied. "Stealing Surtur's sword would do just that."

Tyr was silent as he weighed what she said. It was true, taking Surtur's sword would far eclipse Thor's triumph over Ymir. That, however, was simple hubris, the urge to assert himself as the eldest son. Not enough to justify the risk involved. But there was another reason. The prophecy of Ragnarok, when Surtur would lead his legions up from Muspelheim to incinerate Asgard. In that battle, the burning sword Twilight would strike down Odin. If he could steal Twilight, perhaps he could defy the prophecy. Even avert Ragnarok. More importantly, at least to him, he would again save his father from a doom that had been foretold for him.

"… but how should we even get into Muspelheim?" Bjorn was asking Lorelei when Tyr stirred from his thoughts. "Surtur's domain is guarded by his fire demons."

"There are ways," Lorelei said. "Though I am not my sister, the mystic arts aren't unknown to me. We could cross the Rainbow Bridge to reach Muspelheim. I have spells that could get us past Heimdall, but it would take valiant warriors to brave what awaits us on the other side." When she spoke the last, she again looked at Tyr. "I know your bravery is equal to the task, but is your ambition?"

Tyr returned his sword to its sheath. "Thor shattered Ymir's beard for his own ambition. Mine is to protect Asgard and all I hold dear. For that, there is nothing I wouldn't do." He bowed his head to Lorelei.

"For that, I would even trust you," Tyr said.

FIVE

Lorelei bade Tyr and Bjorn accompany her to her castle out on the Plain of Ida overlooking the Sea of Marmora. The structure could be seen from afar, shimmering in the sunlight. It had been raised from blocks of stone saturated with deposits of mica and quartz so that when the sun struck the fortifications they seemed as though they'd been crafted from the light itself. Tyr found the effect to be magnificent and was impressed by the planning and engineering it must have taken for Lorelei to construct her home in such a manner. There was also a certain symbolism about that impression of a castle built of light, for did they not seek to range across a bridge woven from the same essence?

To ensure their passage across Bifrost, the Rainbow Bridge, Lorelei said she needed certain apparatus she kept in her castle. A deep moat surrounded the walls, and Tyr was surprised when he drew near to it that the bottom was as ablaze with light as the castle walls. Where shadows had reached down into the depression, he found the reason. The moat was lined with jagged shards of crystal.

"A notion of my sister's," Lorelei explained when she noted the subject of Tyr's interest. "She has, on occasion, sought refuge with me and has prevailed on me to take certain precautions." An awkward look squirmed onto her face. "At times she has made strong enemies."

Tyr tried to repress a snort of laughter. There was an understatement! Through her intrigues and enchantments Amora had made enemies of nearly anyone of consequence in Asgard at one time or another. Thor and Loki both had been caught in her manipulations on different occasions, and it was said the rock troll champion Ulik was still howling for her head after being exploited by her.

"It is to be regretted that the beauty of your castle must be tarnished in such a way," Bjorn said as the three circled around the moat to where the drawbridge stood. The gates were open, and the portal lowered when they approached.

"Necessity must always compromise beauty," Lorelei pouted, running her hands across her rough hunter's garb. "Still, you always have to be practical about such things and accept them as they are." She directed the last remark at Tyr. "You see, I've gotten rid of that naivety that made me think charms and potions could win your brother's heart." She shrugged her shoulders. "We live and we learn."

Tyr scratched his chin, giving consideration to that sentiment. "Some of us learn slower than others, maybe." He knew he could be intransigent when it came to adapting new ideas. Or reconsidering his opinion of someone. People did change, but often the impression they'd made on others didn't.

"Welcome home, Lady Lorelei," a brawny guard greeted

her as she started across the bridge. The man gave Tyr and Bjorn a wary study. "Your hunting went well?"

Lorelei dismissed her guard's concern with a wave of her hand. "I gave up the chase when I found some old friends in the Greenfirm," she told him. "They will be my guests, Gunter. Tell the kitchens to prepare dinner for three."

"Is there time for that?" Tyr asked her when Gunter was out of earshot.

"We should make time," Lorelei answered and laughed. "You might be grateful to have a big meal in your belly before we start. I doubt we'll find any fit fare in Muspelheim."

"She makes a good case," Bjorn said. "I don't think Surtur will ask us to sup with him before we steal his sword."

Tyr shook his head as they passed through the castle entrance. "And I'm supposed to be the tactician. The dullest giant knows an army marches on its stomach. Here we are about to start a bold campaign and I forget the most basic element of them all."

Lorelei gave him a lingering stare. "Perhaps you've had other things on your mind," she said before quickly turning away and hurrying ahead of them into the entry hall.

"What did she mean by that?" Bjorn wondered as they followed after her.

"She knows the prophecy of Ragnarok. She knows that Twilight is fated to slay my father," Tyr said. "There's no magic if she guesses this weighs upon me, what I risk by failure and what I may gain by success." While Bjorn accepted his explanation, Tyr only wished that he could be as certain that it was the meaning of what Lorelei had said. There was something about the way she'd looked at him.

Lorelei claimed to have put aside her desire for Thor. Was that because she was now interested in Tyr?

The inside of the castle was no less astounding than its exterior. The entry was a vast hall of marble pillars and winding stairs. The mosaic on the floor was fashioned from alternating tiles of green and blue to create the impression of a river coursing through woodland. Tyr found that this theme was repeated throughout the home, lending itself to the suggestion that a visitor was following the path of the waterway as they moved from room to room. A bronze brazier standing at the middle of the hall illuminated the rich tapestries hanging from its walls depicting amorous scenes from the sagas. Tyr recognized one of them as representing the Midgard tale of Tristan and Isolde.

"A palace in truth," Bjorn proclaimed to their hostess, "but how could anything less be a suitable setting for someone as pretty as you." Had there been less sincerity woven into his awkward speech, Tyr would have smiled at his friend's discomfort. A rustic wolfhunter from Varinheim, Bjorn was always out of sorts among finery and riches. Tyr'd often joked that if he stumbled on a dragon's lair, he'd be more frightened of the hoarded treasure than the fire-breathing worm.

"That's sweet of you to say," Lorelei replied. She extended her arms and waved them at the many doorways opening into the hall. "Please, accept the liberty of my home. Dinner will be ready within the hour." She plucked a finger under the sleeve of her tunic. "If you'll excuse me, I'll change into something more appropriate to the occasion."

"You've yet to explain how you intend to get us past Heimdall and across Bifrost," Tyr reminded her as she started to ascend the stairs.

"We'll talk about that over dinner," Lorelei answered. "Comfortable circumstances allow one to think more clearly."

The two warriors watched Lorelei withdraw into her rooms upstairs. When she was gone, Bjorn turned to Tyr, a hint of irritation in his eyes. "You're still suspicious of her?"

"It is hard to trust someone who cast a charm over my brother," Tyr confessed.

Bjorn pulled at his beard. "If you're so distrustful, then why are we here? Wouldn't the smart thing be to stay far away from Lorelei and whatever she's planning?"

Tyr traced the edge of the mosaic river with his foot. "That would be the wise course, but not the brave one." He laid his hand on Bjorn's shoulder and lowered his voice. "I appreciate your devotion, my friend, but know that if you decide to defer to wisdom and return to the city, I won't think less of you."

"But you intend to press on," Bjorn said. "Even if you think Lorelei is trying to trick you."

Tyr's expression was somber. "She's a good hunter. She knows the right bait to put in her trap. To catch me, she offers Twilight and the chance to lift my father's foretold doom from off his shoulders." He thought again of when he'd put his hand in the wolf's mouth and defied fate to protect his father from a different prophecy. "Even if I was certain it was a trap, I couldn't stay away with such an opportunity before me." He locked eyes with Bjorn.

"That explains my foolhardiness, but it doesn't demand that you join me in it."

"No," Bjorn said, taking hold of Tyr's arm and clasping his hand, "but the bonds of friendship do. We've stalked giants in the mountains and routed draugr from their barrows. I'll not shun your company now that something a little more challenging looms before us." They both chuckled at the understatement. Of all the Nine Worlds, perhaps only Hela's deathly realm was regarded with more dread than fiery Muspelheim.

"Still," the huntsman continued, "I can't share your doubts about Lorelei. She isn't Amora. She doesn't have that thirst for power her sister has. What would she gain by trying to trick us?"

"If I knew that," Tyr sighed, "I would know better what to watch out for."

They spoke no more on the subject as they walked through Lorelei's castle. Each room was more splendidly appointed than the last, and Tyr thought their tour was far too brief when Gunter suddenly appeared in a doorway and summoned them to dinner. Bjorn's tastes might be too rude to appreciate the artistry of her palace, but Tyr found himself impressed by the elegantly carved furnishings, the intricately woven rugs with their colorful patterns, the luxurious tapestries that stretched across the walls. He'd have liked a bit more time to contemplate the long gallery lined with magnificent statues sculpted from equally magnificent stones gathered from across the Nine Worlds.

The dining hall was richly appointed, candles shining from hundreds of silver stands arrayed all around the long table of dark oak. Such was its size that Tyr thought only Yggdrasil could have been large enough to provide the wood. Perhaps Amora had used some spell to meld different boards into each other to create the material for Lorelei's table. There was a note of the ridiculous when Gunter escorted them up to the head of the table. It was big enough to seat two hundred, yet here it was to serve only three.

Tyr and Bjorn took places to either side of the high-backed gilded chair that stood waiting for their hostess. Servants in bright liveries of blue and gold circled around the table, setting vessels before them. Flagons of ale, steins of beer, bowls of a dark soup with spicy broth, plates of broiled venison and steamed pheasant. It was a test of will to refrain from the meal until Lorelei joined them. Indeed, Tyr had to deliver a sharp kick to Bjorn's shin when the wolfhunter would have started in on the soup.

The wait, however, was not a long one. Tyr suspected Lorelei could have preceded them to the table but had lingered off in one of the halls until they were settled. She made a grand entrance as she swept into the hall. The dress she wore was bright azure, complemented by a belt of gold and a necklace with a ruby set into it big enough to choke a bear. Gold combs adorned her hair, sweeping the scarlet locks away from her powdered face.

"It gladdens me that you've accepted my hospitality," Lorelei said as she took her seat at the head of the table. She made a little frown when she saw that neither man had started in on his meal. "Oh, you needn't have waited for me. I know you must be hungry after your hurried departure from Odin's hall." Her eyes sparkled as she looked at Tyr. "You didn't exactly get a chance to finish your meal."

Tyr acknowledged the comment with a wave of his hand. "I'm hungry for the details of your plan to cross the Rainbow Bridge. Other appetites can wait."

Lorelei motioned one of her servants to pour wine for her. She lingered over the crystal goblet, watching the play of its ruddy color within the sharp facets of the glass. "I know you distrust me, Tyr. I know my past hasn't been as ideal as it might have been and I know that my sister's legacy is still less of a recommendation. But please believe that my motives are pure."

"I would very much like to," Tyr said. "Is there anything you can tell me to lessen my suspicions?"

"No," Lorelei said, sipping at her wine. "Indeed, what I must tell you will only make you more suspicious." She set down the goblet and folded her hands before her on the table. "You've asked me how we will get past Heimdall and cross Bifrost? The answer is one that will hardly convince you of my sincerity. My sister has, as you know, taken refuge in this castle with me at times. Some of her arcane apparatus has been left here. Among them there is a certain powder that when cast into someone's face will make their mind turn back upon itself and forget all that has happened over the previous hour."

"This is what you plan to use to get past Heimdall?" Bjorn asked.

"He will forget we even approached the Himinbjörg," Lorelei said. When she saw the stern expression on Tyr's face, she hurried to reassure him. "The powder will do him no harm, only make him forget that we were there. It will hold him immobile for a time and while he is stunned, we'll be able to cross Bifrost."

"Do you think to use this powder on Surtur when we go to steal his sword?" Tyr prompted. His distaste for such a trick was only exceeded by his distaste for leaving Twilight in the fire giant's hands. In war, the most dishonorable tactics had to be considered if it would ensure victory.

"Would that I had enough for such a purpose," Lorelei said. "But my sister left only enough here for us to employ on Heimdall. Even if we were to find another way to Muspelheim, I don't know if there's enough powder to affect Surtur. Or even if something like him can be affected by it."

"It will need stronger magic than a pinch of powder to fight Surtur," Bjorn observed between bites of venison.

Lorelei stared down at the table, a flush rising into her cheeks. "There are other enchantments Amora left," she confessed. "I haven't focused myself on studying magic the way she has, but I have watched her at work. I might not be able to conjure the devices she uses to invoke her magic, but I know enough to be able to make use of what she left here."

Tyr tapped his finger on the table. "Before we devise a strategy to sneak into Muspelheim, I must know the nature of these devices. How they work. What they can do. How dependable they are." He could see his talk was making her uncomfortable. "When we cross Bifrost we'll be entering a hostile land where the very air is an enemy seeking to stifle us. It's important to know the potential of every weapon at our disposal. That includes the magic you can draw upon."

"On your first point I can offer little," Lorelei said. "I know how to work these spells, but not why they work. To the second, I can say there is much they can do. A veil of smoke drawn from the breath of the dragon Fafnir to hide us from the denizens of Muspelheim. A sliver of ice from the glaciers of Niffleheim that can freeze even a fire demon's ire." She paused a moment, weighing her words. "These worked well enough in Amora's hands. But there is one that even she considered erratic in its moods. The Wayfarer's Mirror, crafted for her by the dark elves."

"What is special about this mirror?" Bjorn asked.

"Could its magic be depended on, we'd have no need of troubling Heimdall or crossing Bifrost," Lorelei said. "It might transport us wherever we wished to go within the Nine Worlds." She shook her head. "But Malekith's elves are treacherous and so too are the gifts they bestow on their 'friends'. I wouldn't want to rely on the mirror, but if we were hard-pressed it would offer the possibility of escape from Muspelheim."

Tyr took a swig of ale and wiped the foam from his chin. "If the mirror is as untrustworthy as you say, then it must be a last resort." He smiled at Lorelei. "The other magic you speak of is certain to be useful. It will only bolster our chances of success to have them at our disposal."

"There is more," Lorelei said, looking across at each of them in turn. "My castle's armory is well supplied. You could both of you benefit from a coat of mail. A shirt of chain crafted by the dwarves that resists even the hottest flame. A breastplate forged by the giants that is impervious to the most crushing pressure. There are weapons too–"

Tyr interrupted her with a wave of his hand. "My sword is weapon enough for me," he said. "But we will accept the hospitality of your armory. It will spare us returning to the city and risk others learning of our intentions." He laughed and clapped his hand down on the table. "All of that can wait! Watching Bjorn gorge himself on these victuals has become more tortuous than anything I expect to find in Muspelheim! Let's eat before he finishes what's on his plate and starts raiding mine!"

Lorelei laughed at Tyr's joke. For a moment her eyes met his and there was in them an unexpected warmth. The instant was fleeting, the connection broken almost as soon as he became aware of it. Lorelei lowered her gaze and focused on her plate. Tyr didn't ask her about the interest he thought she'd shown. It was just possible he was mistaken and that it was merely his imagination that had created the impression.

"We'll need more than your sword," Lorelei finally said. "It will take the tactical prowess for which the God of War is so famed." When she returned her attention to Tyr, the warmth was gone, subsumed by a stony resolution. "We can depend only upon our own resources. There isn't anyone else we can call to for help."

Tyr nodded. "Because of the great danger, I am certain Odin would try to stop us." His slapped his hand against the table, causing the cutlery to rattle. "But the very danger is why this could work. Surtur would never expect so small a group to trespass into his domain, much less try to steal Twilight. Surprise is a potent factor in our favor, one that cannot be underestimated." He smiled as he thought about the advantage. "Yes, I think we stand a very good chance, more than those who would dissuade us would credit us with."

Tyr raised his stein and saluted Lorelei and Bjorn. "To Twilight's last hours in Muspelheim," he toasted. "May the fire giant's sword never return to his hand!"

SIX

The renowned Rainbow Bridge that connected the Nine Worlds projected outward from the very edge of Asgard, just beyond the walled city of the Aesir. At its foot, connecting it to the realm, was the dome-shaped bastion of Himinbjörg, home of Bifrost's guardian, the Vanir Heimdall.

Tyr felt uncomfortable as he approached Himinbjörg, a feeling that owed nothing to the thick breastplate he wore, or the heavy shield tied to his left arm. He had the utmost respect for the unwavering loyalty of Heimdall. Tasked by Odin to guard Bifrost, the sentinel performed his duty with an indefatigable sense of purpose. He'd stared so long upon the Rainbow Bridge that now his eyes could peer into other realms, his gaze augmented by the mighty powers of Mimir, observing those Asgardians he concentrated upon. It was that power which made it so necessary to employ the sorcerous powder on him. Even if they did bluff their way past Heimdall, all it would need would be for him to concentrate on any one of them to discover where they'd gone and what they were doing. Tyr's worry was that his father would find out and Odin would try to stop him. Or, worse, venture into Muspelheim to save him. Should that happen, he would be responsible for provoking the battle between Odin and Surtur instead of preventing it. The prophecy was vague on precisely when Ragnarok would unfold, and even the best tactician in Asgard couldn't repulse an attack if he didn't know when it would be unleashed. The nebulous ways of divination always ran the risk that by trying to avoid an outcome, one would ensure it came to pass. Tyr couldn't take that chance, so, as distasteful as it was, they had to employ Lorelei's magic.

She presented a starkly different appearance than she had either at their dinner in her castle or their meeting in the Greenfirm. Lorelei wore armor that had the pebbled pattern of snakeskin but the hardness of diamond. She said it was shed from the ravenous Nidhogg, the fierce dragon who gnaws the roots of Yggdrasil, a gift to her by an adventurer whose name she no longer remembered, a failing of memory that Tyr found disturbing. A satchel slung over her shoulder held the various arcane devices her sister had left behind. At her waist was a long dirk of Uru metal, a provision Tyr had insisted upon. In case both magic and companions failed her, he didn't want her to be defenseless. An Uru dagger in its gizzard would soon settle any fire demon.

Bjorn had liberally availed himself of the proffered armor, though he presented a strange appearance in the coat of dwarven mail when he still had his wolfskin cloak drawn up over it. Tyr had joked that more than ever his friend looked like he was trying to fight his way out of the animal's belly.

He still carried the tried and trusted axes that had served him so well in Varinheim, but to them he'd added a hunting bow and a quiver of arrows from Alfheim. As he put it, he wanted any enemies to know they were in a fight as early as possible.

The city walls loomed behind them as Tyr and his companions approached Himinbjörg. The bastion's inner gate stood open. He could see through to the edge of the realm and the starry void beyond. The brilliant hues of the Rainbow Bridge shone in their chromatic panoply, stretching away into the infinite. Standing upon Bifrost was a towering figure wearing a horned helm and leaning upon a massive sword.

"We must bide here a moment," Lorelei warned Tyr when he would have marched ahead. "Too soon and we may leave evidence of what we've done. The powder will remove his memories of the past hour, but not those of anyone he may have spoken to." She turned her head and judged at what point they would have been visible from Himinbjörg. Tyr knew she'd been making careful calculations as they walked.

"How long must we wait?" Bjorn wanted to know. The wolfhunter had never ventured from Asgard before and with Bifrost so near Tyr imagined that excitement was rushing through him, more intoxicating than the strongest ale.

"Not long," Lorelei decided. She gave each of them a severe look. "You'll have to talk with Heimdall. Distract him so I can cast the powder in his face." Her hand brushed the satchel she carried. "Ten minutes, no more. Otherwise there's a risk he will remember that we approached

Himinbjörg and wonder what happened to us."

"If that happens, he is certain to divine where we've gone," Tyr said. "I've no liking for this trick, Lorelei, but there's no choice if we're to see this through."

"There's no turning back now," Lorelei emphasized. "Once we're upon Bifrost you must keep to the fiery bands of color and focus your minds upon Muspelheim. Keep that focus, and the gate will be open to us."

Bjorn nodded his understanding. Tyr had made the journey before, though usually it was to Midgard or Jotunheim. He knew how easy it was to lose the concentration needed to cross. An undisciplined traveler might walk the Rainbow Bridge forever if they forgot where they were going.

They started down across the rocky ground toward the bastion's open gate. Once they stepped within Himinbjörg, the sentinel on the bridge turned around. Tyr was a tall man, but Heimdall loomed over him, his height magnified by the horned helm he wore. The Vanir's black beard spilled down across his armored chest while his hands clasped the pommel of the great sword Hofund, an Uru blade capable of harnessing the cosmic energies that swirled about Bifrost. From his belt swung the Gjallarhorn with which he would alert Asgard to threats moving across the Rainbow Bridge.

"Hail and well met, Heimdall the Vigilant," Tyr greeted the sentinel.

Heimdall regarded him for a moment with his gray gaze before responding. "Well met, eldest son of Odin," he said at last. His gaze shifted to Tyr's companions. "The Lady Lorelei and Bjorn Wolfsbane." He nodded to each in turn.

Bjorn started at the mention of his name. "You know me?"

The question brought a gusty laugh from Heimdall. "There is no Asgardian who I haven't seen during my long vigil," he said. "I may never leave my post, but not so my vision. When you hunted the rogue wolf Frosthowl, I observed the deed. Your courage stood you in good stead after the beast broke your axe and you brought it down with the splintered heft." He nodded at the pelt draped over Bjorn's back. "I see you continue to wear his skin. A fine trophy and well earned."

Bjorn basked in this compliment from the mighty Heimdall. "Frosthowl was a worthy foe. There are times I regret killing him, but he'd gone fierce and mean, slaughtering man and animal alike for the sheer pleasure of it. For the sake of the villages that shivered when his howl filled the night, I had to take up the hunt." He glanced over at Lorelei. "They called me the greatest huntsman in Varinheim when I came back with his pelt."

"I understand there are more wolves than people in Varinheim," Lorelei said, irritated by his boasting... or that he'd drawn Heimdall's attention to her. Tyr tried to divert the Vanir's focus.

"There was a feast to celebrate Thor's victory over Ymir," Tyr said. "I was surprised you allowed him to pass you to undertake such a reckless venture."

It was the right subject to occupy Heimdall with. His expression darkened and his voice lowered to a grumble. "Your brother misled me as to his intentions. He was meant to journey to Midgard, not Niffleheim. It was to undertake this supposed task that I allowed him onto Bifrost, not to seek the King of the Ice Giants."

"Odin was pleased with the results," Tyr pointed out. "My brother returned with a tuft from Ymir's beard."

"Had he not borne such a token I should have barred him from returning to Asgard," Heimdall stated. "But I knew that because Thor was successful that Odin would overlook his foolhardiness." Again, the Vanir gave Tyr a studious look. "The All-Father is wise, but his heart exults in brave deeds and causes him to quickly forgive boldness when it is triumphant."

Tyr smiled at the comment. He hoped Odin would be as quick to forgive this journey into Muspelheim when he brought back Twilight and laid the fire giant's sword before his throne.

"The All-Father wrested the souls of the brave from Hela that they might dwell in the golden halls of Valhalla rather than the gloom of Hel," Tyr said. "He has ever been eager to exalt those who have courage in their hearts, even when he must steal them from the realm of the dead."

Heimdall leaned forward on Hofund's pommel. "My eyes can see Hela in her dark palace. She considers that Odin has poached what rightly belongs to her. It's a point of contention that festers like an open wound." He arched an eyebrow. "Thor was fortunate not to draw her notice when he went into Niffleheim. What brings you here, God of War? You would be well advised not to follow your brother's path. Thor has tested the luck of the Aesir enough for quite some time."

Tyr shook his head. "I've no intention of visiting

Niffleheim," he said, grateful he could tell the sentinel the truth. "Even if you've forgotten, I can't help but remember it is at the gate of Hel that Garm is kept. Perhaps I must feed the hound's jaws at Ragnarok, but I've no intention of hastening our meeting."

"To know the doom of tomorrow is both blessing and curse," Heimdall said. He started to say more, but at that moment Lorelei interrupted him.

"All-seer, you've yet to ask me why I wish to cross Bifrost," she said. When the Vanir turned towards her, Lorelei blew the powder cupped in her palm full into his face.

For just an instant, Heimdall reeled back and started to raise Hofund. Anger was on his face, but it dripped away like wax from a candle. His expression became blank, his eyes glazed and dull. The great sword hung slack in his hands.

"Quickly!" Lorelei snapped at Tyr and Bjorn. "We have only a matter of minutes before he will recover. By then we must be through the gate and away in Muspelheim. Otherwise he is certain to spot us on the bridge and follow us with his realm-piercing gaze."

Lorelei had no need to further emphasize her point. All three of them rushed past the stunned Heimdall and out onto the colorful beams of Bifrost. The solidified light that composed the Rainbow Bridge always felt strange under Tyr's feet. It was like trudging through shallow waters, a resistance without solidity, cool and crisp as it rushed about his boots. There was no sensation of support beneath him, only a nebulous impression of buoyancy. Crossing the span was neither walking nor swimming, but a fusion of both.

Tyr pressed his way to the crimson and orange beams that would best facilitate their passage into Muspelheim. The varied colors of Bifrost were each attuned to one of the Nine Worlds, and by following those with the greatest affinity for the desired realm it was easier to keep the mind focused upon it and open the proper gate.

The converse was doubly difficult, passage from another realm onto Bifrost, and impossible in many circumstances. Powerful enchantments kept the denizens of other worlds from reaching the Rainbow Bridge without an Asgardian to convey them.

"Concentrate," Lorelei enjoined them as they hurried along the prismatic span. "Keep focused."

Worry for Bjorn threatened to break Tyr's concentration. He chided himself for being so undisciplined. He wouldn't do his friend any good if he were to let himself go wandering away along the Rainbow Bridge. He redoubled his efforts and focused upon the fiery realm that was their destination.

Abruptly a shimmering haze formed ahead of Tyr, redolent of the same colors as those he was walking through. His hand dropped to his sword and he clenched his teeth. He wasn't sure what would be waiting for him on the other side of the gate, but he was determined it wouldn't catch him unawares.

"For you, father," Tyr whispered as he plunged into the haze.

SEVEN

Heat was the overwhelming sensation when Tyr emerged from the portal. The rush of hot air into his face was like sticking his head in an oven. Even the Aesir's brow was drenched in sweat within heartbeats.

The heat was the most immediate of Tyr's observations, but there were others equally dismaying. He'd traded the weird viscosity of the Rainbow Bridge for barren, rocky ground so hot that he could feel it through his boots. The terrain around him was lifeless and grim, without a speck of grass or hint of tree. Just gray, cheerless stone rising in great pillars and columns. The sky was starless and so black it might have been the roof of some gigantic cavern. No moon cast its rays down on the land, but it was well lit anyway. Everywhere it seemed to Tyr there was some vent in the ground belching sheets of flame into the air. Pools of lava bubbled and hissed, throwing off a menacing red light on whatever was near to them.

Several of those pools were close to where Tyr stood. He could see the distortion in the air above the bubbling pits as they added to the ghastly heat. Muspelheim certainly lived up to its reputation as a world of fire and flame.

Tyr turned about to look for his companions. He saw Lorelei beside him, her hair already damp from the withering atmosphere. She gave him an exasperated look, as though to say she was already regretting the plan she'd proposed to him and Bjorn.

Bjorn! Tyr tried to find the huntsman, but saw no trace of him. Behind them was the Muspelheim side of the gate, a great slab of volcanic glass set into the side of a rock wall. The reflective surface gave off only fragmentary suggestions of what might lie beyond or within it. Tyr thought he saw Bjorn, but he couldn't be sure.

"Concentrate!" Tyr urged his friend, though he knew there was no way his words could carry to him.

"Tyr!" Lorelei cried out, alarm in her voice.

He turned to see her pointing at the lava pools. Their bubbling had intensified, changing into churning undulations that sent liquid fire spurting up from their brims. As Tyr watched, an ashy gray arm reached up and took hold of the lip of the pit. It was followed by another. Pressing down on the ground, the arms drew a monstrous shape up from the pool. Craggy shoulders and a squashed, almost apish head appeared. Eyes like chips of obsidian stared from the brutish face. The rocky texture of the visage peeled back in an ugly snarl.

"Magma troll," Tyr cursed, giving name to the creature. Unlike the rock trolls of Asgard and others of their breed, those that dwelt in Muspelheim were utterly bestial in nature, without the capacity for rational thought. They had a certain cunning, though, and could be trained for specific tasks, much like a dog or horse. Watching more trolls draw themselves up from other lava pools, Tyr could easily guess the task these had been given. They'd been set here as guards to watch over the gateway.

The first troll emerged fully from its lair, molten rock oozing from its body. It glared at Tyr with its dark eyes. The snarl expanded into an angry hoot as it clashed its huge fists against its chest. Standing twice as tall as the Aesir, it made for a formidable display.

"If you want to fight, then fight, don't talk about it," Tyr taunted the troll. The stoneskinned beast charged at him, its great arms spread wide, its hands poised to rend him limb from limb. Tyr remained where he stood, waiting until the last moment to pivot to one side. The grasping fingers scraped against the shield tied to his left arm as he spun. As the troll's momentum took it past him, he swung about and brought his sword chopping down. The stroke caught the brute's arm at the shoulder and sheared it away. Molten, fiery liquid bubbled from the wound. The injured troll bellowed its fury, but a second sweep of the sword sent it crashing to the ground.

"Who's next?" Tyr shouted as he turned to face the other sentries. His confidence faltered when he saw that at least a score of the monsters had already climbed from the pools, with still more trying to rise. It looked as though their numbers might be limitless. "Now might be a good time for some of your magic," he yelled to Lorelei.

She'd drawn the piece of glacial ice from the satchel, the fragment stubbornly defying the heat of Muspelheim. It was also stubbornly defying her efforts to command its magic. "I told you, this is my sister's magic. I'm only borrowing it," she yelled back as she pointed the ice at the trolls and made arcane gestures with her other hand.

"Borrow faster!" Tyr shouted as he intercepted a troll charging for her. A cleaving swing of his sword knocked its leg out from under it, while the following thrust settled its menace for good. Even as he rose from the fallen beast, another lunged at him. He smashed his shield in its face and caused it to stagger back. Before it could recover, his blade pierced its chest and sent it toppling to the ground.

Three down, but there were still so many more. The twenty had grown to thirty, with still more climbing from the pits. "I can't stave off this many," Tyr warned Lorelei. "Use that mirror if you have to, but make ready to escape."

"Just a moment more, and I'll freeze them all in their tracks," she vowed.

A bellowing troll charged at Tyr. A cleaving stroke to its side spilled it to the ground, but another followed close behind. He had to duck beneath its grasping arms and stab it in the belly. Narrowly he avoided being crushed under its bulk as it plunged forwards. "We don't have a moment!" he exclaimed.

More magma trolls rushed towards him, an entire clutch of the brutes, their dull eyes filled with malice. By ones and twos, Tyr could fight the monsters all day, but en masse they were too much to overcome. Caught on open ground like this, the trolls' numbers must eventually prevail.

Before the rush of brutes could close with him, Tyr was

stunned to see one fall with an arrow in its head. A second pitched over as another arrow slammed into its chest. From the corner of his eye he saw Bjorn draw and loose a third arrow and send it speeding into another troll.

"Better late than never!" Tyr called to his friend. Though they still faced overwhelming odds, a sense of relief rushed through him. If they were fated to fall here, at least Bjorn would die fighting instead of lost on the Rainbow Bridge.

The unexpected arrows sowed confusion among the bestial trolls. For an instant they faltered. Tyr seized the moment and threw himself upon them. Before the monsters knew what was happening, his sword left three more lying in their fiery blood.

Still there were too many. Tyr was forced back as the monsters remembered their anger. Even with Bjorn's arrows to aid his sword, he knew they couldn't prevail. For every troll he dropped, another climbed out from the lava pools.

Suddenly the heat of Muspelheim vanished. Tyr saw his breath turn to frost and felt the sweat on his brow freeze. A broad smile stretched across his face. Lorelei!

From the shard of Niffleheim ice, a blast of intense cold rippled away from Lorelei. Many of the magma trolls caught in the surge were frozen solid by it, transformed from vicious beasts into immobile statues. More importantly, the magic inundated the lava pools, cooling them instantly and coating them in a layer of solid rock too thick for more of the monsters to break through. The freezing tide pushed onward, turning plumes of fire into crystallized formations and plastering the walls with frost.

Tyr wasn't certain how far the magic had spread, but it

was enough that its power had engulfed the gate's guardians. Some of the magma trolls had been spared the worst of the blast; he thought perhaps Lorelei had focused the power away so that he wouldn't be frozen as well. Though a half-dozen of the brutes remained, their bodies had been slowed by the spell, their molten blood cooled by the ice of Niffleheim. When Tyr met their attack, he found them easily vanquished.

Lorelei shivered in her armor as she returned the shard to her satchel. Bjorn hurried over to her and set his wolfskin over her shoulders to warm her. She smiled at him. "Could you imagine someone catching cold in Muspelheim?" she quipped.

"There's a good many magma trolls thinking the same thing right now," Bjorn told her.

Tyr turned away from the last of his adversaries and nodded to Lorelei. "Your spell might not have been as speedy as I'd have liked, but I'll not argue with its effectiveness." He waved his sword at the frozen trolls.

"You were splendid," Lorelei told him. "Your bravery was the equal of Thor's." She beamed. Tyr saw a flash of resentment in Bjorn's eyes. It was only there for a moment, as though he immediately realized how unreasonable it was to envy the attention she was showing him.

"I'd have traded bravery for a defensible position," Tyr said.

Lorelei laughed. "You make light of your courage, but you've shown me your mettle just the same." She shrugged out of Bjorn's cloak and came towards Tyr. "Why, your sword isn't even stained!" she gasped, pointing at the weapon. "That is no Uru blade. Surely a son of Odin would carry no lesser sword. What manner of weapon is this?"

Tyr hefted the gleaming sword and held it high. "This is Tyrsfang," he said. "Fashioned from a tooth lost by Fenris when it took my hand. Frigga took it to the dwarves to tool into a blade and then brought it to the light elves to weave their spells upon it." He flourished it in a sweeping display. "There is no other like it in the Nine Worlds. The people of Midgard have patterned their best swords after this one and prize them more dearly than a chest of gold."

Lorelei smiled at him again. "Yes, there is no other blade like it," she said. "Nor is there any other like the warrior who bears it."

"We should be going." Tyr awkwardly tried to change the subject. "Magic can be capricious, and we don't know when the trolls will start to thaw. When they do, it would be best if we were well on our way to Surtur's fortress."

Lorelei bowed her head in agreement, but there was a strange sparkle in her eyes when she looked at Tyr. Not so those of Bjorn. As he retrieved his cloak from the ground, the resentment was back in his gaze.

This time it was much slower to fade.

EIGHT

As he walked beyond the area frozen by Lorelei's spell, Tyr felt the withering heat slam into him like a physical force. His lungs felt like the bellows in a forge, drawing in the mephitic vapors of the flame. The ground was hot under his touch, and when he brushed against any of the rocky outcroppings that dotted the landscape, he found them almost blistering in their intensity. For absolute hostility, he doubted anything could match Muspelheim's vicious atmosphere.

The gate to Bifrost proved to be situated in a winding maze of jagged fissures, and as the three Asgardians progressed, the passages became narrower and with many divergences. Each time they took a turn, Bjorn made certain to score the rock with his axe and mark their path so they would know if they'd doubled back on their own trail.

"We'll not be led astray," Lorelei assured them. She drew from the satchel a curious object. It resembled a jewel box, but was fashioned from some ruddy, opaque stone unlike anything Tyr had seen before. Her fingers plucked at some hidden catch and the top of the box sprang open to reveal a sliver of black metal far stranger than the material of the box. It seemed to smolder with an inner fire, little ripples of orange glowing deep within it. The sliver was kept fast to the box by little chains. As he looked on it, Tyr was intrigued to see the sliver struggle and twist against the chains. Lorelei turned, moving around until the black metal was quiet.

"That is the direction we must follow," she declared, snapping the lid shut.

"You seem certain of that," Tyr commented. "Was it not you who warned that magic was unreliable?"

Lorelei rapped her finger against the box. "This we can depend on. A tiny shard from Twilight stolen by a dark elf sorcerer long ago. It strives to rejoin Surtur's sword. Now that we're in Muspelheim, it can be trusted to always point true to where the blade is."

Bjorn turned from marking the wall with his axe. "Then all we need do is let that box guide us," he said.

"Keep at your work," Tyr told the huntsman. "If anything happens to that box, we'll be grateful for those marks." He frowned as another idea occurred to him. "We'll need to come back this way once we've taken the sword. The enchantment will be useless to lead us after we've got what we came here for."

"I hadn't thought of that," Bjorn said. He dragged the edge of the axe against the stone, striving to leave a mark deep enough that it couldn't be missed.

Tyr glanced at Lorelei. He was surprised that she hadn't thought of this problem. "We have to be prepared for the journey back as well as the one ahead."

She nodded. "Quite right. I'm fortunate to have your foresight here to help me." She pointed to the defile before them. "When Bjorn is finished leaving his mark, we should head this way. You'll forgive my urging haste, but I don't know how long my spell will hold the magma trolls."

It was a valid concern to have, but Tyr couldn't shake a feeling that Lorelei was being evasive. Trying to cover an error in judgment on her part, or was it something more? Whatever the reason, he knew he wasn't going to learn anything standing around in these sweltering fissures. "I'll take the lead," he told his companions. "When we come to the next crossroads, we'll consult the box again." He locked eyes with Lorelei. "To ensure we stay on the right path," he added.

The trio continued deeper into the winding maze, stopping frequently so that Bjorn could scratch the walls. Tyr began to wonder if there would ever be an end to these forlorn passages, but at last they turned a corner and saw the land open up before them.

"So this is Muspelheim," Bjorn muttered, dread in his tone.

Indeed, the vista ahead of them was a forbidding sight. Great mountains loomed against the horizon, their slopes black as pitch and barren of life. Volcanoes ejected fiery spumes into the sky, illuminating the range with a hellish light. Enormous clouds of smoke blotted out most of the stars, swirling about like aerial tempests as the eruptions below pulled and pushed them. Between themselves and the mountains was a vast plain, its surface gouged by deep valleys and mottled with clumps of jagged stone. Glowing rivers of lava coursed through the desolation, steam seething from the streams as they gnawed at the rocky banks that enclosed them. Tyr noted an eerie phenomenon at once beautiful and horrible. In a parody of rainfall, cinders drifted down across the land, each flaming mote sizzling as it lighted upon the ground.

"Glory is a prize that belongs to the brave," Tyr encouraged his friend. "The more dangerous the road, the more glory waits at the end of it."

Lorelei consulted the fragment of Twilight, watching until it grew still. "In that direction we'll find Surtur's stronghold," she said, pointing off to their right. Her expression was apologetic when she explained one thing the imprisoned shard couldn't tell her. "I don't know how far we have to go."

"We might get a better idea if we tried to fix the exact position," Tyr suggested. He waved his hand off to their right. "Track along this way and gauge any difference in the shard's bearing."

"A tactician's notion," Lorelei said. "But I think you misjudge how much the shard can reveal. Think of it as a lodestone on Midgard, ever pointing northward, but never telling how far north is." She gazed out across the bleak, forbidding waste. "We know the direction we must follow. We would only squander time trying to tease the shard into telling us more."

"The time will grow no shorter if we stand here and talk about it," Tyr replied, irked to have Lorelei reject his idea out of hand. His annoyance troubled him more than the rebuff, for he couldn't explain why so slight a thing had irritated him. "The sooner we find the sword, the sooner we can be quit of this infernal place."

Bjorn nodded his agreement. "I'm truthful enough to say I'll be glad to breathe the clean air of Asgard again." His eyes darted to the side, his mouth curling with embarrassment. When he looked at Tyr again, he had a request to make. "You led the way through the passages, let me take over now."

Tyr could guess the reason for Bjorn's awkwardness. Truth could be injudicious, and he repented exhibiting anything that might be confused for timidity before Lorelei. It wasn't lost on Tyr that she'd made a definite impression on his friend, and Bjorn was eager to make the best show of his mettle that he could. His only fear was that Bjorn was deluding himself in his ambitions. He didn't want to see Bjorn hurt, but neither could Tyr think of a way to turn the wolfhunter's heart from the hope that had planted itself there.

"Take the lead," Tyr said. "Keep your bow at the ready. There are worse things than magma trolls that prowl Muspelheim."

Bjorn almost beamed with gratitude as he tucked his axe under his belt and took up his bow. He glanced back once at Lorelei and then set off at a jog across the burning plain. Tyr wanted his friend to get far enough away that they'd be able to react to any danger he discovered before it was upon them, yet not so far that they lost sight of the huntsman.

"He's most eager to help," Lorelei said as they watched Bjorn.

"He's young," Tyr replied. "The young are always eager.

They haven't let cynicism rot their enthusiasm. They haven't seen enough of life yet to be jaded by its disappointments." He gave her a sharp look. "I think he's smitten with you."

Lorelei laughed. "I think half the men I meet are smitten with me, whether I encourage them or not."

Tyr's expression grew more severe. "Don't encourage him," he cautioned. "Remember that he's young and the young are more easily injured by such things."

She touched her fingers to her lips and held them against Tyr's chest. "For your sake, I promise this." She lowered her eyes and her voice grew soft. "My own heart is already swayed by another."

Tyr thought of her long pursuit of Thor, but the way she spoke now made him doubt it was his brother she was referencing. For a moment he wondered, but he quickly dissuaded himself of the thought. Gently he drew her fingers away. "We need to start after Bjorn before he gets too far away," he said.

Lorelei gave him another of her enigmatic smiles. "You know best what needs to be done," she said. "I can only point out the path. It is you who must show the way."

NINE

Hours passed, and the infernal land of Muspelheim grew, to Tyr's mind, only worse. Even for an Aesir it was an effort to sustain his lungs with the searing air. His shoulders were blistered by the cinders that drifted down from the sooty sky, the smell of his own singed hair was ever in his nose now. He suspected Lorelei had some sort of enchantment that reduced the malignity of the atmosphere for her, as her hair and skin bore no blemish from the flaming rain. He didn't ask her about it, however. If it was any kind of magic she could or intended to share, certainly she would have offered to extend its influence onto her companions. Perhaps, he considered, it was a finite resource and to bestow it on them all would stretch the sorcery too thin to be of use to anyone.

Bjorn was maintaining the same loping trot regardless of what Muspelheim threw at him. Whether his boots carried him over a blasted plateau of black sand or over rugged ground strewn with volcanic rock, he didn't let his pace falter. Tyr was impressed by his endurance, for he knew his friend was used to the wintry forests of Varinheim and must be feeling the withering attentions of Muspelheim even worse than he was.

The range of grim mountains seemed just as distant as ever, something that made Tyr's heart heavy with frustration. "Surtur is of the race of giants," he said to Lorelei. "The fire giant, they call him."

"This is well known," Lorelei replied. "Of old it is said he fought Ymir and in their struggle they created the Nine Worlds." She gave him a curious look. "You speak as though it is important that he is a giant."

"It is," Tyr said. "Whether in Jotunheim, Niffleheim, Asgard, or Midgard, giants favor mountains to make their homes in." He gestured with his shield at the distant peaks. "I think the shard is leading us to those. I think that is where Surtur has built his stronghold."

The theory was obviously not to Lorelei's liking. "Then we've much farther to go," she said with a sigh.

"And just as much ground to cross on our return," Tyr reminded her. "Only the going back will be even harder. So far, we've not run into any of Surtur's fire demons, but they're certain to pursue us after I've wrested Twilight from their master's grasp."

Lorelei frowned at his statement. "Perhaps there will be no need to face Surtur," she said. She winced when she saw the surprise her words provoked. "Is it so very important that you fight the fire giant as your brother did Ymir?"

Tyr couldn't hide the disappointment the question provoked. Of course it would be a proud moment to return to Odin's hall and proclaim such a mighty feat. Then it would be Thor who would be envious of *him* for a change. At the same time, there were more important concerns than his own pride. "Whatever promises the surest way to take Twilight," he said. "If it can be done without alerting the fire giant, so much the better."

"It can," Lorelei insisted. "Twilight has been broken and reforged many times. Surtur ever seeks to make the sword more deadly for his eventual battle with… your father. When it is being forged anew, his minions kidnap smiths from among the dwarves to labor over the weapon. Dwarves have been disappearing from Nidavellir. That could mean Twilight is once again being worked upon."

"So we might sneak into the forge and steal the sword before Surtur knows we're there." Tyr found the plot anything but valiant. It was the scheme of a thief, not a warrior. But the thought of what it would mean to Odin if Twilight were brought up from Muspelheim was more than sufficient to overcome his repugnance. Just as he'd agreed to using magic to get past Heimdall, he now agreed to Lorelei's strategy. "It would have been best if you'd told me this at your castle."

"Yes," Lorelei conceded, regret in her voice, "but I couldn't take the risk that you'd say no."

Before Tyr could speak, his attention was drawn to Bjorn. The wolfhunter was heading into an area of thick fog. The sight set a tremor of alarm rushing through him. Where in Muspelheim could there be moisture enough to cause such a fog? The question vexed him, and his uneasiness only increased when Bjorn walked further and his shape was lost in the thick mist.

"We need to close the distance with Bjorn," Tyr said. He started jogging toward the fog, Lorelei keeping pace beside him.

"What's wrong?" she asked, some of his alarm passing into her.

"I don't know... yet." Tyr encouraged her into a brisk run when they still failed to spot Bjorn through the curtain of mist.

When they reached the fog, Tyr found the answer to at least part of his question. Though it seemed like some sort of mist, there wasn't any moisture to it, only a bitter heat. Yet it felt heavy and stifling, not dry and smoky like a fume. He thought only a place such as Muspelheim could produce such a contradictory emanation, both humid and parching.

Lorelei reeled back from the withering miasma. She tried to draw Tyr away. "I have to find Bjorn," he told her, pulling from her grip. "Stay here," he added before marching deeper into the fog.

Every step was more painful than the one that preceded it. Compared to the atmosphere within the mephitic mist, the normal heat of Muspelheim was like a cool spring morn. Tyr felt as though he were being cooked from without and within, each breath scorching his lungs. He could only imagine how Bjorn had been impacted and he bemoaned the foolish bravado that had made his friend press on when he should have relented and turned back.

"Bjorn!" Tyr called out, wincing as he drew a measure of the searing mist into his mouth. He kept looking at the ground, certain the huntsman must have collapsed under the boiling intensity of the steaming mist. "Bjorn!"

The sound of footsteps behind him brought Tyr spinning around. Until that moment it hadn't occurred to him that anything might be lurking in the miasma, that some denizen of Muspelheim might use the mist to hide itself while it searched for prey. But the sounds he heard didn't belong to some monstrous fiend. Instead he found himself looking at Lorelei. It was obvious from her appearance that whatever spell fended off the falling cinders wasn't doing her any good in the boiling fog. That made him appreciate her following after him even more.

"Did you find him?" she gasped.

"Not yet," Tyr said, shaking his head. "He's here," he declared, "and I will find him. I'll not leave a friend to cook in this inferno."

Bold words and a bold intention, but as they continued Tyr thought them foolish. The heat was only getting worse and the deeper they went the more trouble they'd have getting out again. Then a thought came to him. "Lorelei, the ice from Niffleheim! When you used it against the magma trolls it turned the air cool."

She reached into her satchel and withdrew the glacial fragment. A dour look crossed her face. "Tyr, I can use this to help us, but without knowing where Bjorn is…" Lorelei shook her head. "He'd take the full brunt of the spell. Frozen as solid as the trolls were."

Tyr blanched at the warning. "Keep it ready," he said. "We'll wait as long as we can. Until we can endure no more." He felt the weight of that decision as he moved deeper into the fog. They could save themselves, but doing so would doom his friend.

The mephitic miasma only grew more intense the farther into it they went. Tyr felt it was impossible Bjorn could have come this far and endured so much, however determined he was. They must have passed the huntsman somewhere along the way. Or else there really was some kind of beast prowling the fog looking for prey.

"Lorelei…" Tyr called to her. He was about to tell her to cast her spell when his eyes caught a dark shape just ahead in the mist. He snapped his mouth closed so quickly he bit his tongue, afraid he'd speak before he could stop the words. He dashed ahead and a sense of jubilation filled him. The shape was Bjorn! The steaming mist had finally exhausted him, but somehow he'd remained standing.

"Keep him close to me," Lorelei told Tyr when she joined them. "And keep yourself near too," she added in a less severe tone. When she was satisfied that both men were close enough to avoid the freezing effects of the ice, she held it before her and made the same arcane gestures with her other hand.

At once a brisk chill wrapped itself around Tyr. Nothing he'd ever experienced was as luxurious as that icy blast after the sweltering torment of the miasma. He breathed deeply and laughed when he saw frost drift away from his mouth. Bjorn revived, stirring in his arms as the wonderful cold surrounded them.

Bjorn gazed up at Tyr. For a moment his eyes were unfocused, dazed by his ordeal. Then an awkward smile flickered onto his face. "I think I underestimated how tough this was going to be." He clasped Tyr's arm, his expression becoming intense. "You took a risk coming after me."

Tyr shook his head. "A risk taken to save a friend isn't a choice," he said. "Besides, we'd have needed to use magic to get through anyway." He gestured to the landscape around them.

The effect upon the miasma was even more amazing. A great swathe of the fog clattered to the ground, transformed into snow. Tyr was stunned by the incredible sight. Snow in the fiery wastes of Muspelheim. So much of the mist had been frozen that they could see through to the other side.

"How long will it remain frozen?" Tyr asked.

Lorelei replaced the ice in her satchel. "Perhaps Amora could tell you. I only know that right now it is the way you see it. Any moment and it could start to melt."

"Then let's get moving," Tyr said. He held onto Bjorn when the wolfhunter would take his place ahead of them again. "No, we'll keep together for a time. Make sure that none of us has been unduly affected by this experience."

"I'm fighting fit now," Bjorn insisted.

"Maybe so," Tyr said. "But you'll be even fitter if you take it easy for a little while."

Bjorn wrested free from him and started trudging through the snow. He kept his pace slow, so Tyr knew his friend wasn't trying to put distance between them. He took that for a good sign, but he was disturbed by the sullen look in the huntsman's eyes.

"You'll have to talk to Bjorn," Tyr whispered to Lorelei. "I'm afraid he'll push himself too far trying to earn your favor."

Lorelei gave him a weary shrug. "If I say anything, it would just make him try even harder."

Tyr sighed. He knew how headstrong Bjorn could be. There was too much logic in Lorelei's argument to discount it.

TEN

Bjorn waited for his companions beside a great mound of broken rock. When Tyr approached him, he saw why the wolfhunter had paused. Before them was a deep canyon that stretched away for miles in every direction. The floor of the canyon was pockmarked with craters, many of which flickered with the glow of fires smoldering in their depths. Around, between, and through the craters molten streams of lava crisscrossed the canyon, distorting the air around them with their heat.

"It'll be a hard thing getting around that," Bjorn said.

Lorelei joined them, once more consulting the sliver from Twilight. "Around or through, we've got to cross it," she said, snapping the box shut and returning it to her satchel.

Tyr studied the terrain, weighing the value of trying to find a way around against the time that would be lost doing so. "Through is faster," he declared. He pointed at great slabs of stone that stretched across the lava streams. "It strikes me that there are too many bridges to be some freak of the elements."

"Surtur's minions?" Bjorn scowled at the idea. "If so then we're well into the fire giant's territory. We'll have to be even more careful of his spies."

"We've run that risk from the moment we entered Muspelheim," Lorelei said. "Surtur might be too confident in the ability of his trolls to keep back any intruders."

"Just the same, we need to be cautious," Tyr took up Bjorn's argument. "These bridges are the first evidence of construction we've seen. Until we have reason to think otherwise, we need to assume the builders are near."

"Do we go around?" Bjorn asked.

Tyr cast his gaze across the canyon, now trying to spot any outpost where sentries might have been placed. He focused on those vantages that would make the most tactical sense to place sentinels. He didn't see anything, but that didn't mean they weren't there. The far side of the canyon was an even better prospect. From there an observer could watch them as easily as they could see the canyon floor from this end.

"That would mean time." Tyr shook his head. "The more time we spend trying to reach Surtur's fortress, the greater the risk of discovery. We might be exposed crossing that desolation, but the time we save will lessen our risk overall." He gave Bjorn a frank look. "Neither choice is a good one, it is simply deciding which carries less danger."

"Then if you think the direct route is better, that is what we'll do." Lorelei shifted the satchel on her shoulder and came to the edge of the canyon. "There seems to be some sort of path over there."

Bjorn looked to where she pointed. "It looks to come

up to this level a couple hundred yards to the right." He removed an arrow from his quiver and nocked it to his bow. "Stay here and I'll see how it looks." There was eagerness in his step as he set off. Tyr knew his friend was hoping to redeem himself from the near disaster in the steaming miasma.

"Just scout," he told the huntsman. "Should you find that guards have been set, come back and tell us." Bjorn made no reply to Tyr's words.

"You don't think he could handle a few guards?" Lorelei wondered as she watched Bjorn stalk towards the trailhead.

"I worry he might not get them all," Tyr stated. "If guards have been left here to watch the path, we can't let any of them slip away and give warning."

Tense moments passed while Tyr and Lorelei listened for the least sound that might indicate that Bjorn had been spotted by some sentinel on the path below. When he dropped below the lip and started down into the canyon, Tyr was even more keyed to the possibility of conflict. Minutes passed and no sound rose from below. Finally, Bjorn popped his head up and motioned for them to join him.

"There are tracks," Bjorn reported, pointing at marks in the scorched dirt. "Something that walks on two legs. Bigger than a man but not as heavy as a troll." He scratched his beard and added, "I don't know how recent they are, but it looks like this trail has seen a lot of use."

"All the more reason for haste," Tyr said. "We move down and across the canyon before whoever is using this path comes back." His decision made, he put action to words and started off down the side of the canyon wall. Lorelei and Bjorn followed his lead. At each bend in the trail Tyr almost expected to see fire demons lying in wait for them. Strangely, he regretted it when his worry didn't manifest. At least a fight would have relieved the anxious expectancy that had sunk its hooks into him.

They reached the floor of the canyon without incident. Bjorn waved his hand at the far wall, picking out for Tyr a trail climbing up it that was very much like the one they'd just left. "No need to consult the box," the huntsman said. "Until we're out of the canyon there's only one way to go."

"I suppose you know the best way across?" Lorelei asked, a trace of irritation in her tone.

Bjorn pointed at tracks in the dirt. "We keep following these. Whatever they did to get across, we just keep in their footsteps."

Tyr would have suggested the same strategy. When campaigning in enemy terrain, it was usually helpful to follow a foe's example. "You're better at tracking," Tyr complimented his friend. "Take the lead."

The bottom of the canyon was even more unforgiving than it had seemed from above. The creatures in whose footsteps they followed had picked their way around the worst of the craters and rock piles, but even so there were many places where, to keep on their track, the Asgardians were forced to climb into holes that reeked of sulfur and scramble up heaps of jagged stone.

Finally, they reached one of the bridges across the lava streams. Closer to the span, Tyr could see that it was unquestionably carved by tools. Rough and raw as it was, the causeway was still an artificial construction, recalling to him the menhirs and megaliths erected by the people of Midgard.

The haze of heat billowing up from the roiling lava was intense. Bjorn recoiled from the searing aura and had to nerve himself before climbing out onto the bridge. He tamped his foot against the stone to test its stability, pleased to find the slab remained firm. It was clear it would take much more than their weight to dislodge it.

"I'll cross first," Bjorn told them. He slung his bow over his shoulder and set off. Tyr watched him intently while also trying to keep his eyes on the other side of the stream. When the huntsman was halfway across, he noted a strange undulation in the lava. Tyr focused upon the disturbance, but it wasn't repeated. A moment later Bjorn was hailing them from the other side. "It's safe."

Some indefinable sense of unease made Tyr less certain of that than his friend. "Keep your bow ready," he told him. "We're going to cross together."

"I can manage for myself," Lorelei started to object as Tyr led her over the span.

"This is a bad place to linger," Tyr said. "If anyone… anything… were intending an ambush, here is where it would offer the best advantage to them. The sooner we put some distance between the bridge and us, the better it will suit me." His eyes kept drifting back to the stream that flowed beneath the span. Once again, he saw a weird undulation. This time it didn't fade away, but instead seemed to multiply. Four different spots below them were writhing, shifting with motion that went against the stream.

"Move! Now!" Tyr shouted to Lorelei, certain that danger would soon be upon them. His fear was almost instantly borne out. Up from the fiery flow an enormous tendril erupted. It shook in the shimmering air, lava dripping from it in blazing blobs that sizzled upon the bridge. The thing was a gigantic tentacle twenty feet long, crimson speckled with yellow, the great suckers along its underside lined with jagged black hooks that might have been carved from obsidian. Soon after the first tentacle emerged, two others surfaced and writhed in the air.

"Lava kraken!" Lorelei shuddered, paralyzed with dread. On the shore, Bjorn was gripped by the same debilitating terror. Tyr could feel a numbing fear trying to overwhelm his own mind. He knew it was more than just his emotions, but some horrible emanation from the beast itself. Stubbornly he shook the influence off. Removing his hand from Lorelei's arm, he snatched Tyrsfang from its sheath.

The sword flashed not a moment too soon. The kraken's tentacles were already reaching out for its paralyzed victims. Tyr swatted aside the coil reaching for him with his shield, hearing the metal sizzle as the lava-coated tendril struck against it. Then his blade was chopping down into the tentacle snaking toward Lorelei. The gleaming edge raked across it, his Aesir strength powering it through the massive trunk. The grasping tentacle was cleaved in twain, its severed end slamming down on the bridge and squirming in mindless confusion.

Tyr's attack broke whatever terrifying influence the kraken exuded. Lorelei rallied at once and reached into her satchel. "The ice of Niffleheim!" she shouted.

"It has me!" Bjorn cried out from the shore. Without someone to guard him while he was paralyzed, the wolfhunter had been caught by one of the tentacles. Only the heat-resistant mail he wore kept him from cooking in the beast's grip. The wolfskin, unprotected by the armor, smoked in the kraken's clutch.

"Get to the shore!" Tyr shoved Lorelei forward. More tentacles were emerging from the stream now and if she remained on the bridge, she'd be easy prey to them before she could work her spell. Nor could he remain to guard her if he were to have any chance at saving Bjorn.

Satisfied that Lorelei was on her way to the shore, Tyr made a standing leap for the tendril that held his friend. The tentacle was already dragging him back to the molten stream. Bjorn tried to reach his axe, but his arms were pinned by the constricting bands of flesh wrapped around him.

"You'll not have him!" Tyr cried as he hurtled down. Tyrsfang ripped into the crimson flesh, slashing through it and sending its severed bulk crashing to the shore. He had a glimpse of Bjorn freeing himself from the dying mass as its strength fled from it. No more than that brief look, however, for almost the moment his own feet touched the shore he was seized, caught in the crushing grip of still another tendril.

The armor he'd taken from Lorelei's castle resisted the constrictions of the kraken, but Tyr was powerless to keep from being lifted off the ground by the beast. His sword was pinned against his side; the best he could manage with it was a slow sawing motion that bit through the monster's pulpy flesh far too slowly. The heat around him was of such fury he knew he would succumb quickly if he couldn't extricate himself.

Even that fate looked doubtful. The molten stream was churning again. Now there were a dozen tentacles breaking the surface and, close beside the bridge, the gargantuan bulk of the lava kraken's body. Tyr could see its saucer-shaped eyes studying him with hungry intensity. The air sacs to either side of its body expanded and popped in a weird parody of a roar. The sharp beak, much like the hooks on its suckers, seemed shaped from obsidian rather than bone. It gaped ever wider, eager for the Aesir morsel that had inflicted harm upon its limbs.

The tentacle gripping Tyr started down towards that greedy maw, but before it could reach its objective, a blast of glacial cold engulfed him. He could see the coil tighten, though his armor kept him from feeling its pressure. The crimson flesh became dull and ridged, the lava dripping from it hardened into a black crust. The rest of the kraken was even more afflicted, quick-frozen by the arcane surge. The surface of the stream was turned into a rock-like scum. The bridge itself creaked and groaned as it shifted between the heat of the lava and the chill of Lorelei's spell.

The freezing surge chilled Tyr to the core of his being. Most Asgardians would have been turned to ice by the shard's magic, but the mighty legacy of an Odinson was within his veins. As Thor had endured the frigid exhalations of Ymir, so Tyr was likewise able to defy the power of Niffleheim. While the kraken froze, its captive remained active. He worked his sword viciously against the tentacle that held him. The freezing blast had made it brittle, and he was able to manage much better than he had before. Still, it seemed much too slow. Held in the kraken's grip, he could feel the strength that still pulsed through the beast. He looked across to the shore. Bjorn had his axe out and was testing the solidity of the frozen stream. It seemed he intended to come across and help him.

"Hurry!" Tyr called to the wolfhunter. "It isn't dead."

His shout to Bjorn appeared to rattle him. He glanced up at Tyr, then at the frozen lava. A moment before, Bjorn had been ready to risk crossing the doubtful surface, now he appeared timid. Or was it something more than that?

"Help Tyr!" Lorelei shouted. At her cry, Tyr saw a look of bitter resentment flash across his friend's face. He drew his foot back from the stream. Then an expression of disgust came upon him and he started running toward the tentacle holding Tyr.

A pulse of animation rippled through the frozen limb. Tyr was nearly halfway through the brittle flesh, but he knew now that he'd never cut completely through. There wasn't any more time. "Get back!" he bellowed to Bjorn. "It's too late!"

The frosty sheen that had encased the kraken steamed away as the monster broke Lorelei's spell. The creature's eyes glared hatefully at her and its entire being shifted in color, darkening to a sooty hue veined with bands of angry orange. The beast propelled itself forward, crumbling the rocky shell that covered the stream and exposing the molten flow beneath.

"You don't learn, do you?" Lorelei taunted the kraken,

raising the Niffleheim ice and repeating the magical gestures with her hands.

She'd made a mistake, however, for the kraken had indeed learned. As she unleashed another freezing blast upon the creature, its body jetted a cloud of smoke and embers into the air around it. Tyr coughed as the blistering fume billowed over him, his body scalded as the burning smog engulfed him. What he suffered was provoked by the least degree of the kraken's expulsion, for the coil that held him was raised above that searing cloud.

From his vantage, Tyr could see what followed. Lorelei was shocked by the lava kraken's resistance. She tried to compensate by loosing another blast from the glacial shard, but before she could, one of the monster's tentacles whipped out from the smoke. It struck her and tried to latch on, but the scaly armor she wore refused the hooks any kind of grip. As the coil sought to lift her into the air, she slipped from its grasp and fell to the ground. When she landed, the impact jarred the chunk of ice from her hand. Panic gripped her as it went rolling away towards the lava stream. Before she could reach it, the precious ice fell into the molten channel, taking with it its invaluable magic!

Bjorn rushed to Lorelei's aid, hacking away at the tentacle as it tried to grab her again. More tendrils were groping towards them now, slithering from the smoke like a nest of vipers. Tyr could see that they would swiftly be surrounded and overwhelmed.

Straining himself to the utmost, Tyr pushed against the tentacle gripping him. The halfsevered flesh was unequal to the god's strength and ripped apart. Tyr was ready for the sudden jolt as he freed himself, stabbing his sword down into the stump and holding fast so that he wouldn't be pitched into the stream below. Bracing his legs against the writhing tendril, he steeled himself for another mighty leap across the chaotic battlefield. He saw an opportunity, though it would expose him to tremendous risk.

Using the kraken's truncated limb as a fulcrum, Tyr sprang back to the stone bridge. Unlike the monster, the span remained brittle from Lorelei's spell, and a frightening groan shuddered through it when Tyr landed upon it. A grim smile filled his face. It was precisely this hazard that his ploy depended upon.

"Ho, slinking monster! Have you lost your appetite for me?" Tyr taunted the kraken. It cared nothing for his words, but when he hurled a chunk of stone he had cut from the bridge into one of its eyes, he had its total attention. Popping its air sacs in rapid, angry spurts, the beast undulated through the molten stream toward him. Tentacles whipped and slashed at him, but he fended them off with his shield and Tyrsfang.

"A little closer, beast," Tyr muttered as the kraken surged nearer. He ducked another cascade of grasping tentacles and brought Tyrsfang slashing down upon the bridge.

Without the strain placed upon it by Lorelei's spell and the kraken's fiery exhalations, Tyr might not have been able to break the massive slab as he did. In its present condition, however, it splintered under his blade. He jumped for the shore as the bridge collapsed beneath him. The monster, its snapping beak poised just beneath the span, wasn't so agile. The severed halves of the immense stone came crashing down into it, slamming into its savage bulk. The central mass of its body was driven back under the molten stream. The tentacles continued to flash and writhe in the air for a time, then they too sank into the flowing lava.

Tyr rose from the ground and watched as the monster disappeared. Lorelei and Bjorn rushed over to him.

"I lost the shard from Niffleheim!" Lorelei cried to him.

"Its magic was powerful, but its loss can't be helped," Tyr said. "We'll find a way to prevail without its enchantments."

"Your defeat of the kraken was spectacular!" Bjorn congratulated him. Tyr gave him a dark look.

"You hesitated to help me when I was in the kraken's grip," Tyr told the huntsman. "I would know why."

"Is this necessary?" Lorelei interjected, but Tyr waved aside her objections. He wanted to hear an answer from Bjorn.

"I was afraid the surface wouldn't hold me," Bjorn said after some hesitance.

Tyr shook his head. "I've seen you dash across a frozen lake to save a drowning dog without breaking stride," he reminded Bjorn. "Don't tell me now that you're a coward."

Bjorn bristled at the word, but he accepted it just the same. "We aren't all gods. My courage isn't without its limits."

The words still rang untrue to Tyr's ears. Whatever had taken hold of Bjorn for that moment when their eyes met while Tyr was caught in the tentacle was something so dark that he preferred to claim cowardice than confess to it. Tyr glanced over at Lorelei. He knew what had stirred that resentment of him. What he didn't know was how deep that jealousy ran, or whether it was wholly a creation of his friend's heart or if it had been placed there by enchantment.

"The hero is the one who strives beyond their limits," Tyr said, his tone sympathetic. "I've seen you do heroic deeds before. I know you will do so again."

Strangely, Bjorn took more umbrage from his sympathy than his scorn. "I'll scout the way ahead," he said as he turned away and started walking across the crater-pocked ground.

"I am sorry a rift has grown between you," Lorelei told Tyr, placing her hand on his shoulder.

"Are you?" Tyr asked. He didn't wait for an answer, but started after his friend. Magic! If it weren't for sorcery he'd be surer of how things were. Whether Lorelei was influencing Bjorn with her spells.

And whether those same spells were slowly working on him, for Tyr was beginning to discover he was developing his own admiration for Lorelei.

€LEVEN

Tyr reasoned that several days had passed before they began to close with the mountains. Time in Muspelheim was a nebulous quality, for no sun rose to illuminate the sky. It was a world of perpetual night lit by the fury of volcanoes and the plumes of flame that flickered up from the earth. The only way to judge how long they'd been traveling was the fatigue that set into their bodies. Even for Tyr, there came a limit to his stamina, though he could push himself far in excess of even many Aesir and Vanir.

Necessity demanded they rest at intervals. Whenever Bjorn found a likely spot that appeared defensible, Tyr would call a halt. Such places were too infrequent not to take advantage of when they appeared. Here they could keep watch for the creatures that roamed Muspelheim. Twice they'd met horrible monstrosities somewhere between a giant crab and a spider that sprang at them from concealed burrows. They'd battled a pack of furless red wolves, huge brutes with fire burning in their mouths. Many times since, they'd heard the seething howls of more packs off in the distance. Then there was the vast crawling thing that looked to Tyr as though a bog of pitch had lifted itself from its mire to seek out a new resting place. Fortunately, that amorphous horror took no interest in them and had simply kept shambling off into the distance.

Their camps were "cold", though that term was itself bitterly ironic. The oppressive heat made the very thought of lighting a fire hateful and the perpetual glow that reflected down off the smoke clouds gave them all the light they needed. Provisions from Lorelei's castle were dispersed, but Tyr had to admonish his companions about drinking too freely of the water. Until they found some way to replenish their supply, they had to be cautious with what they had. Enough to maintain survival but not enough to quench thirst. Their food, at least, was a different matter. Bjorn had tried a steak cut from one of the wolves and while it had a burnt taste, he found it to be edible.

"At last we near Surtur's fortress." Lorelei sighed with relief as the mountains loomed before them.

"Aye, there is the fire giant's home," Tyr said. He pointed to a great volcano, its caldera aglow with the lava within, steam venting into the air. Around the lip of the cone, black walls and spires could be seen. "You can see his castle if you look a little down the mountain's slope."

Bjorn whistled. "The stronghold must be enormous if we can see it this far away."

Tyr was silent, his face somber. Bjorn's words worked both ways. "If we can see the castle, then those in its towers may see us. The closer we get, the more apt they are to spot us." He looked aside at Lorelei. "You spoke of a magic veil that could hide us."

Lorelei nodded slowly. She reached into her satchel and drew out a long bone flute. "The breath of the dragon Fafnir is trapped within here. When I blow into the flute, it will expel a cloud of smoke to hide us."

There was an anxiety in Lorelei's voice that disturbed Tyr. "Is there some weakness in the spell that worries you?"

Again Lorelei nodded. "The smoke will hide us, but I don't know for how long. I don't know if it will be enough to hide us until we reach the castle." Her fingers tightened about the enchanted flute. "There is a way to strengthen it, but I fear it would be unpalatable to you. I can draw the essence of living things into it to heighten the magic."

She was right. The idea was unpleasant. Sorcery wasn't viewed with suspicion by the Asgardians without good reason. There was always a price to be paid for magic. Sometimes the cost was minor, at other times it fell into abomination. Tyr wasn't sure where Lorelei's proposal fit into that scale. Only the prospect of saving his father prevented him from immediately rejecting the idea.

"Don't look at me." Bjorn meant it for a joke, but the laugh that followed his words was strained. It pained Tyr that his friend would have any doubt that he'd consider the wolfhunter's life as an option.

"The essence needn't come from a rational being," Lorelei assured them. "Anything with a life force. Bird, beast, or reptile, as long as its heart stirs blood through its veins." She tapped the flute against her palm. "Or whatever fiery ichor it is the denizens of Muspelheim possess." She looked up into the smoky sky. "Even those should suffice."

Tyr followed her gaze. Until she'd pointed them out to him, he'd been unaware there were birds soaring in and out of the smoke. At least he thought they were birds. Without anything to gauge how high above them they were, he couldn't judge their size, but it was still unsettling to know they'd been up there without his knowing.

"I could entice one down here," Lorelei offered. "In that school of magic, I surpass my sister. But I'll need both of you to be ready to strike the creature when it dives." She frowned and gave each of them a warning look. "My spell will fascinate only one of them, but I can't say how many others might follow it of their own accord."

"I won't let any of them touch you," Bjorn vowed. He nocked an arrow to his bow, ready to meet the descending birds.

"Let's hope the whole flock doesn't come down," Tyr said as he watched the clouds. The longer he looked, the more birds he spotted. "Or that those 'birds' don't turn out to be dragons when they get down here." He thought the chance of that was remote. He didn't know if Muspelheim had dragons, but if it did, he couldn't imagine them behaving any different to those of Asgard, Midgard, and Jotunheim. Dragons in those worlds despised the company of their own kind as keenly as they did a hero's sword.

Lorelei lifted her head and turned her face to the sky. She closed her eyes and squeezed arcane words from her pursed lips. For a moment there was no change, but then Tyr saw one of the soaring shapes wheel about and start to descend. This was the one enticed by her spell, but its movement was noticed by two others that turned and dove after it, perhaps thinking it had spotted some kind of prey and were eager to join in the meal.

"Three," Tyr called to Bjorn in case he hadn't spotted the diving birds. He braced his legs and tightened his hold on Tyrsfang, ready to meet the descending fliers.

As the creatures dove, Tyr saw that they weren't birds at all. They resembled bats more than anything, but their wings seemed to be formed from smoke and their bodies made of flickering flame. Each was as big as a horse and their mouths bulged from the sharp fangs jutting from their jaws. Their dangling feet were tipped with claws as long as knives and streaming behind each of them was a long, whip-like tail studded with bony spikes.

"Hai! See how an Asgardian fights!" Bjorn shouted at the bats. He loosed an arrow into the foremost of the creatures. The missile slammed into the chest, causing the flier to shudder in midair. But it didn't fall, and a moment after the arrow struck it, the shaft was burned away by the intense heat of its flaming body.

Bjorn sent a second arrow up at the monsters. This time he hit one of the shadowy wings. There must have been some physical structure behind the billowing smoke, for the bat screeched and its wing folded back against its body. The creature fell from the sky, slamming into the ground in a plume of black dust.

Tyr had no opportunity to see if the bat had been killed in the fall, for at that moment the other two were upon him. Long claws scraped against his shield as he met the attack. His sword lashed out, hacking a foot from his enemy. What spurted from the wound sizzled like acid on his armor and he wondered if all of this weren't in vain, if the essence of these beasts would be of any use to Lorelei's magic.

The other bat came at him from behind, its long claws raking against his armor, its barbed tail whipping around his leg. He was jerked from the ground as the creature climbed back into the sky, the tail snapping taut and lifting him away. Tyr hung beneath the monster while it ascended. With the ground growing more distant below him, he acted more by instinct than strategy. Bending in half, he brought his sword within reach of the bat's neck. A stroke from Tyrsfang sent the head leaping away. The tail grew slack, releasing him. He hurtled earthwards, the slain bat falling beside him as both crashed to earth from a height of some hundred feet.

The God of War landed in a plume of dust, the impact driving him several feet into the volcanic sand. He coughed as the gritty cloud filled his nose and mouth, spitting the taste of Muspelheim from his tongue. The shield lashed to his left arm had been utterly crumpled by the fall, crushed around the limb in a misshapen snarl of metal. To free himself from the impediment, he used Tyrsfang's keen edge to cut away the straps. It was a moment's work, but even that slight delay was repugnant. There was at least one more bat and neither of his companions were as hardy as a son of Odin.

Tyr scrambled from the crater left by his fall. He saw that Bjorn was vying with the bat whose foot he'd cut away. The huntsman was swinging his axe, trying to fend off the creature, but even keeping it at a distance wasn't enough to be safe from its ire. From its sizzling maw, the bat ejected molten blobs that splashed against Bjorn's mail. Tyr could see his friend's beard was burning from where some of the spatter had landed. It was only a matter of time before the bat's spittle struck a part of him that wasn't protected by enchanted armor.

Lorelei too was beset. Limping across the sand, hissing its malice, was the bat that had its wing broken by Bjorn's arrow. The injured creature whipped at her with its tail, trying to snag an arm or leg in its grasp. She kept circling around the beast, trying to keep its injured side towards her so that at least she would avoid being knocked flat by the bat's smoky wing. The Uru dirk smoldered from the fiery ichor she'd drawn from her foe.

Tyr made his decision quickly. The bat attacking Bjorn was the greater enemy, for it could carry one of them up into the clouds where the rest of the monstrous swarm flew. Even so, he recognized that a dirk was a poor weapon for Lorelei to be using against her adversary. The solution he saw was to strike each bat in turn from an unexpected quarter. Though it would mean exposing his friend to grave danger if he miscalculated.

"Bjorn! Help Lorelei!" Tyr shouted. The huntsman's devotion for her made him turn without a second's hesitation and rush to her aid. The moment he did, the bat darted at him. It was the last thing the creature did. Rushing at it from the side, Tyr drove his sword into its chest even as it charged at Bjorn's back. The massive brute crumpled to the ground, its smoky wings decaying into a skein of ash.

Bjorn dove upon the one-winged bat from behind in a leap that buried his axe deep in its back. The thing flailed beneath him, trying to dislodge him with the claw on its wing. Distracted by the man on its back, the creature left itself vulnerable to the woman at its fore. Taking her dirk in both hands, Lorelei lunged at the monster and slashed the tendons of its wing. A shiver rolled through the bat and it sprawled on the ground, writhing in pain.

"They know they've been in a fight now," Bjorn declared, standing over the injured bat.

"So do we," Tyr said as he glared down at the thrashing beast. He looked from Bjorn to Lorelei. "Do they possess what you need? If it can be helped, I'd rather not go through a repeat of this."

Lorelei had the bone flute in her hand again. She stepped over the dying bat and brought the flute to her lips. Swaying above the creature, she played an eerie melody on the instrument. From the beast's body, Tyr could see ribbons of smoke being drawn into the flute. Though it didn't actually change in size, he had the impression of the bat diminishing as Lorelei drained its essence. In a matter of moments, it was just another carcass sprawled in the ashy sand.

"This will suit our needs," Lorelei stated when she'd finished playing and the first bat was completely drained. She looked over to where the two killed by Tyr lay. "Once I've drawn off the essence of all three, then we'll be ready."

Tyr caught her arm as she started towards the second carcass. "All three?"

Lorelei shrugged. "If I act quickly, before their vitality completely evaporates, I can still harvest them." She fixed

Tyr with a stern look. "You seemed unsettled enough by the thought of enticing one down, I didn't want to disturb you even more by telling you I needed three."

"Then the other two didn't come down by accident?" Tyr demanded.

Bjorn slapped Tyr's hand from Lorelei's arm. "Of course Lorelei didn't plan for the other two to come down. Just because she needed three doesn't mean she wanted them all at once."

Lorelei showed Tyr an indulgent smile. "Since there are three, it would be foolish not to take advantage of them."

Tyr returned the smile with a scowl. "Accidents like this, Lorelei, are why I wonder how much you take after Amora."

"If I were at all like my sister, I wouldn't have to ask for your assistance," Lorelei snapped. "I would command, and you would obey." She turned from him and strode towards the second bat.

"You're unfair to say things like that," Bjorn growled at Tyr.

Tyr watched while Lorelei played the flute and called out the bat's essence. "Just keep watching the sky," he told the wolfhunter. "In case she decides she needs four bats."

TWELVE

Tyr judged they'd been marching for some hours since Lorelei harvested the essence of the bats. The mantle of smoke, the breath of Fafnir, surrounded them from above, below, and on every side. Except for the feel of solid ground beneath his feet, Tyr might have believed himself cast aloft in some dark and noxious cloud, for the musky and unforgettable stench of dragon was all around him. He wondered if the smell would seep into his hair as it had when he'd battled the worm Grafvinti. The smell had lingered so long that he'd shaved his mustache to limit the immediacy of the reek.

"The smell is a part of the smoke and will vanish with the smoke," Lorelei assured Tyr. She calmed his other worry, "Though we can see through the veil, there are none outside it who can see through to us."

"Even so, we must be wary," Tyr insisted. "A sentry might grow curious and come to investigate. Muspelheim is so filled with fire and smoke that it would be no deterrent to the beings that dwell here."

"On the contrary, it is precisely because smoke is so rife in Muspelheim that we'll be unnoticed," Lorelei insisted. "A sentry won't look twice at a bank of smoke billowing across the land. We will be dismissed as one of the rolling fires that sweep across the plateaus."

"We've seen many of those as we've traveled these lands," Bjorn pointed out. The huntsman was more ready than ever to take up Lorelei's cause in any debate.

"This spell is indeed our best way to approach the fortress," Tyr said to Lorelei, "but as you warned when we were still in your castle, it is reckless to depend too much on magic. Should the dragon's smoke fail us, should we be discovered, then you must try to make it back." His hand curled about Tyrsfang's grip. "I'll hold them back for as long as I can."

Bjorn shook his head and glowered at Tyr. "Even should the spell fail, it is I who should act as rearguard, not you. You are the son of Odin–"

"Which means I have the best chance of holding Surtur's minions if it comes to it." Tyr cut him off.

Lorelei stepped between the two. "This bickering over who will play at being the hero is pointless," she snapped. "The spell will *not* fail. We *will* enter the fortress." Her eyes stared past them, peering through the translucent smoke at the fire giant's castle. "I've not trekked across Muspelheim only to be defeated now."

Lorelei's reproach was like a dash of cold water in Tyr's face. Of course they had to anticipate success. He was puzzled by the defeatism that had risen to darken his hope, for it had seemed to come upon him with the suddenness of a gale on Asgard's Sea of Fear. Was it simply the atmosphere of Muspelheim dragging at his spirit or was it something more? When he looked at Bjorn he saw that, whatever the malicious influence, it was taxing the wolfhunter too. That bold resolution that had always been such a part of his friend was gone, replaced not by cowardice but by a grim kind of fatalistic resignation. Only Lorelei seemed unchanged, but Tyr had to admit he didn't know her well enough that he could be certain her own personality hadn't undergone some alteration too subtle for him to notice. Or perhaps it was that, just as she'd defied the falling cinders, some enchantment protected her from the oppressive blight that preyed on his own mind.

"To victory, then." Tyr gestured for Lorelei to proceed, for it was with her that the dragon's smoke moved. He strove to drive down the dour mood that worked upon him. He tried to rationalize everything as he would a military campaign, weighing what was risked against what could be gained. No, even if the odds against them were a thousand to one, they had to try. Taking Surtur's sword would change the doom foretold for Odin, perhaps even avert Ragnarok itself. To achieve such a goal, Tyr knew even the most remote chance had to be taken.

Long hours fell away as the three marched ever closer to the glowing volcano and the stronghold poised above its cauldron. Tyr thought he'd never seen a structure of its like before. The walls and battlements were built from colossal blocks of dark basalt. Towers reared above the main structure, their spiky roofs making them look like clawed hands tearing at the sky. A central keep, immense and foreboding, squatted between the clustered towers, its facade sculpted into the image of a vast and fiendish face. Windows set into the eyes of that face flickered with internal light, lending the fortification an eerie sense of vigilance and awareness.

Several gates opened from the curtain wall. These too had seen savage ornamentation, stone fangs jutting out at every angle so that each conveyed the impression of a twisted maw rather than an entryway. Ahead of the exterior wall was a deep trench, a moat from which plumes of smoke arose. In front of each gate was a wide bridge that spanned the gap. Tyr could see that though the gates themselves stood open, the bridges before them were guarded.

The sentries were fire demons. Tyr had faced their kind before in Asgard and Midgard. Taller than a human, but built in the same rough design, they presented an unlovely aspect. Their faces were almost bestial in their cruelty, with squashed noses and wide, fang-filled mouths. Their eyes were more like hot embers than anything else and from the pores of their charred skin, where another creature might sport hair, there was only a fiery discharge, a nimbus of flame that clung to them so long as there was life pulsing through their bodies to fuel it. These guards carried glaives made from obsidian and thick shields forged from some manner of shiny red metal.

"We must cross one of those bridges," Tyr stated, waving his hand at the fortress. "The most lightly guarded would still see us outnumbered eight to three."

"We've faced worse than that," Bjorn reminded him.

"It isn't enough to simply fight our way across," Tyr said.

"We must do so without alerting the whole stronghold. If the guards on one of the other bridges or some sentry patrolling the walls spots us before we're inside…"

"The smoke will hide us." Lorelei's expression was confident. "We've come this near to the fortress and none of the fire demons have given us a second glance. Under cover of this veil, we can steal right up to the guards without them being aware."

Tyr shook his head. "They might not be able to see into the smoke, but can they hear what happens inside? Does your veil confound sound as well as sight?" He glanced over at Bjorn. "Yes, we've faced more numerous enemies, but we would have to vanquish these before a single one of them could cry out."

"Perhaps not," the huntsman said. He drew his wolfskin close about him. Before Tyr could make a move, Bjorn dropped to all fours and darted to the edge of the dragon's smoke. He hesitated for only a moment, then crawled out from the area of the spell.

"Impetuous pup," Tyr grumbled. "He means to test your enchantment," he told Lorelei. Too late to stop Bjorn, he decided that at least the effort shouldn't be wasted. He watched the huntsman crawl, the skin drawn over him. Up close his antics wouldn't deceive anyone, but from a distance it was just possible he'd be mistaken for one of Muspelheim's ash-wolves. With that in mind, Tyr suited the test to the deception. From deep at the back of his throat he started to growl in perfect mimicry of an angry wolf.

Bjorn came scurrying back after a minute. Once he was

within the smoke, he straightened from his crouch. His face was anxious but eager. "Well?"

"Unless you heard a Varinheim cur defending its bone while you were out there, then no sound leaves Fafnir's breath," Tyr told his friend. The smile that stretched across Bjorn's visage told him that he hadn't heard anything.

"Your stupid antic has undone everything!" Lorelei cursed. She spun around and glared at Bjorn with such intensity that he wilted under her gaze. "Look!" she commanded, pointing towards the bridge. One of the fire demons was moving away from the span and marching towards the smoke. "They spotted you while you were outside my spell!"

Tyr clapped Bjorn on the shoulder. "You may have been rash, but you were also crafty," he told him. "They saw you, but your ploy worked." He looked at Lorelei. "If they suspected there was anything more than a lone wolf sniffing around, they would send more than one guard to investigate."

"If he steps inside the smoke, he'll see us," Lorelei said.

"He'll get inside, but he won't get out." Bjorn ran his hand along the head of his axe.

"There's no other way," Tyr agreed, watching as the fire demon marched ever closer. The guard was eyeing the smoke with more than a little caution, doubtless worried the wolf hiding within would suddenly dash out. Through the veil they could see him warily circle the roiling mass. Tyr knew that there was one fault nearly every fire demon had. They weren't a patient people.

Lorelei had to remain at the center of the smoke, for it

was with her that the mass would move. Tyr and Bjorn, however, had the freedom to match the guard's steps, to move with him and poise themselves to act.

The moment the guard stepped through into the smoke, Bjorn and Tyr were upon him. Tyrsfang ripped across the heft of the glaive, cutting it in half before the fire demon could recover from his shock at finding three Asgardians behind the veil. Bjorn struck at him from the other side with his axe. Even if the dragon's smoke didn't muffle sound, the fire demon was dead before he could cry out.

Tyr sheathed his sword and picked up the broken glaive. He handed it over to Lorelei. She gave him a puzzled look. "When you move, the smoke moves with you. We can leave no trace of the guard on the ground. His comrades might wonder what has happened to him, but if we leave a body behind, then they'll know what happened."

"I suppose that means you want me to lug this one around?" Bjorn asked as he knelt beside the guard. The flames had flickered away, and the eyes had taken on the quality of fading coals.

"Your armor is better at fending off heat than mine is," Tyr told him. Once Bjorn had the fire demon slung across his shoulder, Tyr motioned for Lorelei to start moving toward the bridge.

THIRTEEN

Their veil of smoke rippled over the landscape, dozens of yards in diameter. When they neared the span, it was broad enough to cover much of the bridge. Tyr could see that the moat below seethed with lava, a churning mass of molten rock. Wide as it was, the bridge had no barrier along its sides. Nothing to keep someone from pitching over its edge and into the annihilating inferno.

Banks of smoke like that conjured by the flute must indeed have been commonplace in Muspelheim, for the fire demons paid it as little notice as a frost giant would the fogs of Jotunheim. Even when it started to spill onto the bridge, they suspected nothing untoward.

Tyr and Bjorn moved to the edge of the veil. The advantage was theirs, for they could ready themselves to meet the enemy while the guards remained oblivious right until that final moment when the smoke closed around them and they were within the spell. Swift and brutal play of sword and axe finished six more of the fire demons, three sets of guards poised at intervals along the span, their bodies hidden beneath the expanding shroud of Fafnir's breath. The easy dispatch of their enemies made Bjorn overconfident. When they reached the fourth pair of guards, Tyr's opponent fell as quickly as the others. Bjorn's, however, managed to turn and strive against the huntsman. A slash of the glaive glanced across his armor as the fire demon shouted the alert.

No sound could leave the veil, but Bjorn was desperate to silence his enemy all the same. His axe slammed down into the fire demon. Then the huntsman made a grave mistake. To free his axe, he kicked his boot against the body. The guard went hurtling off the side of the bridge. There were only a few feet of smoke before the fire demon became visible on the long plunge to the lava. The sight was seen by a guard farther along the span.

"Ragnalf's fallen!" the cry went up. There was an almost jeering emotion to the shout. Cruel in their hearts and bored in their duty, the guards along the bridge rushed ahead, eager to watch their former comrade be consumed by the lava.

"Lorelei! Stay!" Tyr hastily called to her, but it was already too late. The smoke spread forwards and drew some of the gawking fire demons within its veil. The Asgardian warriors threw themselves upon the guards, dropping two more in a blaze of violence. There were more, many more. And when they saw Tyr and Bjorn suddenly appear almost in their midst their caustic wrath was roused.

A dozen fire demons against two foes. Under other conditions, Tyr might have appreciated the thrill of such a fight. This, however, was no mere test of arms. Too much depended upon victory. He made no boisterous shouts or taunting japes as he battled the guards. Each swing of his blade brought another crashing down, but there always seemed to be another to replace the one he'd vanquished. His mind descended into the vicious cadence of the fray, striking and parrying more from instinct than thought.

"Lorelei, they seek to flee!" Bjorn shouted. It was only when the huntsman yelled that Tyr was aware their enemies had been whittled down to four. These had turned and started racing towards the castle. As soon as they emerged from the smoke, they'd be visible and audible to the guards on the other bridges.

Lorelei rushed forward, shifting the reach of the veil. Even this wouldn't be enough. Then Tyr noted that the smoke was spilling ahead faster than she could run, overtaking the fire demons. He also thought it was more transparent than it had been. Through his mind flashed an answer. She was stretching the smoke to hide the guards but by doing so she was lessening its consistency.

Bjorn settled one of the fire demons by hurling a hatchet into the guard's back. Tyr sprinted past his friend to close with the remaining enemies. On his side he had the godly power of an Aesir, but the fire demons had the terror of destruction snapping at their heels. It was a perilous race, and one he narrowly won. The guards were only a dozen yards from the gate when he caught up to them. He barreled through them, knocking them down and placing himself between them and the fortress.

"Nowhere to run to now," Tyr told them. It was a credit to their martial pride that the fire demons didn't try to flee back across the bridge. Aware that their only chance was to fight past Tyr, the guards didn't hesitate but came at him together. Or at least so it seemed. When two of them fanned out, he guessed their strategy. It only needed one of them to get into the fortress and raise the alarm.

Tyr lunged at the enemy directly before him, running the guard through with his sword. Leaving the blade in his dying foe, he ripped the glaive from the fire demon's grasp. Hefting the heavy weapon as though it weighed nothing, he spun and threw it at the guard trying to slip past on his left. His enemy dropped in a heap right at the end of the bridge.

Wasting no time, Tyr tore Tyrsfang free and sprang at the last of the fire demons. The guard was nearly at the gate when he caught him. A slash of his blade threw his adversary against the basalt wall. The fire demon struggled for a moment, then the blazing eyes darkened into dull coals and he fell still.

"Lorelei! Above you!" The shout was Bjorn's. Tyr turned from the gate to see his friend dive at the woman, knocking her flat. As he sprawled, he cried out. An obsidian javelin crunched down into his leg.

Tyr cast his gaze upwards. Her spell weakened and the opacity of the smoke stretched thin, Lorelei had been spotted from above by a lone sentry walking the walls. Tyr snatched up the glaive from the last fire demon he'd vanquished. He made ready to cast it, but he knew it would be a desperate throw even for an Aesir. The javelin the guard threw down that struck Bjorn was designed for such work. The glaive simply wasn't.

The matter was resolved before Tyr could act. The fire

demon was reaching for a second javelin, his mouth open to shout an alert, when suddenly the flames flickering around him were snuffed out. Tyr knew what that sudden extinguishing meant. A moment later the guard pitched outward and fell down onto the bridge. He could see Lorelei continue to make arcane gestures with her hands until she was certain the fire demon was dead.

Tyr rushed to her side. He gave Bjorn a worried look, but what he had to say to Lorelei was too important to brook even the slightest delay. "The spell's faltering! They can see into the smoke!"

Lorelei nodded wearily, looking more exhausted than Tyr had seen her before. He wondered just what toll that last spell had taken upon her. Even so, he had to demand even more from her magic. "Is there any way to condense the dragon's breath again?"

"That would serve no purpose," Lorelei said. "To draw it back would reveal the absence of guards and the presence of bodies to the others." She drew out the bone flute. "What I must do is strengthen the veil."

Tyr left her to the macabre process of drawing out the essence from the fallen fire demons. He turned to Bjorn. The huntsman was sitting with his legs stretched out, blood seeping from where the javelin was stuck in his calf. "Did you see?" Bjorn asked with exuberance. "I saved her."

His friend's fawning admiration for Lorelei concerned Tyr. Whatever Tyr's own feelings might be, Bjorn's attitude was making him put himself at risk. One glance at the wolfhunter told him it would do no good to broach the subject. Not with that reckless devotion shining in his eyes.

"This is going to hurt," Tyr warned Bjorn as he took hold of the javelin. He glanced around at the smoke. It appeared much thicker than it had been before. "Cry out all you like. We're the only ones who will hear."

Bjorn took the largest of the fangs he wore and bit down on it. He wasn't going to show weakness when Lorelei was around. He nodded for Tyr to proceed. Such was his determination that not even a moan rose from him. Tyr studied the wound. "You'll be able to walk on it, but not very well," he concluded.

Lorelei came over to them at that moment, having decided she'd foraged enough essence from the fire demons. "We will need to move fast when we're inside the stronghold," she said, overhearing Tyr's statement.

"He won't," Tyr told her.

Bjorn managed a smile and shook his head. "I'll manage," he said.

"You'll do better than manage." Lorelei set the flute on the ground and reached into her satchel. She removed a small jar. "Milk from Audumla, the Great Ice Cow," she pronounced. Crouching beside Bjorn, she peeled back his bloodied leggings and started to knead the pasty material into his wound. "This won't heal your hurt," she warned him. "But it will strengthen your leg and make you forget your pain."

"Strength is all I need," Bjorn declared. "Pain is only the absence of strength."

Tyr shook his head. "Any moment and more guards will be on us. We need to get moving."

"We've time," Lorelei corrected him. "I dispatched the

fire demon on the wall before he could alert anyone. The rest who've seen us…" She nodded at the guards strewn along the bridge.

"Then the two of you must stay here," Tyr decided. "If the smoke leaves the bridge then the stronghold will know what has happened. You'll have to maintain the veil." He looked down at Bjorn. "I know I can trust you to protect Lorelei."

"No need to be so dramatic," Lorelei said. She drew her hands away from Bjorn and replaced the jar of milk in her satchel. Her fingers brushed against the bone flute. "This is what conjures Fafnir's breath. It is to this that the spell is tied." She scowled at the instrument. "I can leave it here and the smoke will remain. The dead guards won't be discovered until whenever their relief arrives. With the stamina of fire demons, that might not be for days."

"Or their relief might be on the way here now," Bjorn warned.

"If so they would find us anyway," Lorelei said. "But if we leave the bodies shrouded by the dragon's breath, they may remain undiscovered long enough to suit our needs."

"That means abandoning another weapon in our arsenal," Tyr said. One look at Lorelei made it clear to him that nobody appreciated the fact more than her. First the loss of the Niffleheim ice to the lava kraken, now the surrender of Fafnir's breath.

"I can see no other way," Lorelei told him. "But we must think on what we stand to gain, not what we lose to gain it."

Her smile as she spoke those words made Tyr think that Bjorn wasn't the only one who would risk everything to keep Lorelei from harm.

Fourteen

The postern gate they chose for their entry to Surtur's fortress opened into a narrow passageway. Walls and ceiling were heavily ornamented with whorls of colored rock that suggested crackling flames against the dark basalt. Tyr gave them wary scrutiny, soon spotting the tiny holes hidden in the decoration. They were too numerous to merely be vantage points for spies. He expected a far more violent purpose.

"Beware here," Tyr whispered to his companions. He went back to the bridge and recovered three of the red shields from the fire demons. Each of them took one. Tyr indicated the tiny murder ports he'd spotted. "If the alarm has been given, we can expect a fierce reception."

Bjorn shook his head. "No archer can send an arrow through a hole that small."

"Those opening aren't meant for arrows," Lorelei said. She glanced up at the ceiling where the ports were even more numerous, then turned to Tyr. "Do you think molten metal is intended to pour through those?"

"Or magma. Or poison gas." Tyr grunted at the irony of still another suggestion. "Perhaps smoke to smother us." He focused on the passageway, straining for the least clue that might betray a watcher hidden behind the walls or peering down at them from the ceiling. "We go," he decided finally. "I'll lead the way."

Tyr still could not find the least hint of a hidden watcher. Each step he took into the passage he expected something to rain down on him from the ceiling or jet out from the walls. If they'd been able to draw the dragon's smoke into the fortress with them, at least a spy would've been blinded.

The sensation under his left foot told Tyr that the presence of Fafnir's breath wouldn't have lessened their danger. He looked down to see the stone under his foot had receded an inch into the floor. If he hadn't been moving with such caution, he'd have removed the pressure from the plate before he was even aware it was there. "Back!" Tyr called to his companions. "The corridor is trapped." He nodded at his foot. "And I've stepped on the trigger."

"Don't move," Bjorn cautioned him. "Nothing happened when you stepped on it, so it must be waiting for you to lift your foot again."

"I should have been suspicious when all the guards were outside," Tyr growled. He glanced at Lorelei. "You even warned that Surtur had kidnapped dwarves to labor at his forge. Our mistake was not thinking he might've set them to other tasks as well."

Bjorn came over and studied the stone under Tyr's foot. He scratched at his beard as he pondered its mechanism.

"The two of you cross ahead," Tyr told them. "I'll try to outrun whatever comes."

Bjorn pointed out the length of the corridor. "I don't think you'd make it."

"Besides," Lorelei added, "dwarves are clever enough to make any trap they design serve two functions. To stop an intruder and to sound the alarm. Even now guards might be rushing here."

"Another good reason for the two of you to get going," Tyr said.

"A reason why we can't," Lorelei countered. "Without the God of War, how long do you think we'd last against the fire giant's forces?"

Bjorn stood and wiped the sweat from his palms on his knees. "I think I've some idea how it works." He picked up the shield he'd taken and rapped it with his knuckles. "We might need these yet, but just now we need one of those glaives." He turned and rushed back to the bridge. A moment later he returned with one of the axe-headed polearms.

"What do you mean to do with that?" Lorelei asked. "It is a certainty that it doesn't weigh as much as Tyr. You'd have been better dragging one of the fire demons in here."

"It isn't a question of weight, but of pressure," Bjorn said. He shook the glaive. "By wedging this between the wall and the stone, it can exert the same pressure as Tyr's foot."

Tyr sheathed his sword and reached for the glaive. "Make your way across with Lorelei. I'll put your idea to the test." He gave Bjorn a reassuring look. "I'm confident it'll work." When the wolfhunter still hesitated, he added to his argument. "You need to lead the way across and make sure there aren't any more triggers. After examining this one, you know what to look for."

Reluctantly, Bjorn accepted Tyr's logic. Guiding Lorelei along the passageway, he paused frequently to score the floor with his axe. "Just ahead of the marks," he called back. Tyr nodded his understanding.

Only when the pair were at the end of the corridor did Tyr start work. Swinging the glaive about, balancing it with his left arm, he brought its end up against the wall. Carefully, inch by inch, he eased it downwards, shifting it until he could bring the obsidian blade against the floor. He eased his foot aside and let the glaive press down on the plate. He looked up at Bjorn and Lorelei. With a grim smile he drew his foot away.

The pressure of the glaive kept the trigger depressed. Tyr exhaled in relief and started down the corridor. He grimaced at the many marks Bjorn had made and the worry flashed through him that perhaps the huntsman had missed one. That concern, however, was overwhelmed when his friend shouted.

"The glaive is moving!"

Tyr turned his head and saw that indeed the weapon was slowly sliding along the wall. A matter of heartbeats and the angle would be compromised and the pressure against the plate lost! He didn't hesitate, but broke into a run, lunging down the corridor.

He just reached the end of the passage when a seething hiss bellowed behind him. Tyr felt the intense heat of the discharged trap. As he twisted around, he saw that glowing magma was pouring into the trap-filled corridor from the ports on the ceiling and in the walls.

"I'm minded of an expression they use in Midgard," Tyr told his companions as they watched the searing flood. "They say 'out of the frying pan...'" He turned his head and looked at the bleak hallway ahead of them, its dark walls lit by smoldering blobs of lava imprisoned in crystal orbs. There was an inescapable feeling of malevolence in the hall, not least because it was built to the scale of giants. It wasn't hard to imagine the colossal figure of Surtur himself striding through these cavernous vaults. "'... and into the fire,'" he completed the saying.

Lorelei opened the box with the sliver of Twilight. It spun around for an instant, then pointed away to their right. "We need to find steps leading down," she stated.

Tyr gestured at the sword fragment. "I thought that talisman only showed direction, nothing more. How do you know we need to descend?"

"It stands to reason that a forge would need heat," Lorelei said. "Surely it would be located lower where the fire of the volcano is nearest." There was an edge to her voice that Tyr didn't like. He was certain she knew more than she was saying and told her so.

"Lorelei's explained why she thinks we'll find the forge lower in the fortress," Bjorn snarled, anger in his eyes. "It seems to me that her reasoning is sound."

"Perhaps too much so," Tyr pressed. He pointed to the left. "If we need to descend, the stairs are as likely to be in this direction as they would in another." He fixed Lorelei with a stern look. He didn't like her keeping secrets from him. As much as he still harbored suspicions of her, it had become important to him to earn her trust.

"Fine," Lorelei surrendered. "You have the right of it. The dark elf who stole the shard from Surtur's sword also made a map of the fortress. At least as much of it as he saw. I memorized that map." She shook her head. "I didn't tell either of you in case you were captured. You can't tell an enemy something you don't know."

Tyr had expected such an answer, much as it discouraged him. "To the right, then, and let's find these stairs before any of the stronghold's denizens come strolling this way."

The three set off down the enormous hallway. Fortune favored them, for they saw no one as they dashed for the steps. Lorelei guided them unerringly to an alcove that branched off from the main hall. A spiral of cut pumice bore its way down into the mountain, lit not by crystal globes, but by the pulsating glow of the walls themselves. The scale was much smaller than that of the main hall. Tyr took some relief in that, until he reflected that the most powerful giants were shapeshifters. The only giant in all the Nine Worlds who could rival Surtur in terms of power was Ymir, though in a pinch Tyr would give the edge to the Master of Muspelheim. If a room was too small for the fire giant, he'd simply change to a size it could accommodate.

"I could almost wish to face Surtur now and get it over with," Tyr said as they started down the steps.

Lorelei's face went pale with horror. "Don't even think such a thing! If it can be helped, we must steal his sword before he even knows we're here." She grasped his arm in a despairing grip. "Please, Tyr, don't squander this chance for the sake of vanity. You... you mean too much to me."

The words were drawn from her almost as a confession. She quickly turned from him and started ahead down the steps. Tyr felt a warmth rush through him that wasn't caused by Muspelheim. Something he'd hardly noticed had happened since they'd left Asgard. He'd come to care deeply about Lorelei. He refused to heed the warning voice at the back of his mind, the one that insisted she couldn't be trusted, that she was holding things from them. In other matters perhaps she was overly cautious, but in this Tyr was certain he knew the truth. Lorelei's heart had opened to him.

Bjorn shot him a bleak look, his face at once angry and pained. The wolfhunter hastened after Lorelei. With his cloak drawn up over him, the resemblance to a devoted dog chasing after its mistress impressed itself on Tyr. He sympathized with his friend, but, after all, how could Bjorn aspire to such ambition. Lorelei was a confidant of the Aesir, not some rough frontierswoman from Varinheim. She'd sought to turn the heart of Thor, did he really think she'd settle for a mere huntsman?

Tyr shook his head as he descended the steps, trying to clear the disparaging thoughts swirling in his mind. He'd never looked down upon Bjorn before, nor any other Asgardian who'd shown their mettle. Why should he harbor these ugly ideas now?

He suspected he already knew the answer. Enchantment, the forte of Amora, and was not Lorelei her sister? If she'd learned other arcane arts from her, why not the one Amora knew best of all? Yes, it rang true to Tyr, this explanation for the influence working upon him.

Yet, even recognizing it, Tyr couldn't shake off that influence. He didn't want to.

FIFTEEN

The lower vaults below the fortress somehow managed to be even hotter than those above. Tyr likened the atmosphere to that of a sauna, blisteringly humid as cracks in the walls and floor vented steam into the corridors. A violent red light dominated everything, pulsing from the walls themselves. These appeared to be unworked for the most part, natural lava tubes that were now employed by Surtur's minions. While there was some consistency to their height, maintaining a ceiling of eight feet, the width of the tunnels varied wildly. At times the halls expanded to twenty feet and more, in other instances they closed in so that the Asgardians were forced to move in single file.

Side branches were frequent as well, veering off at random intervals. Most of these, Tyr noted, were simply diversions of the old lava tubes. Sometimes, however, there was evidence of deliberate construction. Lorelei was careful to divert them away from these sections. "Barracks and guard rooms," she explained. "Places more likely to harbor fire demons."

"I'm surprised we haven't already run into a patrol," Tyr said.

Bjorn, in the lead, turned to give his friend a sour look. "You underestimate my ability as a scout. I'll hear any fire demons long before they hear us."

As if conjured by the wolfhunter's boast, a group of six fire demons rounded the corner ahead of them. They stopped, surprise on their faces. Before the guards could make a move, Tyr heard Lorelei invoke an incantation and gesture with her hand.

Their confusion evaporated in an instant, replaced with a murderous rage. The fire demons came rushing down the tunnel, brandishing their swords and spiked maces. Bjorn made to meet their charge, but he was struck by the slash of a burning sword. He slammed against the wall, flung aside by the blow. Had any of them paused, the fire demons could have made short work of the defenseless man. But their ire was fixated on a different target. Howling their fury, they ran straight for Lorelei.

"Stay behind me and keep your shield raised," Tyr ordered as he stepped forward to meet the charge.

"That was my intention," Lorelei quipped, drawing the shield off her back while replacing the box in her satchel.

The next instant Tyr was engaged by the fire demons. They tried to swat him aside as they had Bjorn, but in their reckless anger they learned too late that the Aesir wasn't so easily bypassed. Tyrsfang flashed, striking down the foremost of the guards as the demon slashed at him with her sword. The demon behind her rushed in with a heavy mace. Tyr intercepted the blow with his shield and thrust his blade into his foe's body. He kicked the maceman away and lunged at a third fire demon as he tried to dart around him and come to grips with Lorelei. A brutal sweep of the glimmering sword spilled the guard to the floor.

Bjorn was up now, staggering back to his feet and shaking his head. He ripped a hand axe from his belt and threw it into a fire demon's back. The cleaving edge crunched through the guard's leathery hide, and the nimbus of flame flickered away as he collapsed. The huntsman groped about on the floor for his battleaxe, obviously still shaken by the initial charge.

The last two fire demons threw themselves ahead with rabid ferocity. Tyr smashed one in the face with his shield and drove his sword into the other. As the one he'd stabbed expired, he caught movement from the corner of his eye. He'd expected the one he'd slammed with his shield to be stunned by the impact, but such was her vicious determination to attack Lorelei that she didn't even stop to recover the sword she'd dropped. Snarling like a tigress, she threw herself at the woman with her clawed hands.

Lorelei staggered when she used her own shield to fend off the fire demon's leap. Then the Uru dagger was in her fist. While the guard clawed at the warding shield, Lorelei drove the dirk over and over into the demon. Only when the flames crackling about the guard's body dissipated did she relent.

"They fought like blood-mad berserkers," Tyr observed as he looked over the bodies. None of them had so much as a flicker of fire crackling across their skin, and the eyes of each had hardened into blackened coals. "No thought to their own protection."

Lorelei sheathed her dirk and slung the shield over her back. "My magic did that," she said. "I put into their minds such antipathy for me that they could think of nothing else."

Bjorn stared at her in disbelief. "You might have been killed," he objected, neglecting the ragged tear in his armor where a fire demon's sword had almost ended his own life. "Why would you provoke them like that?"

"It was the only way to ensure none of them broke away to spread an alert," Lorelei answered. Though she addressed Bjorn, her eyes were on Tyr, much to the former's chagrin. "I was depending on you to stop them before they could reach me."

Tyr frowned at the explanation. "A gamble… and the wager was your life."

"Not much of a gamble when I had you to defend me," Lorelei chided. She patted the dirk on her belt. "Even when the last one got past you, I was under your protection."

Bjorn gave an annoyed grunt as he stomped over and recovered his hand axe. He glanced around. "I don't see anywhere we can hide these guards," he said. "When the next patrol comes through, they're certain to sound the alarm. All we've accomplished here is to buy ourselves a little time. We'd best make use of it." He turned to start off down the tunnel, but Tyr motioned for him to wait.

"We can't use the main passages now," Tyr said. He turned back to Lorelei. "That map you studied, did it show any routes that are more neglected? Less likely to be patrolled?" He was thinking of the dark elf and how that intruder, at least, had been able to slink through Surtur's stronghold and get out again.

"There are paths we could take," Lorelei replied. "But there are reasons the fire demons avoid them. The dark elf noted that the walls are thinner in such places. More apt to split and spill lava into the tunnels. Sometimes the volcano will tremble and cause rockfalls that seal off passageways."

"We'll chance it," Tyr decided. "Once the alarm is given, the main corridors will be swarming with guards. They'd bar our advance as completely as any cave-in could."

Bjorn pulled at his beard. "So which way do we go?"

Lorelei was quiet for a moment. She closed her eyes. Tyr could imagine her visualizing the dark elf map in her mind. "Two more turns to the left ahead of us," she stated. "We'll have to pass close to a guardroom, but after that we'll have a little-used tunnel." A pause as she added a note of worry to her voice. "At least, if the volcano has left it there."

"If it isn't, we'll dig our way through," Tyr said. He stepped in front of Bjorn when the huntsman started to lead the way again. "I'll go first," he told him.

"What's this?" Bjorn demanded.

Tyr fixed him with a stern look. "You should've heard those guards before they got that close to us. The Bjorn Wolfsbane I've hunted beside for so many years would never have let himself be surprised like that. I don't know what's distracting you, but until you figure it out, I'm going first."

Bjorn bit down on whatever reply he was going to make. Tyr could see in his friend's eyes that the reprimand stung all the more sharply because it was justified. He knew he'd failed them. What made Bjorn angry was to have that fact expressed in front of Lorelei. Maybe, if the huntsman were thinking more clearly, he'd realize it was thinking about her that made him inattentive.

Tyr wouldn't make that mistake.

Sixteen

Just as Lorelei had warned, the abandoned tunnels proved dangerous to navigate. The walls pulsed with the barely restrained molten flow of the volcano, the glow they emanated swelling from the red of the main corridors to burning white. Tyr was thankful that only the widest parts of the path had displayed such intensity. At least so far.

The floor was littered with pumice that had been expelled into the tunnels at one time or another. Steam vents spewed their boiling vapor in infrequent spurts. Several times one or another of them had been scalded when one of the fissures suddenly became active. Even Tyr's Aesir skin was tender where a blast had spewed directly in his face. He could imagine that a man of Midgard would have been cooked in his boots by the discharge.

The rumble of the volcano was a perpetual din, a low roar that was ever pressing in upon their hearing. Too irregular, too menacing to deafen his senses to, Tyr conceded that at his most vigilant he'd likely miss a whole company of fire demons marching ahead of them in the tunnel. In that, at least, the infernal passages were proving their worth. There'd been no evidence that the stronghold's garrison ever ventured into these halls.

"If the whole place doesn't come down about our ears, we'll have made a lot of progress," Lorelei said, consulting the box once again. "These tunnels should get us very near to the forge."

An angrier than usual tremor rolled through the mountain. Debris drifted down from the roof. Bjorn snarled in surprise and drew away from the wall as a little trickle of magma seeped out. "We'll be roasted if this goes on much longer," he said, wiping sweat from his brow.

"Not much farther," Lorelei told him. She gestured at the fiery passage ahead of Tyr. "The map indicated this should reconnect with the main corridor. We only need to stay to the course."

Tyr raised his shield as a chunk of rock fell from the ceiling. "If the mountain lets us," he said. A long blast of steam erupted from the floor a dozen feet away, spreading across the passage. "Hurry through!" he urged the others. "There's no saying when it'll stop!" He clenched his eyes shut as he sprinted through the boiling vapor, uncomfortably reminded of the miasma that had so nearly overwhelmed them on the plateau.

When he felt the dripping heat lessen, Tyr opened his eyes again. He saw, only five feet ahead of him, the wall of the tunnel. It curved away to his right before turning once more to the left. He thought he heard a sound from that direction, a cracking grating noise. "Quick!" he shouted to his companions as they emerged from the steam. "It sounds like the tunnel is coming apart up ahead."

Hoping they could slip through before the way was blocked, Tyr ran. Strangely, the sounds he'd heard fell away, though he could still feel tremors rolling through the mountain. If the noise was caused by strain upon the tunnel, its volume should have increased, not gone silent.

The second turn opened into a wider passageway. The first thing Tyr noticed was the bones that littered the floor. He could tell at a glance they belonged to fire demons. The splintered, broken state of them was explained by the creature that stood amid the litter. A mammoth lizard as big as an ox, its hide purplish flecked with black. The reptile had its jaws clamped around a femur, and Tyr realized the cracking sound had been the animal gnawing at its meal. Now, having heard him shout, the lizard stood immobile, its yellow eyes watching him as he rounded the corner.

The scene held for just a moment, god and reptile staring at one another, neither prepared to make the first move. It was when Lorelei and Bjorn came upon the tableau that the lizard made its choice. Seeing more Asgardians turn the corner, it hissed angrily. The bone fell from its jaws and shattered on the floor. With its eyes fixed on Tyr, the reptile charged at him.

It should have been impossible for anything as large as the lizard to move as quickly as it did. The scrambling, somehow frantic gait brought the reptile upon him before Tyr could even raise his sword. The scaly weight of it threw him back against Bjorn and Lorelei, pressing all three of them against the wall. Long claws raked against Tyr's armor while the blunt snout shoved against him, trying to turn him so it could bite his head.

"Filthy scavenger!" Tyr growled at the hissing reptile. He brought his arm around, shoving the shield in its mouth as it finally tried to snap at his face. "You'll not make a meal of me!" He brought Tyrsfang chopping against one of its clawed legs, breaking it and leaving the limb dangling at its side.

The lizard appeared to give no notice to its hurt, but continued to rake at him with its other claws. The powerful jaws locked about the shield, exerting such force that the red metal began to crumple. Tyr raked his sword across the lashings and slipped his arm free a moment before it was crushed in the reptile's maw. Tyr whipped his left arm around and drove the cup covering his stump into the beast's eye.

The hurt to its eye wasn't so easily ignored. The lizard whipped back in pain, lashing the ground behind it with its long, whip-like tail. Tyr stepped forward, letting Bjorn and Lorelei push away from the wall. His advance, however, only rekindled the reptile's agitation. Hissing once more, it ran at him, now with a flopping, flailing motion since one foreleg hung useless at its side.

Prepared this time, with the lizard's erratic speed compromised by its injury, Tyr met the charge with a sweep of his sword. The blade cracked against the blunted skull, cutting through the scaly hide. The fanged jaws snapped at him, but the reptilian teeth slid harmlessly down his breastplate, unable to find purchase. He struck again, this time slashing the beast in the neck.

Sizzling blood pumped from the wound, but the reptile was still capable of fight. It whipped about, shifting its massive body so that its entire weight drove against Tyr. He realized it was trying to whip him with its tail, but instead it smacked him with the equivalent of a hip. The impact threw him to the floor and sent him tumbling away.

"Stay off him!" Bjorn cried, driving his axe into the lizard's flank. The reptile was too intent on Tyr to be turned aside by another enemy. Hissing its rage, the brute flop-scurried at him once more.

Tyr grappled with the lizard as it flung itself upon him. He winced as he felt one of the claws sink into his thigh. There was no room to bring his sword into play, so he locked his arms around the beast's neck and squeezed. The scaly hide felt hot under his grip and he gagged from the stink of its blood. It jerked its head back and forth, trying to twist free of his grip.

"Don't ignore me, drake!" Bjorn snarled as he returned to the fray. The axe bit down into the lizard's flailing tail, severing several feet of it. The reptile scurried away from the injury and the one who delivered it, sprinting toward the other end of the tunnel.

"Let it get away!" Lorelei was shouting, running after the lizard as it carried Tyr with it. Tyr could only smile at her words. There was no way for him to release his hold on the brute, not unless he wanted to be kicked or trampled.

The lizard carried him onward through the passageway. Tyr felt the heat of the walls as they ran past them, then the gradual lessening of that heat as they emerged into a much broader tunnel. It was here that the reptile's endurance finally exhausted itself. A shudder went through it and with a last stagger, it crashed to the floor.

Tyr could hear Lorelei and Bjorn running after him. He pushed the scaly carcass away and raised his arm to greet them. It was only then that he noticed where the lizard's last dash had brought him. He was back in the main complex, the tunnels that were used by Surtur's minions. More stable in their construction than the neglected warren of tunnels they'd been following and lit by flickering torches. And they were far from deserted.

SEVENTEEN

There were at least a dozen fire demons staring at Tyr, their weapons at the ready. Two of the foremost held the leashes of gigantic dogs with furless red hides and flame dripping from their fangs – hellhounds. Guards brought here by the sound of fighting. They looked surprised to see him, but surprised or not, there was no mistaking the hostility in their fiery eyes.

Tyr smiled at the glowering fire demons. "I don't suppose one of you lost a lizard?"

The fire demons holding the leashes released their hellhounds. The snarling dogs barreled towards Tyr, flames crackling about their sharp fangs. He dropped his sword and spun around, seizing one of the lizard's legs. Using his other arm for leverage, he swung back around, dragging the reptile off the floor. Whipping the heavy carcass as he spun, he sent it crashing into the beasts. The hellhounds yelped as the lizard smashed into them and sent them rolling along the floor.

The guards cursed Tyr's feat and charged across the hall.

He recovered Tyrsfang from the ground and made ready to meet them. "Please tell me you have something left in that bag of yours," he shouted to Lorelei as she came sprinting over to him.

"Maybe. If it works," she replied. Again her hand dropped into the satchel, this time emerging with a prism of amber-colored glass. She pressed it to her forehead. "Stay here," she ordered Bjorn when he would have rushed ahead to meet the enemy. He drew back and stood beside Tyr while she wove her spell.

"From the peaks of Jotunheim, I call you, giants of frost!" Lorelei's voice thundered through the passageway. "Attend my conjuring, for your mortal foes are here, the slaves of Surtur!"

Her incantation only incensed the fire demons still more. Tyr thought it was going to be a repeat of her earlier enchantment, driving the enemy into enraged abandon. Only this time he'd need to protect her from three times as many maddened guards!

Then the air began to shimmer. Tyr blinked in amazement as four enormous shapes appeared. Each was several feet taller than the fire demons, with pale blue skin and long white beards. They wore armor of dragonscales covered in clumps of ice and in their hands they gripped massive double-headed axes. By what incredible process, he didn't know, but Lorelei's spell had drawn frost giants into Muspelheim!

The fire demons faltered, their eyes flickering with wonder as the giants appeared before them. They drew back, anxiously muttering among themselves, even their hot tempers cooled by the prospect of fighting the hulking warriors.

Lorelei caught at Tyr's arm. "We've got to go quickly," she hissed, trying to draw him away. Tyr resisted. He didn't know how the frost giants were here, but they were allies against Surtur and he refused to leave even a temporary friend in battle. Lorelei must have guessed the reason for his hesitance. "They're not real," she whispered. "It's an illusion. Now let's go before the guards figure it out for themselves."

Tyr nodded in agreement, but the trick was already doomed to be undone. One of the hellhounds he'd knocked over was back on its feet. The dog limped towards the frost giants, growling at them, its hackles raised. Before one of the fire demons could call it off, it leaped at the nearest giant. Instead of sinking its fangs in an icy throat, the hellhound sailed through it and crashed to the floor.

A heartbeat later and the fire demons were shrieking in outrage, furious they'd been tricked by the illusion. By then, the Asgardians were already running down the passageway.

"I'll look for another lizard you can throw at them," Bjorn puffed as he ran beside Tyr.

Tyr smiled at the jest. "I think we'd need at least two lizards to slow that mob down, but maybe they'll get tired if we keep them chasing us long enough."

"They've been living soft," Bjorn said. "Garrison duty. Nothing to do but sit around and get fat."

"Save your breath and look for a room with pillars," Lorelei advised them. "The forge will be in that direction."

Tyr saw a side tunnel opening into the passageway. He ducked as one of the pursuing fire demons threw a mace at him, then diverted so that he could look down the connecting tunnel. He'd taken only a few steps before he hastily backed away. Another group of guards was hurrying through the side tunnel, a brace of hellhounds at their fore.

"Not that way," Tyr told Lorelei, steering her ahead down the main corridor. He ground his teeth when he suddenly heard the baying of the hellhounds. The second batch of guards had set them loose. The dogs came loping out from the tunnel. They would have been on them in an instant, but their course brought the hellhounds crashing into the original group of guards. Livid curses and angry snarls rang out as the beasts collided with the fire demons.

For the moment the Asgardians were able to put distance between themselves and their enemies. Tyr knew it would only be a few heartbeats before the fire demons recovered and sent the dogs charging after them again. On a straight course, there was no chance of outdistancing the hellhounds.

"Down there!" Bjorn shouted, waving his axe at another side tunnel up ahead of them. There was no hesitation this time to investigate. All three of them rushed for the diversion, putting on as much speed as they could muster.

Tyr was relieved to see that the passage, though wide, took many turns. That would slow the hellhounds and favor them. A slight advantage, but he'd take whatever they could get right now.

Bjorn was up ahead and just a little farther beyond the next turn when he suddenly stopped. Tyr and Lorelei almost crashed into him as they cleared the corner.

It wasn't hard to figure out why he'd stopped. The tunnel

opened into a cavernous hall, cut from the mountain and supported by dozens of pumice pillars. Several corridors branched away in every direction, making the chamber a kind of nexus point, an intersection for this part of Surtur's stronghold. Tyr thought all the main passages must eventually connect to this room. It was a supposition supported by the fact that the hall was occupied.

Arrayed around the pillars was a mob of furious fire demons. Beyond them, standing on the bottom steps of a stairway leading upwards was a being far more imposing. Fifteen feet in height with a head framed by four curling horns, was a giant woman with bright red skin and a long, bifurcated tail. Flames billowed all around her and her eyes were yellow pits of fire. In her hands she held the obsidian leash of an armored hellhound so big it might have used the colossal lizard Tyr had fought for a chew toy.

"Found the room you were looking for," Tyr told Lorelei.

The flame-wrapt giant smiled, her face splitting in a fanged grin. "I too have found what I was looking for," she said, her voice seething like a boiling cauldron. "Lay down your weapons and surrender to Sindr Surtursdottir." Somehow her smile managed to become even more menacing. "Or don't. It has been too long since I spilled Aesir blood."

EIGHTEEN

The daughter of Surtur! Aside from running into the fire giant himself, Tyr could imagine no greater adversary within the stronghold. Tales had reached Asgard of this ruthless monster, the enforcer of her father's tyranny over Muspelheim. Sindr was said to be the first of Surtur's progeny to survive the cruel tests by which he evaluated their worthiness, the first to show some ember of the fire giant's eternal malice. She was a bold, vicious warrior who'd ventured across the Nine Worlds to strike at Surtur's enemies and carry out his schemes to hasten the hour of Ragnarok.

Tyr met Sindr's fiery gaze. The huge hellhound beside her snarled at him, its fangs striking sparks as they clashed together. As its mistress towered over the fire demons, so was the dog a giant among its kind, as big as any whelp of Fenris that stalked the forests of Varinheim.

Sindr lost the domineering smile, her expression dropping into a scowl. "I told you to lose your weapons." Her eyes blazed when Tyr's hand only tightened its hold upon his sword. "Surrender, fools." A rattle of laughter steamed over her lips. "Odin is pretentious indeed to send this trash," she told the fire demons. "The Leavings of the Wolf," she sneered at Tyr. "And two lesser idiots," she added with a dismissive wave at Lorelei and Bjorn. "There's a reason Odin didn't send Thor on this errand. He could foresee it was suicide and didn't want to lose his *favorite* son."

"Are you going to fight, or try to talk me to death?" Tyr snapped. He brandished Tyrsfang, letting the light from Sindr's body play across the gleaming blade. "Care to take a closer look at the 'leavings of the wolf'?"

The flames billowing from Sindr flared angrily. Her body expanded in size, increasing a few feet in height and several inches in width. "Arrogant cur! I am Sindr Surtursdottir! With these hands have I pulled Nidhogg from the roots of Yggdrasil and plucked fangs from the dragon's mouth! Twenty champions of Malekith fought with me and none so much as scratched my skin! I broke down the walls of King Eitri's castle and–"

"As I thought," Tyr interrupted Sindr's boasting, "you mean to talk me to death."

Sindr's entire being was engulfed in a nimbus of white-hot flame so intense even the fire demons recoiled from her. "Kill them!" she roared. The leash in her hand melted from the heat of her body. The huge hellhound bounded forward to ravage Tyr with its fangs.

For just an instant Tyr felt fear flash through him as the enormous beast came for him. His mind shuddered at the image of Fenris, the Great Wolf's jaws gaping to devour the rest of him as it had his hand. The nightmarish vision itself broke his fear. Compared to Fenris, Sindr's hellhound was a feral mongrel sniffing for scraps.

Tyr met the dog's rush, his blade flashing out and gouging the black armor that protected it. The hellhound's charge faltered as it whipped around, the armor across its foreleg hanging by a mere shred and fiery ichor bubbling from its slashed shoulder.

"Come and fight!" Bjorn yelled as the fire demons swept in to attack. His axe hewed through the sword arm of the first to close with him. A second stumbled back with a gash across his stomach. Other guards charged towards Lorelei, but she snapped a hasty incantation that sent whorls of light jumping from her fingers and had the demons clutching at their blinded eyes.

The wounded hellhound lunged for Tyr once more. He dodged the beast's attack and chopped at it with his blade. More of the dog armor was shredded by Tyrsfang's keen edge, but the brute kept coming. This time it slammed into him and sent him sprawling. A fire demon rushed in to exploit his distress, but the hellhound jerked its head around at the sudden motion and bit at him instead. The guard jumped back as the fangs narrowly missed his arm. Satisfied that the fire demon wouldn't trespass again, the hound turned back to its prey.

Only now that prey wasn't so helpless as he'd been only a moment before. Tyr drew his legs close to his chest, and when the hellhound sprang at him, he kicked both feet into its muzzle. The impact against its nose stunned the hound. While it was dazed, Tyr rolled onto his feet and pressed his attack. He brought his sword crashing down, striking the beast at the center of its back. A sickening crack echoed through the hall, and the brute sank to the floor, its spine broken by the god's blow.

"You will suffer as none of my enemies have suffered." Sindr's threat came in a sizzling growl. Tyr spun away from the hellhound as the giant leaped down from the steps. Her clawed fist slammed into his breastplate and threw him back a dozen feet. Tyr could feel his bones shiver from the impact. When he glanced down, he saw the imprint of her knuckles in the metal.

Tyr shook his head and tapped the metal cup against the dented armor. "You call that a punch? I've taken worse hits from Thor… when he was still a child."

The mockery made Sindr even more livid. She shoved aside the fire demons converging on Tyr. "The braggart is mine!" she hissed at them. Stomping forward she glared at him. "We'll see how funny you are after I cut that wagging tongue from your mouth." She held her fist out. One instant it was empty, but in the next a sword of flickering flame billowed into her grip.

Tyr glanced aside to see how Bjorn and Lorelei were faring. They were on the verge of being overwhelmed, their backs brought up almost against the hot wall. If they were to have any chance of living through this, Tyr had to exploit the only thing that could help them now: Sindr's volatile temper.

"Prove it," he scoffed. To heighten Sindr's fury, he didn't give her the chance to initiate the attack, but instead sprang at her. Tyrsfang flashed, sweeping for the giant's leg. She parried with her blazing sword, sparks flying as the two blades strove against one another.

Tyr could feel the giant's awesome strength as it pulsed through the weapons at the moment of impact. She was over twice his height, at least five times his mass. In a contest of sheer brawn, Sindr would overwhelm him. But the Aesir were old enemies of giants, whatever realm they stirred from, and they'd prevailed not by trying to match their foes on their own terms but by exploiting their weaknesses. Tyr might not be able to outfight Sindr, but he might outthink her.

He whipped aside, throwing himself to her left, away from the sword clenched in her right hand. As he dove, Tyr struck at Sindr, his blade raking across her leg. Molten liquid that smelled like brimstone oozed from the cut. The giant snarled and whipped at him with her tail. He ducked beneath the sweep of the bifurcated lash and it battered the floor instead, driving with such force that the rock split.

"Careful," Tyr chided Sindr. "Your father won't be happy if you start breaking his castle."

Sindr spun about and lunged at him with her flaming sword. Tyr darted back, letting it flash only a few inches from him. He slashed his own blade across her extended arm, cutting her from wrist to elbow. She reared back, roaring in pain.

Sindr's injury incensed the fire demons. Several charged at Tyr, determined to avenge their mistress. Tyr slammed the metal cup covering his stump against the head of one howling guard and sent the creature spilling to the floor. His sword slashed a second, ripping through his glaive to smash his chest. The force of the blow threw the stricken enemy backwards, knocking three of his comrades to the ground. Another fire demon, a wicked mace clenched in her fist, charged at him, but a sidewise thrust of Tyrsfang turned her attack into a lifeless slide that ended when she crashed against the wall.

More fire demons were close behind the first that Tyr vanquished. He turned from them as Sindr returned to the fight, her wounds sealing themselves and showing now only as glowing scars on her crimson flesh. He met the descending sweep of her sword, catching it with Tyrsfang and using the giant's own strength against her. Instead of resisting the force of the blow, he let himself be propelled by it, only using his blade as a barrier between himself and the searing edge of Sindr's weapon. Tyr's feet slid across the floor as he was driven back. A twist and he used the stolen momentum to add speed as he dashed across the hall between the furious giant and the outraged demons.

"Coward! Stand and fight!" Sindr bellowed as she stormed after Tyr.

"Laggard! Come and catch me!" Tyr jeered back at her. The flames crackling off her body became still more intense as his barb added to her anger. Sindr's pace increased as she sought to make him regret the insult. One of her strides was the equal of three of his. He could only win a sprint by putting obstacles between them.

A veer to his right provided the first such impediment. Fire demons were moving to cut Tyr off and hold him for Sindr, but the Aesir was faster than they were. He rushed past them, and when they turned to pursue it placed the guards between himself and the giant. A demon shrieked as he was trampled under her pounding feet, the others scattered to give her room and avoid their companion's doom.

Ahead, Tyr saw what he was striving towards. One of the massive pillars that supported the roof of the chamber. A pair of fire demons blocked his way. Tyrsfang met the lunge of the first, cleaving his skull as he struck at him with an obsidian axe. The second guard drove at him with a glaive. She fared no better than the first, felled by a sword blow of such force that it sent her body flying twenty feet across the room.

Tyr braced himself against the pillar and spun to face Sindr. He smiled at her as she ran towards him. "Very good," he cheered with mock approval. "You aren't as clumsy as you look."

The insult achieved its purpose. Tyr worried that Sindr might wonder why he'd suddenly stopped to face her, but he drew her temper to the fore. Anger blotted out any caution she might otherwise have shown. Snarling in almost bestial rage, she swung for him with her blazing sword.

Tyr waited until the last moment before moving. Using his left arm as a fulcrum, he swung around and aside. The mighty slash intended to sunder him from crown to hip instead slammed into the pillar. The searing heat of the blade and Sindr's tremendous strength combined to bite through the toughened rock. A gouge several inches thick now marked the pillar.

"Thanks," Tyr shouted as he swung back around and raked his own sword in the groove made by Sindr. His maneuver was the reverse of the giant's, slashing from bottom to top. Already weakened by her, his thrust expanded on the damage. By the time Tyrsfang cleared the cut, only an inch of rock maintained the pillar's cohesion.

An inch wasn't enough.

With a loud groan, the pillar came crashing down. Sindr was smashed beneath the toppling span, crushed to the floor under tons of broken rock. Rubble spilled from the ceiling, striking several fire demons and sowing panic among the others. A gruesome tremor shuddered through the hall, the remaining pillars visibly shaking as they struggled to adjust to the redistributed weight. Debris clattered downward from cracks that snaked across the roof.

NINETEEN

Tyr coughed as the gritty dust and ash from the fractured pumice filled the air. Covering his face with his arm, he plunged through the noxious cloud. He swung Tyrsfang as a reeling fire demon almost stumbled into him, the blow finishing the guard before he was even aware of the Aesir's presence. He drove himself onward through the blinding murk, making his way to where he'd last seen his embattled companions.

A disoriented fire demon lurched into his path. Tyr struck with his sword, the power of the impact hurling the enemy aside. The cloud was thinner here, and he could make out the ring of foes that surrounded Bjorn and Lorelei. Four bodies on the ground told that the pair had done their part in the fighting, but there were a dozen more opposing the Asgardians.

Tyr offered the fire demons no warning. While they were disoriented by the collapse of the pillar, he hurled himself into their midst. A clubbing strike of his metal cup dropped one where he stood, a sideways slash of his sword threw another across the hall to slam into the wall and wilt to the floor in a broken heap. Two more quickly followed, cut down by Tyrsfang. They were the last to be caught helpless by him. The others turned to confront the opponent who'd appeared on their flank.

An obsidian sword bit into Tyr's breastplate, tearing at the metal. He felt the ragged edges scrape his skin, so nearly did the attack punch through to his flesh. The Muspelheim swordswoman didn't get a chance for a second stroke. Tyrsfang caught her in the midsection and flung her body over the heads of the other fire demons. A glaive chopped at his belly, deflected at the last second by a sideward slap of his arm and the metal cup encasing his stump. The wielder of the glaive stumbled forward, putting himself within easy reach of Tyr's sword. It was the last mistake of the fire demon's life.

"Save a few for me!" Bjorn thundered, throwing himself at the enemies who only a moment before had dominated the field. In their haste to confront Tyr, the guards neglected to watch their original foes. The huntsman's axe crunched into a fire demon's skull. He ripped the weapon free and went after the one beside him as the warriors remembered the enemies at their back. For an instant, Asgardian axe crashed against Muspelheimer sword as the two pitted their strength against each other.

"Shield your eyes!" Lorelei cried out. Tyr covered his face as she made arcane gestures with her hands. Even with his eyes shielded, he could feel the chilly sparks that flared across his vision. For the fire demons, the effect was far more pronounced. They shrieked as their eyes were singed by the icy burn of her spell. While they were reeling in pain, Tyr and Bjorn swiftly dispatched them. Tyr regretted the crisis allowed no measure for mercy.

For the moment, no foes menaced the Asgardians, but Tyr knew it was but a momentary respite. There was no time to rest, they had to either brace themselves to fight more guards or try to lose their pursuit in the winding passageways. The God of War knew the quickest way to squander a victory was to engage in pointless battles. While they had the chance, they needed to escape.

"Which way?" Tyr gestured at Lorelei and then to the corridors branching away from the main chamber. The debris falling from the roof had lessened to a mere trickle of dust now as the remaining pillars took up the weight of the halls above. "More of them will be on us in an instant." Across the room, the survivors of Sindr's entourage were being joined by those the Asgardians had been pursued by. The hellhounds turned in their direction and started dashing over the rubble.

Lorelei consulted the box. She frowned at it for a moment, trying to urge the sliver of Twilight to come to rest. Finally, she pointed a finger to one of the corridors. "That one! Try that one!"

Tyr scowled at the passage Lorelei indicated. Its walls seethed with heat, glowing from the lava that undulated just beneath the surface. After the tremors, he wondered how sturdy the corridor was, or if it would burst the moment they started down it.

"Go for it." Tyr waved at her and Bjorn to make for the passage. "I'll keep the dogs from nipping at our heels." He turned to face the pack of hellhounds. There were four of the beasts, each baying its fury as it loped towards him, fiery froth spilling from their jowls.

Before the hellhounds reached Tyr, the chamber was again shaken by a tremendous force. Splinters of rock sprayed in every direction, pelting dogs, fire demons, and Asgardians with equal malice. Tyr wiped at the blood that dribbled from a cut along his brow. Looking to where the splinters had emanated, he saw a monstrous shape rise from where the pillar had fallen, chunks of the ruptured rock strewn all around.

The flames that roared around Sindr's body were a searing yellow, more furious than the face of the sun. Her body had swollen in keeping with her ire. Now she stood thirty feet tall, her horns brushing against the ceiling. She stretched out her hand and the fiery sword reappeared, now twice as massive as before. Her tail lashed the ground, sending a boulder-sized fragment rolling across the floor.

The hellhounds whined and recoiled, forgetting all about Tyr as the giant started towards him. "I'll make you wish the rest of you was in the wolf's belly!" Sindr hissed as she advanced across the room.

Tyr risked a glance at Lorelei and Bjorn. They were almost at the passageway she'd pointed out. If he could keep Sindr from noticing them a little longer, they at least would have a chance of reaching Surtur's forge.

"Just you?" Tyr scoffed and waved his sword at the fire demons. "Or do you need help?"

Sindr's flaring eyes remained fixed on him. "The goblin who dares interfere will wish they'd never been born." Her threat echoed through the chamber. A malignant smile spread over her face. "I need no help settling one of Odin's lesser sons."

"We'll see about that, won't we?" retorted Tyr. He made a show of rushing at Sindr as he had before. She swung her gigantic sword to thwart the attack, but the moment he saw her arm start to move, he was already changing tactics. His charge became a dive, a scramble for the corridor a few dozen yards to his left. He heard the giant's frustrated howl as she realized she'd been tricked. The smell of burnt hair was in his nose and the floor under his feet seemed to leap beneath his toes, so nearly did Sindr strike him with a second thrust.

Tyr gained the corridor and hurried down it. He smiled as he glanced up at the ceiling, only ten feet over his head. At her current size, Sindr couldn't follow. But escape wasn't his plan. He stopped and turned to face the chamber. The giant appeared at the mouth of the passage, crouching down to peer inside. She thrust her sword down the hall, jabbing and swiping, but he kept beyond her reach.

"I've seen rock trolls try to fish badgers from their burrows like this," he jeered. "Surely the daughter of Surtur is smarter than a troll!"

Sindr's face contorted with renewed fury. She drew back, humiliated by Tyr's jibe. Her next action was less impulsive and more calculating, but it was precisely the tack he'd been counting on. Steeling her resolve, the flames around the giant cooled. Her body condensed, reducing in size and mass, shrinking to a scale that would allow her to pursue him.

Tyr acted the moment he judged Sindr was at her most vulnerable. Her body's reduction didn't keep pace with that of her sword. When she was a third of her previous size, the weapon remained two-thirds its enlarged size. He judged it would be impossible for her to lift, much less swing, the sword.

"For Asgard!" Tyr shouted as he charged down the corridor. He was shocked when Sindr tried to strike him with the over-sized sword, amazed by the tremendous strength that must be in her arms to manage such a feat. Yet, though she had strength enough to swing the huge blade, it remained unwieldy. Tyr was able to dodge past the cumbersome swing and bring his metal cup slamming down on the giant's hand.

The blow numbed Sindr's fingers, and the flaming blade fell from her grip, evaporating into smoke and embers before it could hit the floor. Tyr pressed ahead, driving his body against that of the giant. Only a fighter with the power of an Aesir could have knocked her prone. He ended his charge poised over the fallen giant with his sword pressed against her throat.

"Curse me all you want," Tyr told Sindr, "but if you make a move or try to ignite your body Surtur will be shy one daughter." Sindr glared balefully at him, but otherwise kept still. "That's a handy trick you have to change your size. Do it again. Small enough that I don't have to stand on tiptoe to keep this sword at your throat."

As he gave Sindr orders, Tyr saw the fire demons creeping across the rubble, intent on rescuing their mistress. "Call them off," he warned. Sindr sneered at him. He pressed his sword against her crimson skin. "This is Tyrsfang, forged from the tooth of Fenris itself. Your goons might get me, but I can assure you it won't be before I get you. Call them off."

"Do as he says." Sindr spat the words. "Keep back!"

Tyr nodded as the fire demons halted, pressing no further than the rubble. A few caught the leashes of the hellhounds and restrained the dogs lest they suddenly lunge and provoke the Aesir. "Good," Tyr said. "Now get yourself down to a more manageable size." He watched the giant as her body again underwent a rapid metamorphosis. When she was reduced to a height a little over seven feet the process stopped. Sindr glared at him, almost daring him to demand more.

"Just had to stay a head taller than me," Tyr quipped. He motioned her onto her feet, keeping the blade pressed to her throat. "We'll take a little walk, and if everyone stays calm, I'll let you go." Sindr kept a sullen silence as they moved across the chamber. The fire demons followed, but made no effort to close the distance.

"Of all the audacity!" Bjorn exclaimed when Tyr neared the corridor. "You caught the fire giant's daughter!" He grinned and shook his head. "But what by Sleipnir's hooves are you going to do with her?"

Lorelei stepped forward, her expression utterly remorseless. "Kill her," she told Tyr as she looked over the giant.

"I agreed to spare her if she called off the guards," Tyr informed Lorelei, stunned by her ruthlessness. "I'll not go back on my word." Again he was surprised, for the anger in Sindr's gaze flickered for a moment, her face showing incredulity at his statement.

Bjorn scratched his beard. "That's fine, but it doesn't answer the problem. What're we going to do with her?"

"You should be more worried about what *I* will do to *you*," Sindr growled. "You can't get away, and whatever you do to me, my father will return to you tenfold."

Tyr stared over her shoulder. The fire demons, never long on patience, were testing their luck now, inching ever closer to the corridor. "You must be pretty tough to live in a volcano," he told her. "Fiery within and without."

"Would you like me to show you?" Sindr challenged him. Just one of her fingers began to flicker with flames.

"Bjorn, Lorelei, start making your way," Tyr said, nodding at the recesses of the tunnel. He could see there was a turn ahead, the wall glowing even hotter than those around them. "I'll follow shortly. Once I've finished my discussion." He watched as his companions started down the passage.

"We've nothing to discuss." Sindr gave him a fierce look. "Unless you want to talk about how I'm going to char your bones after I take that sword away from you."

Tyr started backing down the passage, prodding Sindr along. "Fire giant's daughter," he commented. "You probably bathe in lava and drink flagons of boiling oil."

"Yes," Sindr said. "And I eat arrogant Aesir after they've been dunked in pitch."

They were at the corner now. Tyr could see that the fire demons were following them into the corridor. At some point they were going to stop trying to be sneaky and just rush in and try to mob him. Tyr turned so that Sindr stood between himself and the guards. He could feel the heat of the glowing wall close on his right. From the corner of his eye, he fancied he could see the lava flowing just beneath the surface.

"You like hot stuff," Tyr said, nodding at Sindr. "But how well does it like you?" He shoved her suddenly with his left arm. Given no warning, the giant staggered away. He gave her no further attention, for as he shoved her he brought Tyrsfang slashing across the wall just where the rocky shell appeared at its thinnest and threw himself deeper into the corridor.

A jet of lava exploded from the rent Tyr created, a fountain of molten rock that gushed into the corridor. Sindr was struck by the cascade. Her body, as she'd boasted, was impervious to the intense heat, but not to the tremendous force of the tide. She was blasted off her feet and sent tumbling back down the passageway. Giant and flood slammed into the fire demons, propelling all of them out from the corridor.

Tyr observed only long enough to be certain his strategy had worked, then spun around and sprinted after his companions. He'd harnessed the volcano's pent-up pressure to confound Sindr and her minions, but as he dashed past the glowing walls, he worried that other weak spots might burst and send lava pouring after the Asgardians.

TWENTY

The roar of the gushing lava was still in Tyr's ears when he was well away from the scene. Gradually the hue of the walls softened, the glow fading in intensity. Even the heat became less caustic, though still bordering on the unbearable. Tyr rounded another corner and saw Bjorn waiting for him, axe at the ready.

"Thought you were a fire demon," the wolfhunter said, relaxing slightly.

Lorelei came out from around the bend and gave Tyr an appraising look. "What did you do with Sindr?" she asked.

"I invited her to take a swim," Tyr answered. "She won't be bothering us for a while."

"Don't be so sure of that," Lorelei said. "If anyone knows the layout of this fortress better than Surtur himself, it would be her." She waved at the tunnel they were in. "This corridor can lead us to the forge. I remember it from the dark elf's map." She scowled and gave Tyr an exasperated look. "You should've killed her."

Tyr fixed the woman with a steely gaze. "I've compromised a lot on this venture, but I'll not break my word."

"Honor," Lorelei scoffed. "I think you've lost sight of what you can accomplish here." She motioned him to be quiet. "Yes, I really think you have. And consider this. Sindr knows this stronghold and she knows where we've gone. If she stops and adds those together, she'll quickly figure out what we're after. Then the only question is whether she tries to stop us herself, or tells her father."

Bjorn's face grew pale. "Surtur," he muttered.

"I expected from the first I would have to face the fire giant," Tyr said.

Lorelei stepped close and laid her hand on his cheek. "I know. You would die fighting Surtur if it meant staving off Odin's doom. But I don't want that. I want you to return to Asgard a living hero, not a dead martyr."

Tyr felt his pulse quicken at her touch, his senses racing with appreciation of Lorelei's presence, her nearness. For the instant, nothing mattered except her. Not Surtur or Sindr or Twilight, only Lorelei. He couldn't fail her. He wouldn't fail her.

"What's done is done," Tyr said. "All we can do is try to limit the damage and ensure our success. The flood will delay Sindr. We have at least a little time to beat her to the forge and make off with Twilight before she or anyone else can interfere."

Lorelei moved away, her eyes sparkling with appreciation. "A sound suggestion." She consulted the box and gestured ahead. "We keep going this way."

Tyr set out to resume the lead. As he did, he happened to glance at Bjorn. There was no sparkle in the huntsman's eyes. Only an enmity that might have matched what he'd seen in Sindr's gaze.

Tyr couldn't blame Bjorn for being resentful. He imagined that he'd feel the same if Lorelei had bestowed her affection on someone else. Only she hadn't. It was Tyr who'd supplanted Thor in her heart. This entire quest had been arranged by her so that he would exceed his upstart brother's fame, so that by giving him the chance to show all Asgard his bravery Lorelei could prove her own devotion.

It was all so clear to Tyr now. The only thing that troubled him was why it hadn't been obvious to him before.

Lorelei became more hesitant the deeper into the passageway they went. At each junction she stopped, a troubled look on her face. Tyr didn't want to put into words what he feared: she didn't know where they were. Now, when there were other reasons to suspect Surtur would guess their purpose without capturing them and finding it, he bemoaned her decision to memorize the dark elf's map rather than bring it along to consult on the way.

The tunnels, after a brief upward slant leaving the chamber where they'd fought Sindr, plunged downwards again at a steep grade. The heat in the air was hideous, though at least the walls weren't aglow from lava coursing just beneath a crust of rock. Tyr knew the temperature would only grow worse as they struck towards the stronghold's lower vaults, ever nearer the molten core of the volcano.

Cracking sounds from up ahead of them made the

Asgardians stop. For a terrible moment Tyr pictured the tunnel breaking apart and magma flooding the corridor just like the torrent he'd unleashed upon Sindr and the fire demons. They paused, waiting for any sign of such a calamity, but nothing transpired. There was only the steady cracking of rock and the sharp ping of metal.

"Sounds like someone working up ahead," Bjorn offered. His eyes brightened. "Maybe it's the forge."

Tyr shook his head. "More like a mine," he said. He took a few steps forward. Faintly, he could hear voices. The gruff, brutal tones of fire demons. "Guards up ahead, at any rate."

"Are they waiting for us?" Lorelei asked, an edge of dread in her tone.

"I don't think so. No, they're too inattentive to be waiting in ambush," Tyr assured her. "It sounds like only two of them. If Sindr had set an ambush for us, she'd use a lot more warriors." He glanced over at Bjorn. "There's no telling how many turns are between us and them," he advised, noting the curve in the passage. "We might have to move quickly to keep them from getting away if they spot us before we can reach them."

Bjorn ground his teeth. "Just show me where they are," he snarled, fingering his axe.

"Don't get ahead of me," Tyr cautioned him. He nodded to Lorelei. "Just in case it is some sort of ambush."

The Asgardians crept down the corridor, the voices and the sound of work growing more distinct. Tyr began to hope that they'd be able to catch the fire demons unobserved with the way the corridor continued to twist and turn. Then they rounded a final bend and saw a long tunnel before them, as straight as an arrow. There was a good thirty feet between themselves and the fire demons who swung around to glare at them.

"So much for doing things the easy way," Tyr swore as he charged into the guards. He'd underestimated their numbers as well. It wasn't two fire demons, but four who stood in the tunnel. They weren't expecting trouble, however, and lost precious seconds reaching for their weapons. Tyr closed with the first of his enemies before the demon had a chance to do more than raise the spiked mace he'd snatched up from where it was leaning against the wall. A slash to the head and the guard sprawled on the floor.

Bjorn was less lucky when he engaged a swordsman. The obsidian blade was firmly in the fire demon's grip when he swung at him with his axe. The two weapons clashed in a display of sparks, and a savage struggle ensued. Back and forth the two strove against one another, until finally Bjorn was able to drive his enemy back against the wall. The sudden contact with the rough rock jarred the guard for a heartbeat. His defense faltered and, in that instant, the wolfhunter's axe bit into him. Bjorn barked with triumph as his foe wilted to the ground.

Tyr contended with the remaining fire demons. One chopped at him with a glaive, but he ducked beneath the cleaving edge to stab the guard in the chest. A kick to the leg sent the dying enemy pitching headlong, and he lunged past the falling body to meet the sword of the last adversary. The Aesir's might swatted aside the fire demon's parry and left him exposed to Tyrsfang's gleaming edge.

"My mistake. Four guards," Tyr said as he turned from

his last foe. The puzzle of why the fire demons had fought instead of trying to run was solved when he looked down the passageway. He'd thought there must be another bend up ahead. In that too, he was mistaken. The corridor didn't turn again. There was nothing, only a wall of raw rock.

Clustered about at the end of the tunnel were four short, long-limbed people arrayed in the most pathetic rags. Their skin was burned and blistered, their hair and beards scraggly and unkempt. Tyr knew them to be dwarves, but never had he seen a dwarf in such a condition as these. He noted the chains that hobbled their legs, the picks and hammers locked to the manacles around their wrists. He felt pity for them as they stared at him with empty, passionless faces. How long had these dwarves been Surtur's slaves?

"Jormungand gnaw Surtur's bones!" Lorelei cursed. Tyr swung around, relieved that she too was outraged by the treatment of the dwarves. She wasn't looking at them. Her eyes were locked on the end of the tunnel and the evidence of recent construction. "The filthy giant has been expanding his stronghold! What good is a map if everything's been changed!"

Bjorn moved over to console her. "The fragment of Twilight can still guide us," he reminded her. The withering look she turned on him made the huntsman flinch.

"These tunnels are piled one over the other," she said. "I can find the direction we need to take, not which corridor will take us where we need to go." She flicked her finger against the box in annoyance.

Tyr shook his head and approached the dwarves. "Don't be afraid. We're friends," he told them. He knew they should be able to understand. The Allspeak rendered the Asgardians able to converse with any sentient people in the Nine Worlds. The dwarves just kept that same blank look. Not even the merest hint of emotion crossed their faces.

"You waste your time with them," Lorelei declared. "Any boldness they might have had has been seared out of them by the fire demons." Her expression darkened. "When their masters find them, they'll tell them we were here."

Tyr returned her dark look with one of his own. "The fire demons will know we were here when they find the dead guards," he said. When Lorelei expressed such ruthless thoughts, it was hard for him to reconcile his affection for her with his conscience. There shouldn't be a way to harbor such conflicting sentiments at the same time.

He shook off his reservations about Lorelei and focused instead on the dwarves. "You're free," Tyr told them. He brought his sword shearing down through the chains that hobbled their feet. Still there was no reaction from the prisoners.

"Lorelei's right," Bjorn called out. "You're wasting your time."

"Wasteful or not, I'll see them free," Tyr vowed. He turned his attention to the manacles, working the point of Tyrsfang under the hasps to break them one after the other. "Besides, if we're lost then there's no advantage to be had by haste. We don't know how to get to the forge."

Tyr's words finally had an impact. One of the dwarves reached out and laid a calloused hand on his arm. "I can show you," he stammered, his voice creaking as though it was seldom that he spoke. The other dwarves slowly nodded their heads. "Sometimes they set us to work there instead of digging tunnels."

Tyr laid his arm on the dwarf's shoulder. "You've been there, then? You've seen Twilight?"

The dwarf shivered and gave the sword a different name. "I've seen Odinsbane," he whispered.

TWENTY·ONE

The dwarf's name was Grokrim, and with his guidance the Asgardians were able to retrace their steps and find the turn they should have made earlier. This part of the stronghold, it transpired, had undergone much expansion over the years since the dark elf spy was here. As much as her knowledge of the map had helped them earlier, in this part of the fortress Tyr knew they could no longer depend on Lorelei. A situation she only reluctantly accepted.

"Do you think we can trust these dwarves?" Lorelei whispered to Tyr when she thought she could do so without any of them hearing. "They might betray us to curry favor with Surtur."

"I think they've been in Muspelheim long enough to know the fire giant better than that," Tyr said. "Surtur doesn't reward those who do him a service, they simply avoid being punished for failure." He shrugged and nodded at the pumice walls, thinking of the many turns and junctures they'd passed. "Besides, I don't see we have much choice in the matter. It's either follow Grokrim or wander this maze until the fire demons find us anyway."

Lorelei took little solace from the stark assessment, but it was clear she saw the logic in it. Instead of raising new concerns about the dwarves, she focused on what they would do when they reached the forge. "Twilight is certain to be protected," she said. Her hand patted the satchel hanging from her shoulder. "I've only a few spells left. We've consumed the best of Amora's devices. If the forge is too well defended, I'm not sure I can render much help."

Grokrim stopped and turned, his eyes filled with fear. Despite her whispers, the dwarf had heard everything she said. Tyr guessed that captivity in the fortress had honed his senses to a razor's edge. "More than guards, maybe," Grokrim muttered. "Surtur sometimes visits the forge. A great black throne sits facing the kiln, and he will spend hours, even days, there, watching the flames lick across Odinsbane."

Tyr's heart pulsed with a mix of fear and excitement. It might yet come to pass that he would face Surtur in battle. He looked over at Lorelei, then fixed Bjorn with a commanding stare. "Should the fire giant be there, I'll handle him. You two get Twilight and get away."

Panic showed on Lorelei's face. She pressed close to him. "You mustn't," she objected. "You'd certainly be killed!" The concern in her voice made Tyr's heart beat still faster.

Bjorn barked an ugly laugh, jealousy in his eyes. "You think you'd last a second against Surtur?" he scoffed. "They say the fire giant is a thousand feet tall. That when he fought Ymir the heavens themselves shook in awe of him."

Tyr favored the huntsman with a thin smile. "I don't know if Surtur is a thousand feet tall or not," he said. He gestured at the confined tunnels around them. "But I do know if he dwells in this place then he must bring himself down to a less formidable size. Just like Sindr, he wears the shape that best suits his needs." He turned back to Grokrim. "Well, what about it? How big is the fire giant when he visits the forge?"

Grokrim whispered with the other dwarves before offering an answer. "Always he comes clad in a frightening aspect, the fury of the mountain hissing around him like a cloak. Looking at him, the power and strength is obvious. As to his size, the throne is built to seat someone ten times as tall as a dwarf, nor is there room to spare when he sits there."

"That would give him a height of fifty feet," Lorelei estimated, worry in her voice.

"A far cry from a thousand," Tyr remarked. He glanced at Bjorn and raised his left arm. "I've met bigger foes," he said.

"But who's going to tie Surtur down for you?" Bjorn replied. At once the wolfhunter's face went pale, shocked by the slight that had left his own mouth. Tyr saw him start to say something more, perhaps by way of apology, but when his eyes drifted to Lorelei, he held his tongue and bitterness crawled back onto his visage.

"The denizens of the stronghold are enemy enough, old friend," Tyr cautioned Bjorn. Whatever Bjorn's reasons, however blinded by emotion, the insult had pierced him like a dagger. "Don't seek to make more." He shifted his gaze to Lorelei, then back to the huntsman. "If you insist, then wait until we've seized Twilight and are on our way back to Asgard before you force the issue."

"I'll wait," Bjorn promised. "By the conditions you've named." His hands clenched into fists at his side. "But I'll not wait long."

It pained Tyr to see Bjorn's anger and to know it was focused on him. Yet he knew there could be no compromise with the delusion that fed such hostility. The love of Lorelei was something the huntsman wouldn't give up, even if it was an illusion that existed nowhere except in his own mind. Time was the only cure for the lovestruck, and right now there simply wasn't enough.

"Lead on, Grokrim," Tyr instructed the dwarf, turning from Bjorn. Whatever hostility, whatever delusion, he knew the wolfhunter would hold to his word. "Let's find this forge and take our leave of Surtur's domain."

By Tyr's estimation, several hours had passed since he'd released the torrent of lava that carried off Sindr and her entourage. It was more difficult to evaluate the distance they'd covered since then. The tunnels were a winding, confused maze, passing over and through each other, sometimes swelling to massive heights, at others becoming so low that only the dwarves could walk in them without bending their backs. Always oppressive, the heat rose and fell as they marched through the corridors. Sometimes the walls glowed with the heat they exuded, at others they were cool enough to touch without burning the skin.

As the journey stretched on, Tyr expected to hear alarm bells ringing. He was confident that Sindr had suffered no harm in the molten flood. He didn't know how far the surge had swept her away, but he anticipated that once she returned the stronghold would be put on alert. Patrols would rove the tunnels, hellhounds loosed to run the intruders down. He almost welcomed the onset of these inevitable attacks, for then at least he'd be spared the tension of waiting for the blow to fall.

Yet with each moment they remained undiscovered, Tyr knew they got closer to the forge. He wondered again if Sindr hadn't guessed their purpose, if the reason why there were no guards hunting for them was because she'd held them back to lie in ambush at the forge. It would be in keeping with what he knew of her cruel mind to hatch such a plan. Let them come within a hand's breadth of victory only to snatch it away from them at the last instant.

"The forge is up ahead." Grokrim stopped and turned to Tyr. He pointed to a branch of the tunnel to their right. The passage grew both broader and higher in that direction and there was a flickering glow playing across it in the distance.

"You sound as though you aren't going any farther," Lorelei accused the dwarf.

Grokrim bowed his head. "We haven't the courage," he admitted. "There was a time when we would've helped you against the fire giant, but that was long ago."

"You'll have to come with us," Tyr told Grokrim. "We won't have the time to come looking for you after we take Surtur's sword." He noted the blank expression of Grokrim's face, saw it repeated on the visages of the other dwarves. "You have to stay with us so we can rescue you from Muspelheim."

Grokrim shook his head. "The time for that too is past. We've been too long under the fire giant's boot. Our honor is withered. Were we to return to Nidavellir, we would see our shame reflected in the eyes of every dwarf we met." He nodded to the other dwarves. "No, it is here we stay, but if you can steal Odinsbane from Surtur, then at least we'll know we've helped strike back at the fire giant."

Tyr started to argue, to try and break the dwarves of their morbid fatalism, but Lorelei motioned him away. "When the mind of a dwarf is set, even the All-Father can't change it. You'll never convince them they're not responsible for being captured. They're ashamed they've let themselves be slaves and lacked the courage to die fighting." She sighed and made a helpless gesture with her hands. "They still lack that courage. Let them be. They've helped us, but they have to find the ambition to help themselves. Even my magic can't give that to them."

"You could still fight," Tyr told Grokrim. "Losing a battle doesn't mean losing the war."

"We'll remember your kindness," Grokrim said. He and the other dwarves turned away and started back up the tunnel. "We'd only be in the way, and concern for us might distract you. If you would do something for us, then fulfill your quest and hurt Surtur where he will feel it the most." The dwarves hastened away into the sweltering maze.

"They want to get away quick so when the trouble starts they don't get caught up in it," Bjorn commented.

"Don't judge them too harshly," Tyr advised. "We don't know what they've gone through, or how long they've had to endure the chains of Muspelheim." He wiped beads of sweat from his brow. "How much valor would you have left after years locked away down here? No, Grokrim took risk enough just showing us the way. Let's prove his trust in us wasn't misplaced."

TWENTY-TWO

Cautiously, the three Asgardians made their way down the tunnel, each step bringing them nearer to the flickering glow and the rising heat. Faintly at first, then louder, the sound of metal striking metal reached their ears. Bjorn wrinkled his nose and sniffed the air. "Even in Muspelheim, it seems a forge carries the same smell," he said.

Tyr's fingers tightened about his sword's grip. "Remember, if it proves that Surtur is there, leave the fire giant to me. Your role is to seize Twilight and escape." He waved his arm to stop the objection Lorelei was going to raise. "This is more important than glory and pride. Without Twilight to wield, Surtur won't be able to carry out his part in the prophecy. We'll have changed the doom that menaces Odin at Ragnarok."

They crept onward, listening for any sound that would betray the presence of Surtur. There was nothing. Only the steady clamor of metal against metal. As their advance continued, the passage turned. Before them, closing off the way ahead, was a set of enormous doors fashioned from the same red metal as the shields the guards on the bridge had carried. The portals were sculpted into the semblance of leering, fiendish heads, horns protruding from their foreheads, fangs jutting from their jaws, lupine tongues lolling from their mouths. The flickering glow they'd noticed from afar was seeping out from beneath the doors, a fiery haze that crawled along the walls like mist. The sound of hammer striking metal was even more distinct now, making it obvious to Tyr that its source was just on the other side of the barrier.

"You're the strongest," Lorelei told Tyr, provoking a scowl from Bjorn. "You'll have to smash open the doors."

Tyr shook his head. He had an idea why Lorelei wanted him to execute the task and why she'd put it in such terms as to feed Bjorn's jealousy. If he forced the doors, then the wolfhunter could rush past him. In his current temper, Bjorn would be certain to make straight for Surtur. By default, Tyr would have to secure Twilight and escape with it. "The door may not be locked," he said.

"We have one chance to surprise whoever is inside," Lorelei replied. "If they hear us fiddling with the latch to see if it is locked, we'll lose that advantage."

Tyr still didn't like it, but he knew there was logic in what she said. He nodded his head and gave Bjorn a reminder. "The fire giant is mine." The huntsman gave him an indifferent shrug. Tyr knew it was the only kind of answer he'd get from his friend.

Steeling himself, Tyr drew close to the doors. When he was ten yards away, he broke into a run. Tightening his grip on his sword, he drove his left shoulder into the metal panels. He could feel the impact shudder through his body. There was the sound of tortured mechanisms bursting apart, the clatter of pins and catches scattering across the floor. The doors were thrown inwards, banging back on their hinges. Tyr stumbled forwards several paces before he regained his balance.

The room he found himself in was immense and illuminated by the red glow of the massive forge at its center. An enormous basin, apparently crafted from obsidian, stretched across the middle of the chamber. It was filled with bubbling lava fed by a chute that stretched back into one of the walls and a flue that carried up into the ceiling. A gate of diamond sealed the flue, but behind its transparent face could be seen a mass of molten lava. Rings were embedded in every side of the basin and to these were fitted heavy chains. From what Tyr could see, the shackles hung empty, saving those that were fastened about a lone dwarf. It was his hammer that they'd heard, and the object upon which he worked was a sight that caught the Aesir's breath.

A gigantic blade, twenty feet long and five feet across, its edge as black as midnight, lay in an obsidian mold. It was a weapon fashioned for a giant, shaped from an ore Tyr couldn't begin to put a name to. Its darkness was mottled by internal sparks, as though a constellation had collapsed into its surface. An aura of distortion flickered about it, coruscating through shades of brightest red to deepest purple. More than its shifting hues, it was the atmosphere of menace that rolled off the sword that impressed Tyr, the condensed horror of a battlefield, impatient and eager to wreak havoc upon the universe.

In the moment it took Tyr to recover, he saw Bjorn dash past him. "Fire giant! Bjorn Wolfsbane has come for you!" he howled as he charged into the chamber, axe held high. Tyr shifted his gaze and saw the huntsman was making for a colossal seat that appeared to have been carved from a single ruby. Sculpted with dragons along its arms and a fanged beast for its backrest, Tyr imagined it was a recreation in gigantic miniature of Surtur's Burning Throne from which he reigned over Muspelheim in his Court of Conflagration. The haste of Bjorn's rush to come to grips with the tyrant before Tyr made the hunter overlook an important detail. The chair was empty.

Not so the room. Bjorn's headlong charge exposed him to the other denizens of the forge, set there to guard Twilight. Four monstrous sentries moved away from alcoves cut into the walls. One had already started towards the doors Tyr threw open, but the other three lumbered after Bjorn. Each was twenty feet tall, crudely human in shape if not proportions. Their skin, if such the shell that covered them could be called, was hardened stone, grinding and groaning as they moved. Though Tyr thought they resembled some manner of ape in body, their heads had a woeful familiarity, evoking the horned visage of Sindr. Revulsion filled Tyr as he asked himself to what use Surtur had put her siblings, those who failed the cruel tests set by their father.

The shambling sentinels bore weapons in their oversized hands, an array of swords and bludgeons larger and more imposing than those of the stronghold's fire demons.

Tyr noted that armor had been riveted directly to the stone bodies, encasing the most vulnerable points with irremovable plates of dull red metal. There was only a dim awareness in their gaze, recalling to him the stare of a trained dog. Attentiveness, even cleverness, but no real comprehension.

"Back, monster!" Tyr shouted at the sentinel as it advanced towards him. The lumbering creature didn't so much as pause, but merely raised its stone club to strike at him. He met its swing with a sweep of Tyrsfang that sent the better half of the bludgeon spinning through the air. The armored brute drew back its arm and threw the remains of its weapon into his face.

The tactic caught Tyr by surprise. The broken heft of the club slammed into him, slashing his nose and cheek. Momentarily dazed, he failed to fend off the sentinel's fist when it drove a punch at his belly. The stony fist had the force of a battering ram. Tyr was lifted off his feet and flung through the air. He crashed against a rack of tools near the forge, spilling them across the room. He heard the horrible sizzle of those that splashed into the basin of lava.

In his fall, Tyr's sword was knocked from his grip. As he started to rise from the wreckage, he could see it lying on the floor but before he could make a move towards it, the sentinel charged him. A second blow of its massive fist drove him back to the ground. Tyr raised both arms to shield himself as the monster made ready to stomp on him with its foot.

Before the blow could fall, sparks flared before the sentinel's eyes. The brute didn't cry out, it simply pawed at its face as though by such means it could regain its sight. Tyr took no chance that the strange creature could. He seized its upraised foot. The stone sentinel must have weighed several tons, but the Aesir's strength was equal to the burden. Gripping with his hand, leaning in with his other arm, Tyr heaved against the creature's mass. This time it was the sentinel that was lifted off the ground, pushed back against the forge. It had enough awareness to recognize its peril, for its hands left its eyes and fumbled at the lip of the basin. The agility to save itself, however, wasn't in the monster's favor and it toppled over into the molten fire.

"Quickly! Get Twilight!" Lorelei shouted to Tyr, pointing at the obsidian mold.

Tyr took one step towards the black sword, then his gaze was drawn to Bjorn. The huntsman was surrounded by the remaining sentinels. His axe had removed the fingers from one and gashed the knee of another, but the creatures were little bothered by such injuries. Steadily they converged upon Bjorn. When he tried to put a stone rack between himself and the enemy, one of the monsters swatted the barrier aside, spilling materials used by the smiths in every direction.

"Get the sword!" Lorelei shouted again.

Tyr shook his head and turned. His hand closed about the grip of a sword, but it was that of Tyrsfang, not Twilight. He couldn't leave Bjorn to be overwhelmed by the sentinels. Ignoring Lorelei's shouts, he rushed to help the huntsman.

TWENTY-THREE

One of the sentinels turned as Tyr ran toward the melee. It had little chance to defend itself before he leaped at it, bringing his gleaming sword chopping down. The brute had just started to lift its own blade to block his blow. Tyrsfang sheared through the weapon and ripped down into the creature's head. The metal plates bolted to its skull split beneath the strike, torn from their moorings in the stony skin. The creature staggered as fiery sludge bubbled up from its wound. It appeared immune to pain, however, and struck at Tyr with the remains of its broken sword. The jagged edge raked across his armor with a metallic shriek.

"The heart! Strike for its heart!" The shout came from the dwarf shackled to the forge. Tyr seized upon the smith's advice and stabbed at the hulking monster's armored chest. The red metal offered no protection against Tyrsfang, and its point punched through to the stony skin beneath. Tyr had to spring back as a spray of steaming ichor jetted from the wound. The sentinel staggered for a moment, clutching at the gash in its chest as though to stem the molten flow.

Then it slammed forward, the ground shaking as its lifeless bulk fell.

Tyr gave a worried look at Tyrsfang, but the enchantments laid upon the Great Wolf's fang were too mighty to be overcome by the sentinel's burning heart. Jumping over its inert form, he hurried to help Bjorn. The remaining monsters had him pressed back near the crimson throne, forcing him up onto the steps of the dais on which it stood. He was bleeding from a gash in his leg, nearly losing his footing as the steps became slick with his blood.

"Stay there!" Tyr cried out in warning. With his back to the throne, Bjorn was unaware of the grisly change that had come upon the chair. Flames were emanating from its depths, slowly growing in intensity. Some dread sorcery was involved, for though the flames became more violent, he noted no increase in the heat that afflicted the room. He wondered what magic disguised the flames, and to what purpose.

Bjorn didn't appear to hear him, for he continued to climb the steps, doing his best to stave off the sentinels with his axe. Tyr sprang over the materials scattered on the floor, ingots of Uru and dwarven steel stolen by Surtur's minions for the continual refinement of Twilight. He came upon the sentinels from behind, lashing out with his blade and slashing each in its turn across its broad back.

One of the monsters swung around, chopping at him with its sword. Tyr managed to fend off the blow, though turning the sentinel aside was like matching strength with Sindr again. He made a quick feint to one side, hoping to trick it into exposing its chest, but the creature refused the bait and he had to content himself with a long cut down its leg. The brute stumbled, the injured leg buckling under it, but the sentinel remained very much in the fight.

The same couldn't be said of the wolfhunter.

"Bjorn!" Tyr cried out. He saw the sentinel fighting his friend drop the Asgardian with a glancing blow from its club. He crumpled on the steps of the dais at the monster's very feet.

Tyr ignored the creature he was fighting and charged instead for the dais. He felt pain shoot through his body and knew he'd been hit in the side by the monster he'd been fighting. It was a sloppy contact, however, for a more telling strike would have thrown him across the room.

Forgetting the closeness of his escape, Tyr leaped at the sentinel standing over Bjorn as it raised its club to deliver the killing blow. The Aesir slammed into the creature from behind and sent it crashing into the throne. The eerie flames, that fire without heat, engulfed the monster, lapping around its stone body in a slithering, creeping manner. Tyr shoved Bjorn aside as the sentinel rose and stumbled away from the throne. The thing was a walking pyre now, flames writhing greedily around it. The armor bolted to its body dripped away in molten blobs, its craggy flesh began to split and fracture as the inferno consumed it. Tyr thought of the awful precision with which the Burning Throne had been named if it too possessed the deadly power of this one. He could readily imagine the fire giant reigning from such a lethal place, a chair whose blazing fury only Surtur could endure.

While the stricken sentinel was being consumed, the

one that Tyr had struck in the leg returned to the fight. It stalked straight towards the two warriors. He tried to rally Bjorn, but the stunned huntsman didn't stir. Tyr frowned when he saw that the last enemy was aware of how its fellows had been struck down. It was coming at them from an angle that would keep it well away from the throne's trap and it had one arm clenched close over its chest to protect its heart.

Tyr ground his teeth. Now would be a good time for one of Lorelei's spells! If the situation weren't so dire, he might find it funny that he should call on magic to help him after warning the others not to depend too dearly upon it. He shot a glance across the room. He saw Lorelei beside the obsidian basin. Though they had not found Surtur waiting for them in the chamber, he took a bleak kind of comfort knowing she was ready to make off with Twilight if the fight with the sentinels went against them.

"Come along and get me," Tyr hissed at the monster, flourishing his sword to hold its attention. He wanted to divert it from Bjorn and, above all, keep it from noticing Lorelei. The monsters had been set here to guard Twilight after all.

The ploy worked. The brute came lumbering after Tyr. Now, as he moved, he began to feel the hurt of his wound. Blood ran down his side from where the sentinel's sword struck him. "You've had a bit of my blood, but that's all you'll have," he warned the guardian.

The sentinel stomped through the spilled materials. Tyr watched as steel ingots were stamped out of shape by the monster's weight. He heard the groan of Uru as it resisted the pressure brought against it. Pursuing Tyr through the debris, the creature shattered jars and pots, spilling more esoteric materials from their vessels. When one pot in particular broke open, Tyr noted a familiar smell.

Perhaps if Sindr hadn't boasted about her venture to Hel, Tyr would have dismissed the connection the odor evoked. He'd also ventured into Hela's deathly domain and while there he'd seen the dragon Nidhogg chewing on the roots of Yggdrasil. The smell of the worm's venom wasn't easily forgotten, nor its terrible effect.

Tyr sheathed his sword and circled around the last sentinel. He was certain the monster had no idea of its peril, otherwise it would never have risked stepping on the pot. Only luck had kept the monster from already suffering the bite of Nidhogg's venom. Tyr was going to change that luck.

"That's it," he goaded the brute. "Keep after me. I'm the one you want." He darted back as the sentinel slashed at him with its sword. Tyr kept one eye on the broken pot, not willing to risk exposing his plan by looking directly at it.

The opportunity finally came. Tyr angled himself so that with one quick motion he could make a grab for the broken vessel. He could see the venom leaking from it, sizzling on the floor. Would there be enough left for his purpose? He didn't know, he could only act and trust that there would be. When the sentinel made another swing at him, Tyr darted to the side. His hand seized the handle of the shattered pot. Wary lest so much as a speck of the venom land on his own skin, he swung the broken vessel at the sentinel.

The monster brought its sword up to block the crude missile, but in doing so it only caused the venom to spatter across more of its body. Smoke bubbled off the sentinel as its stony skin crumbled, dripping to the floor in bits and pieces. The brute's face cracked and where the venom sizzled its features began to slough away.

Tyr drew Tyrsfang once more and charged the stricken monster. He thrust the blade into its chest, easily penetrating its crumbling skin. He was prepared this time for the gout of molten ichor that jetted from the wound, twisting so that he was clear of the fiery spray. The sentinel made a last, feeble swipe at him before collapsing to the floor.

"And then there were none," Tyr said. He turned and hurried back to Bjorn. The wolfhunter was recovered enough that he was sitting up, one hand pressed against his bleeding scalp.

"Couldn't save one for me?" Bjorn grumbled. "Had to show off in front of Lorelei."

Lorelei! A sudden dread took hold of Tyr. He spun about and faced the forge. Unbidden, rising up from deep inside him, was an overwhelming fear. Though he'd urged her to escape with the sword, Tyr now feared that he would find both her and Twilight gone.

Twenty-Four

Tyr found that Lorelei was still beside the forge and Twilight was still resting in its mold. What he couldn't be certain of was whether either situation was of her choosing. She was backed up near the basin, her dirk in her hand. The satchel of arcane apparatus was lying on the floor at her feet. Preventing her from reaching it, or from stepping away from the forge was the dwarven smith, his hammer clenched in his fist and raised to strike her if she made a move.

A tremendous sense of relief rushed through Tyr, blotting out the fear that had come over him. Here was the explanation to why Lorelei lent them no aid in the fight. She'd been set upon by the dwarf. She was still true to her friends and to Tyr. It had been shameful of him to suspect her, even for a moment, of treachery.

"Peace, swordsmith," Tyr called to the dwarf as he stepped closer. The shackles fastened to his chains made it clear he was no willing helpmate of Surtur, but a captive like Grokrim and his group. "Lorelei is a friend who has led us through many a danger to reach this place."

The dwarf shifted back so he could see both of them at the same time. When Lorelei made a move to recover the satchel, he gestured menacingly with his hammer. "I recognize you for Tyr Odinson," the smith declared in his gravelly voice. "That is why I called out to you in the fight. *Her* I don't know."

Lorelei glared at the dwarf. "It should be obvious to you that I'm not a fire demon or one of Surtur's brood," she snapped.

"The obvious is the most deceptive of all," the dwarf said with a shrug. "We've been forced to craft many things for the fire giant, among them a jeweled belt that allows the wearer to take on the seeming of whatever they choose. For all I know, I bandy words with Sindr at this moment."

"You would be wrong," Tyr assured the smith. He gestured with his sword at the dwarf's chains. "Would you accept that we're friends if I freed you?"

The dwarf's eyes were wary, and became more so when he spotted Bjorn limping across the chamber toward the forge. "I trust nothing until I know why you've come here." He gestured at Twilight in its mold. "Obviously you've come for Surtur's sword, but with what intention? What use do you hope to make of it?"

"No use at all," Tyr said. "Merely to keep it from the fire giant's grasp. We will bear it back to Asgard and seal it away in a vault where it can harm no one."

The answer brought visible relief to the dwarf. He lowered his hammer and bowed in apology. "Forgive me, but I had to be sure. I trust the word of Tyr Odinson that you'll do what you say." He nodded at the obsidian basin. "I've labored long over these flames, giving shape to Twilight. I know only too well the evil power that has been infused into the sword. The only thought that gave me any comfort at all was that its evil wouldn't be unleashed until Ragnarok and the end of all things." He turned and bowed his head to Lorelei. "When you reached to take Twilight, I panicked, fearing you'd come to bear it away and set its evil loose."

"The only thing I'll set loose is you," Tyr said. "And I do so now." He brought his sword shearing through the smith's chains.

The dwarf stepped back, massaging his wrists, a jubilant smile on his face. "You've the fellowship of Nilfli for this deed," he said. "If there's any favor a dwarf too long held by the chains of Muspelheim can render you, you've but to ask and it shall be done."

Tyr smiled at the smith. "I've but one favor for now," he said, nodding at the forge. "What wards have been laid on Twilight to prevent its theft?"

"None," the smith said. He jabbed a thumb at one of the lifeless sentinels. "Those were set here to watch the dwarves who labored over Twilight, to guard against sabotage. In his arrogance, Surtur never believed anyone could be so brazen as to enter his stronghold and try to steal the sword." Nilfli waved his hand at the mold. "You've but to reach in and pluck it out. It was made to resist the hand of Surtur. There's no fire that can warm it unless it has been anointed with the proper unguents first. Don't be daunted by its size, for just as the fire giant can expand and reduce, so too must his sword. Twilight will alter to suit the one who holds it."

Tyr sheathed Tyrsfang and stepped toward the forge.

"It will need do so only one more time," he vowed. "After that, no other hand will touch it." He could feel the wickedness of the sword when he came close to it, sense its destructive malignance. Twilight was a weapon made for no other purpose. A blade to bring annihilation to gods and mortals.

"Stop!" Lorelei called out. Her face was filled with concern, her eyes at the verge of tears. She came toward Tyr and laid her hand on his arm. "Let me weave a spell to protect you against the sword's malice. I should not bear it if anything were to happen to you now, at the moment of your great triumph."

"My courage has brought us this far," Tyr said, patting her hand, feeling energized merely by her touch. His injuries from the sentinel faded from his awareness. All he could think of was her and how pleased she would be when he brought their quest to an end. "My courage is enough to see us through to the very end."

"Is my courage any less than yours?" Bjorn growled. Despite his wounds, he raced to the forge. There was a desperate, feverish look upon his face as he stared at them. His eyes were filled with devotion when he looked toward Lorelei and the most bitter jealousy when he gazed at Tyr. "The honor is mine!" Bjorn insisted, reaching into the mold.

Tyr knew the wolfhunter wasn't thinking clearly, that the only thought in Bjorn's mind was to impress Lorelei and earn her favor. The realization gave him momentary pause, for hadn't his own mind been filled with the same obsession? In the moment it took him to reconcile the thought with his emotions, he lost any opportunity to stop Bjorn. The huntsman's hand closed about Twilight's raw tang and raised the weapon from its mold.

Nilfli cried out as the sword shrank to fit Bjorn. Sight of the evil blade raised high was too much for the smith and with a scream he ran from the forge, striking at a section of wall that pivoted inwards. Tyr had only a momentary glimpse of the dwarf as he fled down a dark tunnel.

Tyr could see the reason for Nilfli's panic. It was written across Bjorn's face. The huntsman's expression was consumed utterly by murderous bloodlust, a twisted malice that went beyond the frenzy of a berserker or the savagery of a beast. It was a face that didn't merely *want* to kill but *needed* to. He knew he was looking upon the power of Twilight. Bjorn wasn't wielding the sword... it was wielding him!

A maniacal laugh like nothing he'd ever uttered before spilled from Bjorn's lips, and the huntsman sprang forwards. Tyr moved to intercept him, to keep his crazed friend from inflicting harm on Lorelei. He started to draw Tyrsfang, but Twilight's power lent Bjorn a strength and speed he'd never displayed before. The evil weapon smashed into him, splitting his armor and throwing him across the room. Tyr landed in a crumpled heap, his body racked with agony such as he'd never imagined.

"Run!" Tyr shouted at Lorelei. He strove to crawl toward her, to at least distract Bjorn long enough so she could get away.

Lorelei didn't move. She just stared at Bjorn, and a cruel smile formed. The mania slipped away from the wolfhunter as though a veil had been lifted. He blinked in confusion, but when his eyes focused on Lorelei, the consuming ardor instantly returned to them.

"Enchantress." Tyr spat the word. As he did, his own ardor for Lorelei evaporated. He was aware now of the magic she'd gradually woven to snare both of them, a magic so strong that its hold over Bjorn was mightier than Twilight's murderous urgings. Lorelei had made a great show of relying upon the devices Amora had left her while letting them forget that in one arena of magic she surpassed even her elder sister, the dark art of enchanting the minds and hearts of others and using their devotion to make them her slaves.

Lorelei turned and glowered at Tyr. "Curse me as you like," she told him, a sneer on her lips. "Fortune favors the brave." She ran her fingers down Bjorn's cheek.

"You've bound him with your spells!" Tyr snarled. "Just as you tried to bind me." He shifted his gaze to Bjorn. "Fight her! The enchantment will weaken if you recognize it for what it is!"

"Of course, in your arrogance you would insist only a spell could make me prefer Bjorn Wolfsbane to Tyr Odinson," Lorelei said, smiling at the huntsman. "You can't conceive that he's the better man. But he is." She pointed at Tyr. "Kill him," she told Bjorn.

Bjorn took one step towards the Aesir and then hesitated. Tyr was amazed to see the turmoil on his face. Lorelei's enchantment had overcome Twilight's call, but it wasn't enough to make his friend murder him.

Lorelei noted the reluctance of her swain to act. An edge of fear crept into her eyes and she hurriedly dismissed the command that provoked the conflict lest she lose control of Bjorn. "Leave him," she countermanded her previous order. "He can do no harm to us here." She reached into her satchel and drew out the Wayfarer's Mirror. She turned it away, letting the light from the forge play across it until it reflected on the floor. "Come, Bjorn. It is time we were leaving."

"Bjorn!" Tyr shouted to his friend. "Can't you see she's just using you? She needs someone under her spell to carry Twilight for her so she doesn't submit to its power! She'll cast you aside as she did me, the moment she doesn't need you!"

The wolfhunter turned and gave him a weary look. "I thought better of you. Can you not be happy for me?" Bjorn didn't wait for an answer, but stepped into the light cast by the mirror. One moment he was there, the next he was gone.

"Goodbye, Tyr," Lorelei said, blowing him a kiss. "You were almost a perfect stooge, but, all things considered, it is better this way. Bjorn will be much easier to deal with than you would be when we reach Asgard."

Pivoting the Wayfarer's Mirror, Lorelei stepped forward until she reached the reflected light. For an instant she stood there, then she was gone.

Tyr was alone. Abandoned to Muspelheim and Surtur's vengeance.

TWENTY-FIVE

Tyr pounded his fist on the floor, staring at the spot from which Lorelei and Bjorn had vanished. The Wayfarer's Mirror! From the very first she'd intended to use its power to escape Muspelheim, begging that its magic was too uncertain to employ in such fashion merely to deceive them as to her intentions. Another ploy to make Tyr and Bjorn believe she needed them to help her return to Asgard when in truth she needed only one of them. The one who was so under her sway that he would even resist Twilight's power to obey her.

It was only now when Lorelei was gone that Tyr understood how much he'd fallen under her enchantment. She'd sent her sorcery into his heart and mind, manipulating him just as she had Bjorn. He wondered if it even really mattered to her which of them would secure Twilight for her. All her insinuations, her appeals to his vanity, had been only deceit. She cared nothing for Tyr, she made that clear when she ordered Bjorn to kill him. He marveled at the great regard his friend must have for him that he'd been able to resist that command. He tried to tell himself that if their roles had been reversed, he'd have done the same, but there was no way to be certain. Indeed, even now, knowing how she'd used him, Tyr couldn't completely banish his feelings for Lorelei. Her affection for him might have been merely deception and enchantment, but she'd evoked something genuine within him. It made her betrayal all the more painful.

Pain raced through more than just his heart. Tyr's whole body was tormented by the wounds he'd suffered, both from the sentinels and from Twilight. It taxed his endurance nearly to the limit simply to stand. He groaned when he thought of the vast network of tunnels winding through the stronghold. He'd have to pick his way through that maze, alone and injured. Even if he made it out of the fortress there would be the trek across Muspelheim's hostile wastes before he reached the gate again. Nor was he certain he could force his way through to Bifrost. After all, Heimdall had been bewitched, made to forget that they'd passed his post. Unless someone else noted Tyr's absence and asked Heimdall to use his Allsight to find him, there was no reason to expect the way to be open to him.

First, though, was the matter of getting away from the forge. Tyr knew when the alarm was raised and Surtur's minions started looking for intruders, this would be one of the first places the fire demons would secure. That they hadn't already done so was a stroke of luck. He didn't want to test the indulgence of fickle fortune still further.

Fleeing when the Asgardians fought among themselves,

Nilfli had left the secret door open behind him. That would be a starting point, Tyr decided. He didn't know how many denizens of the fortress knew about the dwarf's escape route, but he was betting it wasn't general knowledge or it would have been sealed up.

Tyr struggled back to his feet. Clenching his teeth against the pain that flared through him, he slowly made his way towards the door. Each agonizing yard of progress felt as arduous as the scorching plains of Muspelheim. Only the Aesir's firm resolve kept him moving. The determination that he would somehow make it back to Asgard and set everything right.

Nilfli's door was still dozens of yards away when the sound of baying hellhounds reached Tyr. He could hear the excited snarls of the fire demons commanding the dogs as the beasts picked up the scent. In a few moments the patrol would reach the forge. In his condition, Tyr didn't know how much of a fight he could give Surtur's minions, but he knew what the end result must be. To remain at liberty and have any chance at all, he had to reach the secret door.

Blood streamed from Tyr's wounds as he forced himself onward. He defied the torment that racked his body as he drove himself across the forge. Yard by yard, the door drew nearer. So too did the sounds of his pursuers. The baying had become frantic, he could picture the hellhounds straining at their leashes, trying to slip free of the fire demons and run their prey down. Any moment and the dogs' handlers might do just that and set the pack on him.

The closer he came to the door, the more Tyr pushed himself. To be undone after he'd exerted himself to such effect was too terrible to contemplate. He had to succeed. He wouldn't allow his struggle to be in vain.

With a last lunge, Tyr threw himself forward and toppled into the tunnel behind the door. The noise of the patrol was louder now. Any moment and they would be in the forge. If they saw the open door he'd be caught. He rolled onto his side and kicked out with his legs, driving his feet against the portal. It spun about on its pivot, locking into place with a barely audible click.

As the door shut, all sound outside became muffled. Only when he pressed his ear to the rough pumice could Tyr hear the fire demons and hellhounds as they entered the room. He had to strain to make out the shouts of the guards as they found the sentinels destroyed and Twilight stolen. There followed the awful moment when his trail of blood was discovered, and a hellhound began to snuffle at the other side of the door.

Tyr crawled away from the portal and drew his sword. Whatever enemy was first through that door wouldn't have long to regret it.

"You can put away your sword, Tyr Odinson." He spun about to see that he wasn't alone in the tunnel. Nilfli was at the mouth of a small niche cut into the side of the wall, a stone jar clenched in his hands. He nodded his chin at the door. "That's dwarf work, and only a dwarf can find it once it has been shut. The fire demons will give up after a time and try to figure out some other way we escaped from the forge."

"My companions did just that," Tyr told Nilfli. "Lorelei used a magic mirror to create a portal to Asgard."

The dwarf shook his head. "And they left you behind." He tutted.

"Had you closed the door, I would have been finished," Tyr said.

"I lingered here to do just that," Nilfli replied, "but when I saw your distress, I left the door open and went to fetch this." He held out the jar. "We're both fortunate you gained the tunnel before the guards arrived."

"What is that?" Tyr asked, pointing to the stone jar.

"Your wounds will need tending." Nilfli tapped the vessel's side. "In here is a salve we use when Surtur's minions become too enthusiastic about disciplining us. This concoction has saved the lives of many dwarves."

Tyr hesitated for a moment to let the dwarf approach. After the way he'd fallen for Lorelei's deceit he was alert for further treachery. Then he considered that Nilfli had given him no reason to distrust him. The smith had been chained to the forge, a slave of Surtur. Had he wanted to, he could have closed the secret door behind him and left the Aesir to be captured by the fire demons. That would have allowed Nilfli to strike against Tyr without exposing himself to any chance of reprisal.

Tyr set his sword down on the ground beside him as Nilfli came forward and removed the stopper from the jar. A musky, pungent smell rose from inside it. The dwarf dipped his fingers in and removed a blob of grayish paste. Tyr undid the clasps of his breastplate and let it slip away. Exposing his injured side, he winced as the stinging unguent was slathered across his wound.

"These tunnels... they're some kind of refuge for your

people?" Tyr asked, trying to keep his mind from his own pain.

"The fire demons can't watch us all the time, and not all their chains are so cleverly wrought as those that bound me to the forge," Nilfli said. "Over hundreds of years dwarves have excavated many bolt holes under Surtur's very nose. The whole stronghold is honeycombed with secret passages and hidden rooms. Some are stocked with useful supplies." He dipped his hand back into the jar and applied more of the salve. "Sadly, few who escape into these refuges remain long. Either they weary of hiding and scrounging and return to their chains or else they try to leave the stronghold and strike out across Muspelheim." The dwarf's eyes gleamed with pride. "I did so once. I made it as far as the sulfur lakes of Dyre before the fire demons caught me."

"And the secret has been held all these years?"

Nilfli's expression grew grave. "Even under torture no dwarf would betray his fellows." He drew back the sleeve of his tunic and exposed a hideous brand on his shoulder. "Sindr gave me that, and worse, when she interrogated me." His hands tightened into fists. "But I told her nothing no matter what she threatened to do."

Tyr could well imagine. The dwarves had a reputation for stubbornness that was exceeded only by their fame as craftsmen. Once a dwarf's mind was settled to some course it might as well be cast from stone. "If the secret has been kept, then could we escape the stronghold the same way you did before?"

The dwarf pulled at his beard and studied Tyr for a moment. "Perhaps we might do better," he said after a time.

"The salve should heal your hurts, and I know where we can lay our hands on some stonebread to recover our strength." Nilfli pointed at Tyrsfang. "A remarkable sword. A blade strong enough to withstand the molten heart of Surtur's sentinels. Could it stand even greater heat, I wonder?"

Tyr reached down and lifted the sword. Already he could feel his pain lessening as the gray salve did its work. He smiled as he turned the gleaming weapon back and forth. "This was made from one of Fenris's fangs. No force could destroy the Great Wolf, neither is there a power in the Nine Worlds that can destroy its tooth."

Nilfli's eyes gleamed with admiration for the weapon. "Then there might be a way," he said. "But first I would know why your companions deserted you when they returned to Asgard."

The request wasn't an easy thing for Tyr to answer. He had to confront how he'd been exploited and deceived, manipulated by Lorelei to suit her own ambition. He understood now the gambit she'd used, her enchantments befuddling both him and Bjorn so they would unwittingly do her bidding. Though Bjorn had left with her, Tyr knew his friend was but another disposable pawn to be discarded once she had no need for him any longer. Lorelei hadn't changed at all. She was still intent on securing Thor as her husband. With Twilight in her possession, she'd finally have the tool she needed to bind him to her. Just as Tyr had risked all to secure Surtur's sword to protect Odin, so too would Thor sacrifice everything if it meant their father could escape the doom foretold for him. Jealousy of his brother had played its part in bringing him to Muspelheim.

Now concern for his brother made Tyr desperate to return to Asgard.

"I fell for Lorelei's deceit and only by undoing what I've done can I rectify that wrong," Tyr stated as he finished explaining to Nilfli the treacherous turn his quest had taken. "My family is endangered by her ambition, for I think she'll not be content merely to be wife to Thor. Through him she would proclaim herself Queen of Asgard were something to happen to Odin… and with Twilight in her grasp, she has the weapon to bring my father's ruin."

The dwarf shook his head. "It is a grim business. This witch has surely caught you in a twisted web." He clapped his hand on Tyr's shoulder. "But there may be a way to spoil her scheme. There's a way to leave Muspelheim without crossing the Rainbow Bridge." He pointed at the ceiling above them. "Within Surtur's castle burns the Eternal Flame, the First Fire shed when he did battle with Ymir at the dawn of time. The fire giant can't make use of it because it is a part of himself, but he has sent his agents into other realms by means of that sorcerous flame."

"Are you saying we could pass through this Eternal Flame?" Tyr asked, hope swelling up inside his breast.

Nilfli paused, as though weighing the idea. "Ordinarily I should say no. The barriers that protect Asgard are strong, and Surtur's agents haven't been able to penetrate its walls." He raised his hand when he saw the despair that flashed onto Tyr's face. "The theft of Twilight makes things different," he hurried to explain. "Long have I labored over that terrible blade. I know the spells and substances that have gone into its forging. When she stole Twilight, Lorelei took a piece of Muspelheim itself into Asgard. That creates a harmony, a resonance that will weaken the barriers." His expression brightened. "Yes, I think it can be done."

Tyr rose to his feet. Though he still felt weak, the pain that had beset him was now only a dull throb. "Then let's get going," he told the dwarf. "The sooner we make our way to the Eternal Flame, the faster we can escape."

"Nothing is that easy," Nilfli warned him. "If it were, every dwarf who slipped his chains would have returned to Nidavellir." His visage turned grave and there was a haunted look in his eyes. "The Eternal Flame is guarded by one of Surtur's most monstrous servants, the fyrewyrm Svafnir. The serpent's breath brings on a terrible sleep that leaves its enemies helpless when it crawls forth to devour them. To pass through the portal, you will need to overcome the dragon."

"Let's find this stonebread of yours," Tyr said, his voice filled with resolution. "I'd rather not face a dragon on an empty stomach."

TWENTY-SIX

The secret tunnels and rooms cut by the dwarves crisscrossed Surtur's fortress at every level. Though they didn't create a unified network, when Tyr and Nilfli were forced to venture through the stronghold's halls there was always another hidden door nearby to bolt into when they heard the sound of a patrol. Tyr was impressed at the craft and care that generations of dwarves had employed to both construct and maintain the network. He wondered if Grokrim and his companions were even now hiding in some spot. If he could have been certain where they were, he'd have liked to bring them along to the Eternal Flame, as well as any other escaped dwarves concealed in the tunnels.

"Too dangerous," Nilfli advised, not without regret. "The more of us there are, the greater the chance we'll be discovered. No dwarf has willingly betrayed the secret of these passages, but there have been times when one was caught before covering their tracks. That is why the fire demons know there are hidden chambers, even if they lack the insight to find them except by accident."

"It is a painful thing to leave anyone behind to Surtur's tyranny," Tyr said.

"Much more for me to do so," Nilfli told him. "Some of them are kindred, a few are even of my clan. It is not easy for me to turn my back on them. But it is even more important that you make it back to Asgard and thwart Lorelei's plans. Were Odin to fall, who can say what other calamities would follow? Even we dwarves know the All-Father keeps the realms safe from Surtur. Without him, what would there be to hold the fire giant back?"

"To win a battle, sacrifices must be made." Tyr shook his head. "But it weighs easier on the mind when those making the sacrifice know what they're giving up and why."

The two continued on in silence. Tyr sometimes took a bite of the gritty stonebread Nilfli had provided. It had the taste of gravel and a texture that could chip a troll's tooth if one wasn't careful, but he had to concede that there was an invigorating quality to it. He was refreshed as though he'd spent a long night in a soft bed, his strength rekindled to what it had been before enduring the rigors of Muspelheim. Unpleasant and rough it might be, but its sustaining properties were unmatched.

Gradually the tunnels were taking them upward, into the great halls of the castle proper. The secret passages became less frequent, narrower and more confined. No longer was there room for Tyr to walk upright and he had to follow Nilfli in a stooped crouch that nearly matched the dwarf's stature. The walls pressed in so that he had to twist himself around and walk sideways to navigate the passages. Only in one respect was there any relief. The further away from the molten core of the volcano their steps took them, the less hideous the heat.

At least, such was the rule for many hours. Then, when they were well into the fire giant's halls, the temperature began to rapidly climb again. Tyr expected to see the walls start to glow from the presence of lava just behind them, but the heat they now suffered was from a much different source.

"We draw near the Eternal Flame," Nilfli cautioned him, his voice dropping to a whisper. "Svafnir is often asleep, lulled by its own breath, but if the fyrewyrm should be awake, even these tunnels won't hide us from its senses." He pointed at Tyr's sword. "You'll have to strike fast, attack the dragon before it can react."

"I've fought dragons before," Tyr said. "You've no need to worry on that score."

Nilfli's face darkened with hate. "I've fought them before too. There's nothing I despise so much as a dragon unless maybe it is a frost giant." He stirred from his dark reverie and gave Tyr an apologetic smile. "Old grudges. You'll have to excuse me. Some of my kindred once tried to slip past Svafnir despite my warnings. I never saw them again. I can only assume the serpent ate them."

"If Svafnir stands in our way, you might have your vengeance," Tyr assured the dwarf.

Nilfli led the way to another of the secret doors. He made a motion again for silence, then pressed his hand against the panel. It swung aside, revealing a stretch of hallway with walls of polished black basalt. A pungent smell at once rushed into the tunnel, both musky and burnt in its stench. Tyr knew that stink from old and had smelled it again when Lorelei employed Fafnir's breath to hide them on their approach to the stronghold. It was the reek of dragon.

Tyr followed Nilfli out into the corridor. After the confines of the dwarf passages, the colossal scale of the castle's hall was overpowering. Surtur might stride these passages a hundred feet tall and yet have room to spare. For a moment, even the God of War was awed by the magnitude of the construction and the power of the being who was lord over it all.

"This way," Nilfli mouthed, tugging at his arm and indicating the juncture ahead of them. Both the heat and the dragon stench increased as they walked down the hall. Tyr braced himself for what he would find when they reached the crossroad.

The hall the dwarf guided him to opened out into a gargantuan chamber. At a guess, Tyr judged it to be five hundred feet across and two hundred feet from floor to ceiling. Its walls were a sinister, ruddy color shot through with veins of gold, all of it polished to an oily smoothness and a mirror-like sheen. At the center of the room a mammoth flame blazed up from the floor as though emerging from a fiery well. The conflagration was at once all colors and none. Tyr was surprised that it reminded him in some strange way of Bifrost, though even the coolest shades were distorted into an angry and volatile hue. This was certainly the Eternal Flame, the First Fire shed by Surtur in the dawn of time.

Coiled around the well was a creature almost as massive in size. Svafnir the fyrewyrm, a serpent as wide around as a longship and coated in dark red scales. Looking on the reptile's hide, Tyr wondered if the shields used by the fire demons hadn't been shed by the dragon, such was their thickness. Though the beast was curled in upon itself, he judged that if it stretched out it would be longer than the hall itself.

Keeping a tight grip on his sword, Tyr advanced into the hall. He couldn't blame Nilfli for hanging back. The dwarf had shown remarkable courage just to lead him this far. Dragonslayer he might be, but Tyr doubted the orms Nilfli had faced before were aught compared to Svafnir. Certainly, Tyr had never raised a blade against its like.

The serpent's head was tucked beneath one of its coils, only the tip of its snout projecting outward. Tyr could see its flared nostrils, a greasy fume rising from them. Its jaws were clamped shut, the scaly mouth sealed tight. Warily he moved deeper into the room, wondering if there was some way they could climb over the reptile without disturbing its slumber.

As he approached, Tyr saw a glimmer of light shining from the shadow of the overhanging coil. He peered closer, his pulse racing when he noted that the shine came from a set of enormous eyes. He urged himself to calm, knowing that dragons of Svafnir's ilk had no lids to shut their eyes and must perforce sleep with them open.

No sooner had that thought come to him than a long, forked tongue rasped out from the jaws and wobbled before the dragon's face, twitching as it tasted his scent in the air.

"Assssgardian," a low, unctuous voice trembled across the room. Tyr took a step back as the dragon's coil slipped down and its head reared up. The snake-like eyes stared down at him. "It hasss been a long time ssssince I sssmelled Asssgardian."

Tyr shifted his gaze to the dragon's snout. Meeting a dragon's stare was a dangerous thing to do and he'd brought enough trouble onto himself already by letting someone meddle with his mind. "Would it do any good to ask you to step aside?"

A hiss of laughter rose from Svafnir. It shifted its colossal bulk and clawed the air with its small, vestigial arms. "Ssstep asssside," the dragon chuckled. "A disssmal turn of phrassse, Asssgardian."

"Slither aside then," Tyr corrected himself. "Whatever removes you from my path."

The forked tongue flickered again. "The only path for you issss to my sssstomach."

Tyr cursed himself for bandying words with Svafnir. The dragon's speech, as much as its stare, had a stupefying effect. He failed to notice that it had uncoiled more of its body until the serpent's tail came hurtling toward him. Instinctively he darted back and took a swing at the scaly member. But Svafnir had no intention of actually striking him. What it wanted was precisely what he'd done.

The wedge-shaped head darted forward, jaws gaping wide. Svafnir's breath exploded across the chamber. Not a blast of fire, but a smog of yellow vapor that washed across Tyr. Only for a moment did he remain standing, then the soporific cloud brought him crashing to the floor.

"Tyr!" Nilfli shouted from where he was poised at the entrance to the hall.

Svafnir twisted its head and looked towards the dwarf. "Ah!" it mused. "I sssee now! Ssso, it'sss you! After I sssettle with the Assssgardian, I'll sssee what to do about you."

The serpent dipped its head forward, mouth open to seize Tyr in its jaws. Before it could reach its prey, Svafnir found its victim wasn't as helpless as he seemed.

"Tyr!" Nilfli cried out, but this time with excitement rather than dismay. The Aesir rolled onto his feet and brought his gleaming blade swinging around. Svafnir started to pull back, but it recognized its peril too late. The sword gashed it just ahead of its eye, biting deep and raking along the snout.

"Coward! Sssneak!" the dragon howled, fiery blood spilling from its head, smoke billowing from a cleft nostril.

Tyr gestured at the reptile with his sword, not rising to the bait of answering its cries. He was still surrounded by the dragon's sleep-inducing smog and wasn't about to risk inhaling any of it. Not after how he'd almost been caught by the sudden attack.

"Isss thisss how Odin'sss ssspawn fightsss?" Svafnir raged. The dragon drew back and made ready to strike at Tyr.

Instead of meeting the challenge of the fyrewyrm's jaws, Tyr swung to meet the battering length of its tail. He'd taken something of the dragon's measure now and found that its heart was rotten with trickery. As he expected, Svafnir reversed its earlier tactic, now feinting with its head while its tail moved in from the attack.

Tyrsfang ripped across the tip of the reptile's tail, shearing through its scaly armor and sending a five-foot length of it spinning across the floor. Detached from Svafnir's body, the severed section crackled and crumbled into brittle ash.

In its fury, Svafnir uncoiled the rest of its enormous body. It reared up, its horned head brushing against the roof. Its gaze bore down on Tyr, trying to compel him to stare into its eyes by sheer force of will. Had one of its eyes not become dull and listless from the smoke spewing from its gashed snout, perhaps he would have submitted, but for now its ambition wasn't equal to its ability.

Across the chamber Tyr charged at Svafnir. The dragon's head dove toward him with the speed of a lightning bolt, but he was ready for its assault. Throwing himself to one side, he drove Tyrsfang into the reptile's jaw and twisted the blade. Fangs and bone were torn away as he wrested the sword free again.

"Sssuffer!" the dragon shrieked. "You'll both sssuffer for that!"

The enormous body undulated toward Tyr. He slashed at one of the scaly coils, but this time he misjudged Svafnir's ploy. The seemingly puny and worthless arm struck at him and caught him in its claws. He could see the digits curl around him as the dragon tried to crush him.

Again, the enchanted armor saved Tyr, defying Svafnir's effort to pulverize him. The dragon stared, incredulous at its inability to crush the Aesir. He gave the serpent no chance to resolve the puzzle. Hewing away one of the claws, Tyr broke free. Using the dragon's paw to brace himself, he lunged at the worm's head.

A roar of pain boomed through the chamber as Tyr's sword struck Svafnir's eye. The dragon whipped away from the Eternal Flame. Its anguished gyrations threw Tyr to the floor. By the narrowest margin was he able to escape the serpent's crawling bulk as it slithered across the hall. His sword flashed out again, raking along the reptile's side and slicing thick scales from its hide.

This last hurt was one wound too many. Blinded in one eye, the other clouded from its own soporific smoke, bleeding from tail, jaw, arm and side, Svafnir regretted the arrogance that had made it challenge Tyr. Heedless of any other concern, the serpent fled from its tormentor, nearly crushing Nilfli as it slithered out through the entrance.

The moment the dragon was past him, Nilfli rushed into the room. The dwarf's face fairly glowed with excitement. "By all the gods, you did it!" he crowed. "You sent that misbegotten snake hurrying from here as though Agnar the Eagle King were nipping at its tail!"

Tyr returned the dwarf's praise with a weary smile. "It was harder than it looked," he informed the dwarf. "Svafnir underestimated me. That's a dangerous thing to do in any fight. Contempt for an enemy can be a mortal error."

Nilfli kicked the heap of ash where the severed tip of Svafnir's tail had lain. "You've settled many a score laid against that snake," he said. "I only regret you didn't settle the dragon itself in the process." He gave a hopeful glance to the trail of blood the fleeing orm had left behind.

"We've more important things to do than chase after wounded dragons," Tyr reminded Nilfli. "Svafnir is sure to have the entire fortress rushing here in no time." He gestured at the billowing column of the Eternal Flame. "We'd better be gone before they get here."

Cries in the distance told them both that the alarm was already spreading. Tyr could hear the sound of rushing feet and the clatter of armor, the angry voices of fire demons vowing revenge.

"Hurry to the flame," Nilfli instructed Tyr. "Take my hand so that my courage doesn't falter," he added.

Tyr sheathed his sword and took hold of the dwarf. "I should think after seeing Svafnir, the Eternal Flame would hold no terror for you."

"The barrier between Asgard and Muspelheim is strong," Nilfli replied. "I've been so long in this realm that I don't know if I can pass through on my own. I need you, Tyr Odinson, to ensure I'm not cast out by the walls and sent back here to endure Surtur's punishment."

"I owe you much," Tyr said. "I'll not let go no matter how hard the barrier strives against us."

"Focus upon someone or something you know is in Asgard," Nilfli instructed him. "Picture it in your mind. Will yourself towards it." The dwarf gave him a sharp look. "Think of Twilight! Then we should be brought directly to Surtur's sword when we cross over."

Tyr nodded, trying to fixate upon the image of the fire giant's blade. His mind kept wandering, distracted by other thoughts. Faces of those who'd wronged them and those who he'd wronged. "Nilfli, I don't know…"

Before he could say anything more, a company of fire demons came charging down the hall into the chamber. A hundred and more, all armored in red metal and bearing obsidian weapons. Hellhounds rushed ahead of the guards, sparks flying from their fangs.

Tightening his grip on the dwarf's hand, Tyr ignored the intense heat rising from the fiery well and plunged into the Eternal Flame.

TWENTY-SEVEN

The enormous heat from the Eternal Flame inundated Tyr's body. For a heartbeat it felt as though everything that made him – flesh, mind, and spirit – was being consumed by the writhing fire. Then that instant of torment vanished, leaving in its place an impression of falling, being flung through an empty void where the only impact upon his senses was the prismatic whirl of colors that filled his eyes. Only dimly could he feel Nilfli's hand in his own.

The dwarf's hand twitched and struggled in his grip. Unable to hear anything as he was hurled through the nothingness between worlds, Tyr didn't know if Nilfli cried out to him in panic, but he knew why the dwarf was filled with terror. His hand was slipping away from Tyr's, being drawn off by the mystical energies of the portal. The Aesir tightened his hold, forcing all of his strength into the fingers that were closed around Nilfli's. He owed the smith a mighty debt and wouldn't let him be dragged away from him, doomed to languish in this eternal void.

Tyr clenched his eyes tight and banished distracting thoughts from his brain. The void, Nilfli, Muspelheim and everything else had to be ignored. To cross into Asgard he had to focus upon what he sought there. Such had been the dwarf's warning.

Again, there came a sensation that was so complete that it resonated through every facet of Tyr's being. This time it was like slamming into a wall, an unyielding barrier that tried to repel him. No, not him, but Nilfli, for the force that strove to rip him from his grip intensified, straining to tear him away.

"You'll not have him!" Tyr roared into the soundless void. Abruptly, the resistance broke, and he felt himself rushing through a breach between realities.

Tyr knew he was again in a physical domain when he felt solid ground under his feet. He could hear the dripping of water and the squeak of rats. His skin felt cold, chilled by the air around him, an almost rapturous sensation after the inferno of Muspelheim. He opened his eyes and saw that he was in a small room, its floor littered with straw. The walls were mortared stone and one end of the chamber was sealed off by metal bars. Beyond, illuminated by flickering torches, was a wide hallway with other barred doors along the opposite wall.

"Where have you brought us?" Nilfli groaned. The dwarf released Tyr's hand and hurried over to the bars. He clapped one of his calloused hands on the barrier and tested its strength. He shot Tyr a furious look. "Out of one prison and into another!"

"Lorelei's castle," Tyr answered the dwarf. He gestured at

the barred door. "I expected she would bring Twilight to her refuge, though I confess I didn't anticipate arriving in her dungeons."

Tyr's attention was drawn to a crude wooden framework piled with straw at the back of the cell. A figure stirred there, peering out from the murky gloom with amazement on his face.

"Tyr? By the All-Father, how can this be?" Bjorn asked. The wolfhunter jumped to his feet. The Uru armor had been taken from him, as had his weapons, but the wolfskin cloak had been left to him by his captors, and he hugged it tight around his body. Like Tyr, it would take time to adjust after spending so long in Muspelheim's heat.

Tyr gave the huntsman a wary look, trying to gauge Bjorn's mood. Then he threw aside caution and embraced his friend. "I was shown a way to escape Surtur's stronghold," he said, nodding towards Nilfli.

"But you botched my instructions," the dwarf grumbled, tugging at his beard as he moved away from the bars. "I told you to focus on Twilight so we might be drawn to where the sword is. Instead, you were fretting about this idiot and brought us to share his dungeon." Nilfli kicked at the straw in frustration.

"Twilight's here," Bjorn told Nilfli. He stepped back and sat down on the edge of the bed. "I brought it across for the witch." His voice was venomous when he spoke, and he hung his head in shame. "I was so determined to earn her approval I laid the most terrible weapon in all the Nine Worlds at her feet." He looked up and fixed an imploring gaze on Tyr. "Can you forgive me for being so blind? I forgot my friendship, even came to hate you whenever she offered you a tender word or smiled at you. I was overcome with anger whenever your deeds outshone mine until–"

Tyr shook his head. "There's no need to apologize. We both fell under her enchantment and she knew just how to play us against one another to suit her plans." He gestured at the cell. "From this, it seems Lorelei has no further use of you."

Bjorn's eyes were like chips of steel. "The moment the Wayfarer's Mirror brought us back to her castle, she threw me aside like an old rag. She took Twilight from me, and her guards brought me down here." A flicker of pride worked itself onto his face. "Not without some doing. More than a few of them will be laid up for months from the bones I broke." Tyr looked over at Nilfli. "That means Twilight is not as far away as you feared."

"What good does it do us if we're locked in her dungeon?" the dwarf snapped. He gestured at the bars. "Those are tough enough to defy a giant, the way they're set!"

Bjorn rose and walked over to the dwarf. "Complain all you like, but keep your voice down. I didn't injure all of her guards, and some of the ones who are left like to come down here and jeer at me."

Nilfli gave Bjorn a sour look, but when he spoke his voice was just a whisper. "They're bound to find out we're here anyway," he said. He turned and looked at Tyr. "A fine thing. You've made a present to Lorelei of us. Let us get caught without her needing to lift so much as a finger. When her guards find us, she'll get a good long laugh."

Tyr looked around the cell. While the corridor outside was well lit, in here it was dark and filled with shadows. "That depends if they find out we're here on their terms or on ours." He pointed at Bjorn's cloak. "I'll need to borrow that. I'm going to set a trap." He nodded to each of them in turn. "You two are going to be the bait..."

TWENTY-EIGHT

Tyr lay beneath Bjorn's wolfskin, curled on the floor in the deepest shadows. His sword was drawn and lay on the ground beside him with straw kicked over it. He doubted the deception would survive close scrutiny, but from a distance he might pass for nothing more than Bjorn's cloak thrown on the floor. And if anyone came close to get a better look it would be precisely what he wanted.

Bjorn and Nilfli slipped into their roles the moment they heard a door open and footsteps in the corridor. "I want to know how you got in here," the huntsman barked, his voice loud and angry.

The dwarf, when he replied, also did so in a tone that would carry. "To tell you that would be to let you know how you can leave," Nilfli wheedled. "I'll not be doing that unless you agree to pay my price. Show me that gemstone again."

The footsteps broke into a run, and it wasn't long before a man appeared outside the cell with drawn sword. From beneath the wolfskin, Tyr recognized Lorelei's castellan Gunter at the door, his face contorted with confused outrage.

"You!" Gunter snarled at the dwarf. "How did you get in there!"

Nilfli turned and smiled at Gunter. "Your prisoner offered me a sapphire big enough to choke on if I tell him that." His tone became unctuous. "What kind of counter-offer will you make me? Rubies? Diamonds?"

"Steel!" Gunter growled, brandishing his sword in one hand while he inserted a key into the lock with the other. Nilfli's brazen avarice had whipped the man into a rage. Though Tyr thought he had no choice except to act as he did even if he were thinking more clearly. If he left to get help, the dwarf might spirit his prisoner away through whatever hidden door let him into the cell. He'd no way of even guessing Nilfli was as trapped as Bjorn was.

"Now we'll get to the bottom of this," Gunter vowed as he threw open the door and stepped inside. He menaced Bjorn and Nilfli with his sword. "Back against that wall."

Tyr waited until Gunter was a few steps away from the door before springing into action. The jailer's face went ashen when he rose up from the floor and threw aside the wolfskin. Before he could recover from his shock, Tyr sprang at him. Tyrsfang cracked against the man's hand, rapping the knuckles with the flat of the blade. The blow was still delivered with enough strength behind it that Gunter's fingers were broken, and his sword clattered to the floor. Bjorn sprang in and grabbed up the weapon while Nilfli wrapped his arms about Gunter's legs before he could try to run.

"It looks as though your mistress didn't tell you to expect me," Tyr said. He lifted his sword and poised it at

Gunter's throat. "Where's Lorelei?"

Gunter swallowed and licked his lips anxiously. Fear dripped off him, but his commitment to Lorelei remained firm. "I... I won't betray my lady. Do what you want, but I won't talk."

Nilfli stepped back, his gaze fierce as he regarded the jailer. "I can make him talk, Tyr Odinson." He drew back his sleeve and displayed the ugly brand left there by Surtur's fire demons. "I don't think this one would've lasted an hour once he was turned over to Sindr's care."

Tyr shook his head. "We don't have an hour." In a blur of motion, he whipped his sword around and drove the hilt against the side of Gunter's head. The man collapsed to the floor, stunned by the blow. Tyr chuckled to see the surprised expressions Bjorn and Nilfli gave him. "What? He said he didn't want to talk." He gestured to the huntsman. "Take his livery and whatever else you can use, then bind and gag him. We'll let him take your place for a while."

"And what then? We get clear of this castle and warn Odin?" Bjorn asked.

"There isn't time for that!" Nilfli argued. "You can't leave Twilight in the possession of this witch a moment longer! There's no knowing what kind of evil she could put it to." The smith thumped his chest. "I've worked on that sword long enough to know its power. Surtur used some of his own essence to bind that blade to him and magnify its strength. I tell you, you don't know the awful things someone could use it for."

"Nilfli's right," Tyr said. "We caused this. We're the ones who have to put an end to it." He shook his head and locked eyes with Bjorn. "That isn't pride speaking, but necessity. Lorelei was cunning in her scheme to steal Twilight; it would be reckless to think she didn't already have a plan for when she brought the sword back to Asgard. We have to find out what that plan is. Then we'll know what we need to do to stop her."

It was a far different experience than the last time Tyr had walked the halls of Lorelei's castle. Then he'd been an honored guest, now he was a slinking intruder. The role reversal was striking. Creeping up from the dungeons, concealing themselves every time they heard a servant moving about, there was little resemblance to that first visit.

"We're in good practice for this sort of thing," Tyr told his companions as they ducked into a lumber room to hide while several servants walked the corridor outside. "Though we can be grateful she doesn't have any hellhounds sniffing around."

Bjorn smiled. "After Muspelheim, that cell I was thrown in was sweet as a palace."

"Fine of you to joke," Nilfli griped, acid in his tone. He fixed Tyr with a sullen gaze. "If you'd done as I said, we'd have been brought right to Twilight." He flicked Bjorn with a calloused finger. "You could've gotten him free any time."

"You do realize I have a sword now?" Bjorn warned the dwarf.

"I've been dragged before Sindr," Nilfli bragged. "After seeing the First of the Flames, I'm certainly not going to tremble because a pup has gotten his hands on a knife. Keep it up and I'll take it away and–"

"Enough!" Tyr came between the two. "We've enough problems without you antagonizing one another. None of us wants Lorelei to make use of Twilight, so let's stop arguing and work towards finding out what her scheme is."

Nilfli pulled at his beard. "If you'd just done as I said…"

"We'd have appeared right where she's keeping Twilight." Tyr repeated the dwarf's complaint. He tapped Nilfli with his metal cup. "Have you considered that we don't know what she's done with the sword? We might have emerged into a sealed vault without any chance of escape, or in a room filled with guards. She might have spells warding Twilight that would destroy us the moment we tried to take it… if we even dared to try." Tyr didn't need to repeat the evil weapon's own malefic influence. Both he and Bjorn had felt it at work. Nilfli, laboring over it for so long in the forge, must surely have noted its dire energy.

However, the dwarf was less intimidated by the sword's power than by the question of where it was being kept. "I'd take my chances," he declared. "Whatever else happens, we can't let Twilight be used by the witch. The damage she could cause is beyond measure. No, to stop her, I'd readily risk my life." He frowned and tugged again at his beard. "More than I already have," he added.

"Finding Lorelei is the first step to finding the sword," Tyr said.

Bjorn lifted his head, his nose twitching as he sniffed the air. "Venison," he said after a moment. He opened the door just a crack to watch the hall. "Five servants carrying platters of meat and victuals. At a guess, I'd say Lorelei's entertaining more than a few guests."

Tyr remembered the dinner she'd laid out for them and the ostentatious display she'd arranged to impress them. It would seem she was using the same tactic again. He wondered if her dinner guest was Thor, if the net she'd cast had already ensnared his brother.

"Let's follow them," Tyr decided.

Nilfli caught at his arm. The dwarf's fingers felt hot on Tyr's skin. "You don't know that she'll have Twilight with her even if she's there. It isn't the kind of sword one wears to dinner."

"She'll be there," Tyr assured Nilfli. "It won't matter if she doesn't have Twilight with her, because if there's one person in this castle who knows where it is, she's the one."

Bjorn's eyes turned cold. "I've a lot of things I'd like to discuss with Lorelei."

"First we find Twilight," Tyr said. "There will be time enough for her to answer for her misdeeds after the sword is secured."

The last of the servants was just turning the corner at the end of the hall when they emerged from the lumber room. They cautiously made their way down the corridor and around the bend. "I'll lead the way," Bjorn told them. "If they catch me, they'll think I escaped the cell on my own. They won't know the two of you are even here."

The wolfhunter slipped around the corner. A moment later his hand beckoned to them. Tyr and Nilfli followed, turning into another passage. Bjorn ranged ahead again, determined to keep the servants in sight. Soon the need for tracking them became unnecessary as they came into a part of the castle they recognized from before. The way to the dining hall where Lorelei had feted them was known to both Tyr and Bjorn.

They were in a corridor that ran along the backside of the dining hall. Bjorn reached an oaken door just as it swung open and a wine steward stepped into the passage. The wolfhunter caught the man and smacked his head against the door as it closed. The stunned man slumped to the floor, and Bjorn swung him to one side. Tyr and Nilfli joined him at the door and listened to the voices seeping out from behind it.

"… this is the chance you've been waiting for, Gnagrak." Lorelei's voice was strained with a note of exasperation behind it.

"Seems to me that I'm taking all the risks." There was no mistaking the deep, growling rumble of a troll's voice. "You get to sit back and look pretty while my warriors do all the fighting."

"I've already taken my share of the risks, Gnagrak," Lorelei retorted.

"*Prince* Gnagrak," the troll snarled at her.

"Really? I understood that King Geirrodur refused to acknowledge you. That's why you can use my help." Lorelei's tone was commanding now, clearly irritated with the troll's pretensions. "There will be little fighting for your followers to do. Just enough to lure Thor into the trap."

"So you can crown yourself Queen of Asgard," Gnagrak scoffed.

"And so you can become king in the Realm Below," Lorelei returned. "We've both of us much to gain…"

Tyr had heard enough of their plotting. It didn't concern

him what the rock trolls did in their internal power struggles, but he wasn't going to have his brother ensnared and his father deposed by Lorelei's intrigues. Surprise was the best tactic to employ right now. Confront their enemies where they thought themselves secure. Driving his shoulder against the door, he burst it from its hinges as he stormed into the room.

"Whatever your plan, Lorelei, it ends now!" Tyr shouted, holding his gleaming blade high. His voice echoed through the vast dining hall, scattering servants with its ferocity.

The creatures seated around the table didn't scatter. Tyr'd heard only Gnagrak, but the supposed prince wasn't alone. Ten other rock trolls were around the table. A glance at Lorelei showed she hadn't brought Twilight with her to dinner, but the trolls had most certainly brought their weapons. The instant they saw Tyr, they kicked away their chairs and produced a vicious assortment of blades and bludgeons.

A shaggy brute with a scarred face and an oversized tusk drew a flail from his belt. From the purple cloak and many rings that circled his fingers, Tyr thought this must be Gnagrak. When the orange-skinned troll spoke, the voice was the same.

"The deal was for one Odinson," Gnagrak snarled, glaring across the room at Tyr. "This one is going to cost you extra." He waved his flail and the other rock trolls surged forward. "Take the Aesir, and she didn't say anything about being gentle with this one!"

TWENTY-NINE

Rock trolls charged toward Tyr, thundering across the hall like a herd of mastodons. Goblets and bowls shattered on the floor as the vibrations from their advance pitched them from the long table. Tapestries shook from their fastening and crumpled at the bases of the walls. Few in Asgard could stand unflinching before a troll attack.

Tyr was one of those few. Instead of waiting for the trolls to reach him, he dashed forward to meet them. His bright sword flashed out and hewed the head from a massive hammer one of the creatures swung at him. The warrior stared at his broken weapon in shock, then went careening into one of the walls when Tyr smashed his head with the flat of his blade.

A second troll tried to chop at him with a huge axe, raising it in both hands for an overhead blow. Tyr dodged the brutal attack and thrust up into the warrior's chest, piercing the scale armor and the thick hide beneath. The enemy stumbled back and clutched at his wound before toppling to the floor.

More trolls converged on Tyr, goaded on by Gnagrak. "Kill him! A barony to the one who brings me his head!"

Tyr's tactic of keeping the trolls fixated on himself now bore rewards. By rushing forward to engage them, he'd given Bjorn and Nilfli the opportunity to dash into the room and give the enemy another surprise. The wolfhunter struck at a warrior trying to flank Tyr on his left, wounding the foe before he could get into position. The dwarf scurried towards the table, the axe dropped by one of the fallen trolls clenched in his hands. He ran at one of the warriors rushing toward Tyr, holding the axe lengthwise like a pole. Instead of chopping at the creature, he scurried between the enemy's legs and tripped the troll with the breadth of the axe. The heavy table was knocked over as the bulk of the unbalanced warrior slammed into it, throwing candles and plates of food in every direction.

Tyr lost track of his companions as the red whir of battle swelled to a maelstrom of mayhem. Enemy after enemy came at him, howling for his blood. He lashed out with Tyrsfang, breaking weapons and bodies with equal ferocity. In his mind he could see the doom that had so long hovered over his father. He saw the chance to drive away the shadow of that doom, and these rock trolls were standing in his way!

A fog seeped into his brain, clouding the images that drove him on, dulling the reflexes that spurred his sword arm. He felt the stirrings of his heart. Why should he fight? There was no reason to. All could be resolved if he would only...

"You overplay your magic!" Tyr laughed as he struck a

troll swordsman in the face and hurled him back into the midst of his comrades. He couldn't take his eyes away from the enemies around him, but he knew Lorelei was nearby. Close enough to hear his scorn. "I fell for your tricks before because you wove your spell slowly over time. Now you reach too far and too fast with your enchantments. Amora should have taught you better than that!" Tyr punctuated that last defiant shout by smashing a troll's ribs and sending him crashing to the floor.

"You'll not threaten Lady Lorelei!" Gnagrak snarled, shoving past his followers to swing at Tyr with his flail. The spiked ball at the end of the chain whipped past his ear, drawing blood as it grazed his scalp. Tyr retaliated with a parry, but the flail's metal handle defied the bite of Tyrsfang. Too late he discovered the prince's weapon was made of Uru, further enchanted by some sorcerer from the Realm Below.

Gnagrak snarled and drove his knee into Tyr's belly, knocking the wind from him and causing him to stumble back. "Fight me, swine! Let me show her ladyship how a prince attends to scoundrels!" The flail whipped around and smashed Tyr's left arm just below the shoulder. The impact sent him reeling away to crack his head against the overturned table.

Tyr shook his head to clear the sparks that danced before his eyes. As his vision cleared, he had a glimpse of Lorelei. She stood at a corner of the dining hall, her hands shifting in arcane gestures, grim determination on her face. Gnagrak's sudden decision to stride into battle rather than keep directing it from behind a screen of his warriors was explained. Unable to charm Tyr's mind, Lorelei had shifted her magic onto the troll prince.

Gnagrak's vicious growl warned Tyr that his enemy was upon him again. Scrambling over the table, he just gained its cover when the flail came crashing down. The spiked ball ripped through the wood, pulling a section the size of Tyr's head away. The prince glared at him and swung again.

This time Tyr's sword met the attack. A fang from Fenris, even after being reshaped by magic, was far tougher than any table. The ball was struck aside, spinning as it was deflected. The chain wrapped itself about the blade, dragging Gnagrak closer. The troll strained to pull his weapon free. Tyr glared back at him and tightened his grip on the sword, slowly drawing the prince towards him.

Hate flared in Gnagrak's eyes, the same expression Tyr had seen so many times when Bjorn was under Lorelei's spell and trying to impress her. The troll snarled at two of his warriors when they moved in to help. "The cur is mine!" he raged. Then he clasped his other hand around the handle of his flail and pulled. Tyr lurched forwards as Gnagrak redoubled his strength. "What will you do now?" the prince chuckled.

"This," Tyr told him, kicking out with his leg and sending the table slamming into Gnagrak. The sudden impact caught the troll by surprise and for just a heartbeat his hold on the flail slackened. It was all the advantage Tyr needed. He pulled Tyrsfang back, dragging the entwined flail with it. Gnagrak reeled over the table, exposing himself to the Aesir.

Tyr struck down with the metal cup on his left arm, smashing the prince's head. Gnagrak let go of the flail and toppled to the floor. The blood dripping down his face appeared to take with it the force of Lorelei's enchantment. Fear, not hate, now ruled the troll's eyes. He shook a fist at the warriors he'd warned off only a moment before. "He's struck your prince! Kill him!"

The troll that came in from Tyr's left suddenly cried out. He dropped his weapon and grabbed his foot where Nilfli had struck it with the axe. The warrior to his right swung at him with a mace from across the upended table. Tyr dodged the blow and struck at the creature's head. The troll ducked down, seeking to use the table for cover. The heavy furnishing was no barrier to Tyrsfang, and a thrust of the blade sent it sheering through the thick wood and the foe sheltering behind it. The warrior collapsed and Tyr jumped over the table in pursuit of Gnagrak.

Except for the injured troll chasing after Nilfli, the other creatures were rallying to their prince. Four of the orange-skinned warriors in various stages of injury stood around Gnagrak and helped him to his feet. Tyr glanced aside to see that Bjorn was trying to hold one of the doors against more enemies. A force of Lorelei's guards was attempting to push its way into the hall.

"I thought you were going to do this yourself," Tyr scolded Gnagrak. The rock troll glared back at him, but there was still fear in his eyes. The warriors around him, however, gave their prince surly glances. They too had heard the bold claim. It seemed they expected their leader to live up to his words.

"Braggart," Gnagrak clenched his fist and shook it at Tyr. "I've no weapon to fight you with."

Tyr made a whipping motion of his sword that sent the entangled flail sliding free to clatter across the floor to Gnagrak's feet. "Any other excuses?"

With his warriors watching him, Gnagrak had no choice but to meet Tyr's challenge. He stooped and retrieved his weapon, making a few experimental swings with it. "You'll regret giving this back to me." His face contorted with malice. "I've taken your measure now."

Gnagrak lunged forward. Tyr was ready to block a swing of the flail. Instead the prince thrust his other hand toward the Aesir. The middle ring flared with light and a sheet of flame shot from the stone at its center. The treacherous attack almost caught him flatfooted. As it was, he felt the heat of the fire wash over him as he darted across the table. He crashed down on his back, hitting the floor with such force that Tyrsfang was knocked from his grip.

"Now you die!" Gnagrak thundered, rushing after Tyr. He paused a moment when he saw the sword lying just beyond the Aesir's reach and a vicious grin spread across his face. The troll hefted his flail, ready to bring it crashing down on Tyr's head.

"You don't learn, do you?" Tyr scolded his enemy. His legs kicked the table, this time knocking it up instead of back. The edge of the table caught Gnagrak beneath the chin. The troll's jaws cracked together with a loud smack. The prince toppled backwards, stunned by the blow.

Tyr rolled over to recover his sword. As he did, he saw the door at the other end of the hall slam inwards and a half dozen Asgardians wearing Lorelei's livery over their armor rushed into the room. Balked by Bjorn at the other door, some of the guards had taken an alternate route to reach the fray. As they entered the hall, Tyr saw confusion on their faces. They'd been drawn by sounds of fighting, but had little idea what they'd find.

Tyr seized on that confusion with a ploy that would have impressed Loki. "The trolls have turned on Lorelei! Stop the trolls!"

The guards were Asgardians and had grown up with repeated threats from the Realm Below. They were ready to believe the worst of the rock trolls and didn't question Tyr's words or who had shouted to them. Swords flashing, they charged Gnagrak's warriors. Had the trolls hesitated, the infighting might have been stopped, but their savage instincts rose to the fore. They met the charge with a rush of their own. Soon the two bands were mixed in a vicious melee.

"No!" Lorelei cried out to her men. "Not the trolls! Tyr is the enemy!" She tried to use her magic to break up the fight, but when one of her guards was seized by her spell, his faltering sword left him easy prey to the rock trolls and he was cut down.

Tyr picked up his sword and turned toward Lorelei. "You still have a chance to surrender," he told her as he advanced.

Lorelei took a step back. "I don't know how you escaped Muspelheim, but you should have stayed there." She reached into her gown and removed what looked like a black gemstone.

Tyr kicked a goblet lying on the floor and sent it careening toward Lorelei. She cried out in pain as it shattered against the wall beside her and fragments slashed her hand. The gemstone clattered to the floor. "No more spells. No more tricks," Tyr warned as he marched nearer.

At that moment an agonized shriek rang out over the bedlam of battle. Tyr spun about to see the troll with the gashed foot staggering about the hall. The warrior was bathed from head to toe in crackling flames. He floundered through the room, pawing at himself in a futile effort to douse the fire. Combatants broke away as the stricken troll stumbled near them. Tyr wondered if the warrior's doom would have been his own had Gnagrak hit him with his ring and a shudder pulsed through him. He looked around for the treacherous prince.

Lorelei gasped, drawing his attention back to her. She was shivering from fright. "How *did* you escape from Muspelheim?" Then her gaze was drawn by Nilfli as the dwarf scurried out from under one of the chairs. The moment she saw him, her face went pale. "What *have* you done?" she muttered.

THIRTY

Before Tyr could move, he saw Lorelei's hands weave in arcane patterns. Gnagrak appeared from the other side of the table, blood streaming from his mouth. The troll's eyes had a glassy, distorted look to them now. This was more than a mere charm to tease control over his mind. Lorelei had blotted out everything except the command she placed there. The prince smashed his flail through the table and shoved the broken halves apart as he stormed through. Tyr readied himself to meet his enemy, but Gnagrak didn't even glance his way. The troll was focused entirely on Nilfli.

Tyr ran after Gnagrak, but it was already too late. In a blinding motion, the prince drew back his arm and hurled the flail at Nilfli. The weapon smacked into the dwarf, bowling him over and sending him slamming against the wall. Tyr brought his sword slashing across the troll's back, ripping through the purple cloak and the orange hide beneath. Gnagrak was tossed aside by the fury of the blow, sent crashing into one of the chairs.

Tyr gave no further attention to the troll, but hurried toward Nilfli, even though he was certain the dwarf had been killed by the cruel blow he'd suffered. He stopped in amazement when he saw the smith stir and unwind the flail's chain from around his neck. The blood that dripped from the dwarf's battered head had a strange color to it.

"What have you done?" Lorelei cried again. She turned and threw herself against a portion of the wall. It pivoted inward, exposing a hidden panel. The mechanism tried to close behind her, but it wasn't fast enough. Managing more haste than he'd seen from the dwarf before, Tyr watched as Nilfli ran after the fleeing sorceress.

Tyr started to follow them, but before he could move, he was seized from behind. Gnagrak's massive arms held him in a crushing embrace. Treacherous and craven he might be, but there was a reason the rock trolls who followed him had taken the brute as their leader. Tyr could feel the mounting pressure as the prince poured all of his remaining strength into a last attack.

"You've killed me, Aesir," Gnagrak coughed, blood spattering Tyr's armor. "But I'll drag you with me down to Niffleheim." He gnashed his teeth and redoubled his effort. He expected to hear Tyr's bones cracking. He couldn't understand why his victim wasn't crying out in pain.

Gnagrak's nose broke when Tyr drove his head back into the troll's face. The crushing grip faltered, and he pulled himself free. He glared at the dying prince and thumped the magic armor he wore. "A gift from your ally, Lady Lorelei," he said. "A kraken couldn't crush me while I was wearing this, much less one of King Geirrodur's whelps." A last flicker of hate in Gnagrak's eyes and the prince crashed to the floor.

The last rock trolls howled when they saw Gnagrak fall. They fought through the remaining guards and fled into the corridor, Lorelei's soldiers chasing after them. Their departure gave Tyr the chance to help Bjorn secure the door where the other group of guards was still trying to force their way in. Sheathing Tyrsfang, he dragged part of the broken table across the room and, with Bjorn's help, wedged it against the wall.

"A giant couldn't break through now," Bjorn declared as he stepped back and admired their work.

"It only needs to hold them for a moment," Tyr said. He led Bjorn across the room to the panel by which Lorelei had made her escape. "This is where she went. Unless I'm much mistaken, she's gone to fetch Twilight before she abandons her castle." He nodded and added "Nilfli is already..." His eyes caught a flicker of motion on the floor. He looked over and saw that there were little specks of flame where the dwarf had fallen after being struck by Gnagrak.

"Nilfli's following her," he said, but now the words had an edge of dread in them. Tyr thought of the burning troll, the one that had been chasing Nilfli. He thought of Lorelei's terror when she saw the dwarf. What, indeed, had he done?

"Hurry." Tyr dashed to the panel and flung it open. "There might still be time!"

Bjorn plunged in after Tyr, following him down the dark passage behind the wall. "We'll stop Lorelei," he assured him. "She's already beaten."

Tyr shook his head. "It isn't Lorelei we have to stop

now," he growled. "It's the thing I brought with me from Muspelheim!"

The winding network of passages eventually opened into a vast underground vault. Tyr was impressed by its scale and the mighty pillars that rose up from it to support the ceiling above. He judged that they must be down under the very foundations of the castle.

Orbs of arcane light bound into crystal spheres illuminated the cavernous chamber. A crypt-like table of stone was at the center of the room, otherwise the place was devoid of appointments. Near the steps that led out from the passage, Tyr spotted Lorelei lying on the floor. He rushed to her and picked her up. Blood stained the back of her head where she'd been struck from behind. More alarming to him, however, was that the hair around the injury was singed.

"Too late," Lorelei shuddered, staring up at Tyr.

"Not yet," Tyr told her. He handed her over to Bjorn. Turning back to the vault, he started towards the stone crypt. His fingers tightened around Tyrsfang's grip. He would still set this right.

Nilfli emerged from behind the crypt. The dwarf's face glowed with wicked triumph. "Just in time," he laughed. "I only now finished undoing the wards." He smiled and pulled at his beard. "She really should have brought in a sorcerer better versed in that sort of magic. It was almost too easy banishing these."

Tyr kept advancing towards the dwarf. "I brought you here. I'm not going to let you win."

"Poor fool," Nilfli said. "There's nothing you can do about it now."

A slap of the dwarf's hand and the slab on top of the table went crashing to the floor. Nilfli rose and reached his hand down into the space beneath. Tyr was surprised by the action, for a moment before the smith had been too short to perform such a feat. Now he saw that the dwarf was growing, a growth that continued when he lifted Twilight from its hiding place. The sword of Surtur flared with coruscating flames as Nilfli held it high.

The growth continued. Nilfli was now taller than Tyr. As he increased in size, so too did Twilight, keeping pace with the being that held it. Tyr had seen this once before.

"Sindr," Tyr whispered as the full magnitude of how he'd been deceived was borne home. As though conjured by her name, Nilfli's body was consumed from the inside by fingers of fire. As the semblance of the dwarf burned away, the flame-wrapped shape of the giant emerged.

The giant continued to increase in size, her fingers tight about Twilight. She was fifteen feet tall now, and becoming larger with each moment. The flames that shone in her eyes had a mocking quality to them.

"Tyr Wolf-tamer." Her voice rumbled through the vault. "I owe you something for all you've done to help me. What shall it be?"

An inarticulate howl of rage rose from Tyr as he charged at the giant. Sindr was twenty feet tall now, and Twilight was increasing its size to match her. Before he could come near enough to strike at her with Tyrsfang, she dealt him a glancing blow with the burning sword. He was flung back across the vault to crash against one of the pillars.

Sindr smiled at the crack that snaked through the masonry where Tyr had struck the column. "I have it!" she said. She continued to grow, now fifty feet tall, her horns almost scraping the roof. Twilight now had a length of thirty feet and more, its flames scorching the floor. "I will give you what any warrior should be happy to have."

Tyr raised his head and stared at the giant. He tried to rise, but found the effort was too much. He slumped back against the pillar, his face filled with anguish. More than physical pain, it was the torment of knowing he'd brought her into Asgard and helped Sindr recover Twilight.

"Such pain," Sindr said as she watched Tyr. She hefted Twilight, letting its fire sear the ceiling. "In my father's hand, this weapon will be Odinsbane." She stared longingly at the black blade, as though to draw its infamy into herself by sheer force of will. Then her eyes shifted back to Tyr. "In the hands of Sindr, it will be Tyrsbane! My gift to you – a quick death!"

THIRTY-ONE

Twilight's flaming edge swept past Tyr's eyes. Too weak to move, he braced himself for death. Instead, a pained cry rang out and Sindr staggered back, pawing at her face with one hand. The fire that rippled about the giant's fingers was snuffed out and a frigid paleness crept into them. Tyr gazed in amazement at her eyes, for they'd turned from burning pits into icy deeps spattered with hoarfrost.

Lorelei's magic! For he was certain it could be no other who could blind those eyes of fire and turn them to ice. Sindr roared in fury and struck with Twilight, lashing the great sword from side to side in her blind rage. The monstrous blade ripped through the pillars around her, hewing through the stone as though it were butter. One collapsed as the giant's swing cleft it in twain. A second swiftly crumbled, the damage rendering it incapable of enduring the strain of supporting the castle above. The whole vault shuddered and shook as the roof cracked and slabs of rock came crashing down.

"This fight is over," Bjorn told Tyr. The wolfhunter appeared suddenly at his side and reached his arms under the Aesir's shoulders. "You might take a hero's death being struck by Twilight, but you'll finish like a worm if you're buried under all this rubble!"

Bjorn dragged Tyr across the chamber, back toward the hidden stairs. After a few moments, Tyr rallied enough that he was able to aid the huntsman's efforts and speed their progress somewhat. Nor was even a slight measure of haste wasted. Huge blocks of stone came crashing down now as Sindr continued to rake Twilight back and forth, hewing through the pillars. Twice they were nearly crushed beneath sections of the castle that spilled down into the vault.

"In here! Swiftly!" Lorelei shouted. She was still bloodied and pale, but she'd recovered at least somewhat from the stunning blow Sindr had struck her. Her hands made arcane gestures, and Tyr thought he felt strength rush back into him. Certainly, he wasn't mistaken that Bjorn's pace increased and the huntsman's grip became stronger.

The flailing giant continued to batter away at her surroundings, intent on bringing down the ceiling to prevent her enemies from escaping. In Muspelheim she'd shown such a collapse would be only a momentary obstacle to her, but if the Asgardians were crushed she wouldn't need to see them to bring their destruction. Not that her blindness would last much longer. The icy hue around her fingers had already burned away. Steam rose as the hoarfrost around her eyes evaporated. Tyr could see the glow of Sindr's fiery eyes shining from behind the frigid veil that covered them and knew that it would be only a matter of moments before her vision was restored. Before that could happen, a swing of Twilight toppled one pillar too many. With a roar more terrible than anything before it, the whole roof came down. The giant was lost beneath tons of crashing stone.

Tyr should have been lost too, but at that moment Bjorn reached the stairs. "This way!" Lorelei shouted and spun about. Her foot kicked against a block in the wall, triggering some hidden catch and exposing a dark tunnel. With the castle collapsing into the vault, this was no moment to hesitate. Tyr stumbled after Lorelei as she ducked into the tunnel with Bjorn hastily following him.

The passage was old and crudely constructed, but it was firm. Tyr could hear the hideous tumult from the vault behind them, but the tunnel's walls barely trembled. He wondered if this might be the work of rock trolls, so stoutly did the place defy the tremors that pulsed through it. Certainly, Gnagrak and his ilk had some way up from the Realm Below.

When Lorelei led them down the tunnel, the slope angled up, not down, relieving somewhat Tyr's worry that they'd trade escape from the collapsing vault for the manifold dangers of the troll kingdom.

"You've ruined everything," Lorelei hissed as they made their way through the dark tunnel, the only illumination rising from clumps of phosphorescent moss clinging to the floor. "Your recklessness brought that monster into Asgard!"

Tyr glared at her. "If you'd not plotted treachery from the first…"

Another shudder rolled through the passageway, mightier

than those that came before. The walls and ceiling resisted the tremor, but the ground under them cracked and split. Tyr caught himself against the wall before he was thrown to the floor by the uneven footing. Bjorn was sent sprawling. He looked up, his face cut by flakes of flint. "We argue later," he said, brushing his hand across his bloodied cheek. "Right now, we've got to get out of here."

Hostile silence held them as they continued along the tunnel. A few more tremors rippled through their surroundings, but nothing like the magnitude of what had come before. Tyr wondered how great the destruction must be to still be producing such shocks. Lorelei's castle wouldn't be quite so beautiful after Sindr's rampage. He knew it was a petty thing, but after what the sorceress had tried to do, he was pleased that her home had suffered because of her intrigues.

How greatly the castle had suffered was yet to be revealed. Not until the steeply angled tunnel reached a set of steps that climbed up to a door in the ceiling. Tyr judged that they must be a mile or more from Lorelei's castle now. She was no fool. Aware that some of her enemies might take it into mind to besiege her fortress, she'd prepared an escape route that would put her well beyond their reach.

"Let Bjorn open the door," Tyr said when Lorelei started up the steps. Her eyes smoldered with indignation, but she acquiesced and moved aside so the wolfhunter could remove the heavy bar that secured the portal. Harsh sunlight streamed down into the tunnel when Bjorn threw the door open. He peeked his head over the lip, then ducked back down.

"I don't see anyone," Bjorn reported, giving Lorelei a wary look. "If any of her swains are lying in wait for us, they've hidden themselves well."

Tyr shook his head. "I doubt you shared this secret with anyone," he said, fixing his gaze on Lorelei. "You'd never be sure that someone wouldn't betray you out of jealousy. That's the pitfall when you play upon someone's emotions. When you bind a confederate to you with wealth, you simply have to make sure they can't do better with another patron. But when you use affection to hold someone in your power, you gamble with the fickleness of the heart. No hate is deeper than that held against someone once loved."

"You think you know so much," Lorelei replied, disdain in her tone. "What experience have you had, Tyr, with the notoriety of your own bloodline? Growing up in my sister's shadow, tarnished with an infamy I had no part in, what kind of chance do you think I had? To always be treated with suspicion by those around me. I learned very early that I had to fend for myself because no one else would help." All warmth vanished from her eyes, supplanted by cold bitterness. "I did whatever I had to do to improve my situation and I didn't scruple about who I took advantage of to get what I wanted."

Tyr returned her steely gaze with a look every bit as cold. "I could almost sympathize with you, Lorelei. I know what it is to be in the shadow of a sibling. That sense that you can't measure up, that quiet envy that is so pervasive you don't even recognize it after a time. But instead of harnessing that feeling to push yourself to great deeds of your own, you've let it fester like a wound. You use the pain you feel to justify whatever you do, no matter who you hurt. Maybe the reason nobody cared about you is because you never cared about them."

Lorelei's face curled in a sneer. "You needed little persuasion to sneak away for the sake of your own pride. It would have been easy enough for you to tell Odin of my plan."

"You told me we would take Twilight to protect my father," Tyr reminded her. "Not that your only interest was in taking it to use in your designs to compel Thor to wed you."

"It wasn't me who brought Sindr to my castle," Lorelei snapped back. "Only a fool would have expected the fire giant's daughter to be overcome by flowing lava. You know the giants can alter their size and shape..."

Tyr jabbed his finger at the sorceress. "Your spells didn't uncover Sindr's disguise when we were in the forge. Then you only had eyes for your prize and nothing else!"

Lorelei's lip trembled with fury. "There had to have been something that warned you what she was! I saw it when the dwarf's boots scorched the floor while fighting the trolls. It was no great feat of magic to pierce her disguise and see what it was you brought into my castle!"

"There's not much of a castle left," Bjorn called down to them. He nodded when Lorelei and Tyr stared up at him. "Come see for yourselves," he invited, climbing out through the door.

Tyr thought he knew what to expect from Bjorn's words, but he wasn't prepared for the destruction that greeted him when he emerged from the tunnel. Lorelei's castle, that beauteous structure, was nothing but a pile of smashed stone gleaming in the sunlight. A cloud of dust slowly rolled away from the rubble, sinking down into those parts of the moat that hadn't fallen in upon themselves. The gatehouse and drawbridge were the only parts of the fortress still intact, though a section of curtain wall and part of a tower on the eastern side were still mostly standing. The rest had fallen inwards, sucked down when Sindr's rampage knocked out the foundations.

Lorelei stood and gawked at the devastation. A tear rolled down her cheek. "All ruined," she muttered. "There's nothing left." She rounded on Tyr and slapped him across the face. "You brought that monster here!"

Tyr wiped the blood from his lip with the back of his arm. "And you abandoned me to rot in Muspelheim." He regretted the guilt he saw on Bjorn's face when he spoke. That had been the subtlety of Lorelei's enchantment, that it made her commands seem things of her thrall's own volition. For the wolfhunter to have resisted her at all was enough to absolve him of any guilt in Tyr's eyes, if not his own.

"I couldn't take the chance that you'd use Twilight against Thor," Lorelei told him. "You say you understand how I feel about my sister, well maybe I know how you feel towards your brother even better than you do yourself." She smiled when she noted the doubt she provoked in Tyr. "Instead you've done even worse. Somehow you brought Sindr into Asgard."

"Without her I could never have escaped," Tyr said.

Lorelei laughed at him. "She used you every bit the way I

did, but with far more terrible intent." She tapped her finger against Tyr's chest. "I brought Twilight across, you brought Sindr. Do you know what that means? The giant and the sword both together in Asgard?"

"It means your castle lies in ruins," Bjorn said, waving at the rubble. "It means they're both down there, buried under tons of stone."

Tyr's gaze lingered over the destroyed castle, doubt gnawing at him. They'd already seen Sindr pull herself free from one pile of stone. Grimly he watched as the fractured stone shifted. A few blocks at the top of the heap fell away. Then a few more. Steadily the agitation spread further and further through the mound.

"I think you spoke too soon," Tyr advised his friend.

The pile continued to tremble until the whole heap was in motion. Shattered towers and collapsed walls broke apart into smaller aggregations of stone, sliding away into what remained of the moat. As the mound shifted, flashes of light could be seen boiling up from below. Tyr was reminded of the molten pits of Muspelheim, and not without good reason.

"Sindr lives." Tyr spoke the words in a subdued whisper. Though he wasn't as weak as he'd been in the vault, neither was he so hale that he could look to another fight against the giant with confidence. And then there were the dark powers of Twilight to take into account. His only hope was that she'd been wounded by the castle's collapse and that in the mayhem she'd lost the sword beneath the rubble.

THIRTY-TWO

The rubble heaved upward and then went crashing down into the moat. Sindr didn't climb from the pit into which Lorelei's castle had fallen, she *grew* from it. The giant's body was wreathed in flames as she emerged from the depths. Clenched in her right hand, still increasing in size to match her own, was Twilight. The very atmosphere around the blade was distorted by the heat emanating from it. When Sindr finally stopped growing and pressed her hands against the ground to lift herself from the vault, where the sword rested the debris bubbled and smoked, stone changing to molten streams of glowing mush.

Lorelei sank to the ground, transfixed by the horrible sight of the giant rising above the rubble of her home. "Tyr, by trying to save Odin from his doom, you've brought doom to all Asgard," she muttered.

Sindr turned her horned head to the sky, and a peal of steaming laughter, like the roar of a dragon, seethed across the landscape. Tyr looked down at his sword and his expression was grave. Tyrsfang had vanquished countless enemies and monsters since it was given to him, but he wondered if it could be enough to contest with the fire giant's daughter and the malignant blade she bore. Still, he wouldn't run. Whatever the reasons for doing so, however he'd been tricked, Lorelei was right. He'd brought Sindr into Asgard.

"You must alert the city and the All-Father," Tyr told his companions. "I'll stay here and hold Sindr at bay."

"If you were so eager for death, you should have stayed in Muspelheim," Lorelei declared. She pointed at Sindr. "Even your brother would be hard pressed against such a foe. What chance would you stand?"

"This once I must agree with Lorelei," Bjorn chimed in. "What could you do alone against that?" He perked up and smiled. "Look! She's walking away!" It was true, the giant had turned and was striding off across the plain to the north. "Either she didn't notice us or she didn't care."

"Or she has more important things to do," Lorelei said.

Tyr tore his eyes away from the spectacle of Sindr marching out into the grasslands, her footsteps smoldering behind her and threatening to set flash fires in her wake. "What do you mean?" he demanded. "You've some idea of what she's after. More than just recovering Twilight. You knew the moment you saw through her disguise. What is it? What is Sindr's purpose here? Does she seek to assassinate Odin with her father's sword?"

"Note the direction she's headed," Lorelei told him, shaking her head. "North across the plains."

"The City of Asgard." Bjorn swore. "With Twilight she could break down the walls. Cause untold damage."

"Not the city," Lorelei said. She hesitated before continuing, fear in her eyes. "Beyond the city is Himinbjörg and Bifrost."

The moment he heard those names, a knot of cold dread formed in the pit of Tyr's stomach. "The Rainbow Bridge! She means to throw open the gate to Muspelheim!"

"She'll set loose an army of fire demons upon Asgard!" Bjorn exclaimed.

"Far worse than that," Lorelei stated. "I had a chance to study Twilight after it was safely stowed in my vault." She looked aside at Tyr. "Believe me, what I told Gnagrak was only what I had to tell him to make use of him. After studying Twilight, after discovering *what* it is, I would trust no one to carry it."

Tyr was unconvinced by her appeal, but he motioned for her to continue. "What did your magic tell you? For I can tell you what I've learned. Sindr revealed to me that Twilight is much more than Surtur's sword! The fire giant has invested the blade with a part of his own essence. It is a part of him, an aspect of the fire giant's spirit."

Lorelei's eyes were wide with shock. Whatever her own study of the sword had exposed, she hadn't suspected this truth. "Then the sword is an externalized piece of Surtur himself. Made still more malignant by the poisons and spells the captured dwarves have added to it with each reforging." The sorceress staggered against the wall, color draining from her face. "It is more awful than I dared fear."

"Twilight isn't merely bound to Surtur," Tyr said. "It is part of him."

"You keep saying that, but what does it mean?" Bjorn

demanded, trying to decipher the exchange. He waved his hand at the distant figure of the marching giant. "We waste time better spent in pursuing the enemy bandying words. Tell me plainly what it is that Sindr plots?"

"I'd never have dared bring Twilight here if I knew what it was," Lorelei stated. She looked from the wolfhunter to Tyr. "Understand, by bringing it into Asgard part of Surtur was brought here. Should Sindr bring the sword to Bifrost, she can use it to draw her father through! The resonance between sword and master will be strong enough to penetrate the barriers that imprison Surtur in Muspelheim!"

Bjorn shuddered at the image Lorelei conjured. "The fire giant set loose upon Asgard even before Ragnarok unfolds."

A ghastly thought came to Tyr. "Surtur let us take Twilight." He looked at his companions. "Sindr noted the passage we withdrew down when we escaped from her. That was enough to suggest to her what we were after. When she reported to her father, he hatched this scheme to break free from Muspelheim." Tyr groaned as he appreciated another factor. "Surtur is bound to the prophecy of Ragnarok as well. A doom hangs over his head as it does Odin. What if he were to force the issue ahead of the appointed time? Just as I thought to spare my father from the fate foretold by stealing Twilight, so Surtur might do the same by storming Asgard before Ragnarok."

"We have to warn them!" Bjorn shouted. "Warn the All-Father so the greatest heroes in Asgard can help Heimdall guard Bifrost and prevent Sindr–"

"It would only delay her plans, or force her to even more devious means," Tyr said. "Sindr deceived me by changing herself into a dwarf. She'll try to use some similar ploy against Heimdall rather than stride past the city in her own giant shape. If she sees that a guard has been raised, then she'll never try for the Rainbow Bridge while they're there – and if we tell Odin what has happened, he is certain to set a guard. She'll lie low and bide her time." He shot Lorelei a stern look. "Or seek allies of her own to help her. The rock trolls would make common cause readily enough if they saw a way to bring down the Aesir."

Bjorn stamped his foot on the ground and shook his fist at the departing giant. "Then what do we do?"

"We go after her," Tyr said. "Just the three of us." He saw the incredulity on their faces. "Three of us are no great threat to Sindr, or so she'll believe."

"She'd be right," Lorelei said. "Perhaps if Sindr didn't have Twilight we'd have a chance–"

"We've got to try." Tyr cut her off, his voice firm. "Each of us is responsible. We've got to set things right." He noted their hesitation. "Then I'll try to stop her by myself." He started to walk away, but Bjorn held him back.

"Many a hunt and many a battle we've shared," Bjorn told him. "If this is to be the last, then I'd share it with you. At least she'll know she's been in a fight before we're through."

"I'll go with you," Lorelei spoke up, rising to her feet. "You may rely upon my magic. I think by now you've seen I'm not quite the novice I wanted you to think I was. My spells can help you." She gave Tyr a pained look. "I ask that you take back what you said of me. I'm not so callous that there aren't people I care about. Nor am I so obsessed with my own ambition that I would betray the whole of

Asgard to Surtur. Whatever I can do, you have but to ask it." She reached into the satchel she carried, showing her companions that she'd retained the Wayfarer's Mirror. "This was enough to escape Muspelheim. Its power can send Sindr back if we can set its light against her. There would be a certain irony in that, don't you think?"

Tyr smiled at her. At this moment, he could almost forgive Lorelei her intrigues. Perhaps she even spoke the truth when she said why she'd left him in Muspelheim. Whatever the case, she was willing to pit herself against impossible odds for the sake of Asgard.

"For now," Tyr said, pointing with his sword at the smoldering footprints across the plain, "the work falls to Bjorn and myself. We'll have to follow Sindr's trail."

Bjorn laughed at the statement. "Following a giant's tracks isn't much a test of woodcraft."

"At the moment," Tyr told him. "But I think before long Sindr will prove much harder to pursue. She didn't make the journey to Asgard only to make herself a target for the entire realm. She'll take a more subtle form soon, and then our skills will be tested to the utmost."

Tyr gestured again at the giant's blazing figure as she strode across the plain. "Just remember, whatever guise she adopts when we catch her, *that* is the reality lurking beneath."

The great smoldering prints left behind by Sindr were so obvious that a child could follow them. The longer they traveled, the more Tyr's suspicions were aroused. He knew Sindr was arrogant and filled with pride, but he didn't think even she would be so brazen when crossing an enemy country.

"She knows someone will eventually find Lorelei's castle," Bjorn suggested when Tyr broached the subject. "Sindr leaves an obvious trail away, showing anyone who finds it that a monster is responsible for all that destruction." He waved his hand at Lorelei. "Anyone who saw that scene would think Amora visited you and conjured up some creature she couldn't control."

"No one would immediately suspect an invader from Muspelheim," Lorelei said, ignoring the reference to her sister. "The barriers preventing that from happening are too strong."

Tyr looked across the plain. Sindr had drawn far enough ahead that she was no longer visible, though the smoke rising from her tracks left no question as to her route of travel. He considered the sameness of the terrain. "She's looking for a place where such a creature might go to ground. A place where those who follow her trail from the ruins would expect her to be. A cavern or a ravine, some place a huge monster could hide."

"And when she finds such a place, she changes her shape and backtracks." Bjorn nodded in appreciation of their foe's cleverness.

"Only she didn't reckon on two old wolfhunters taking up her trail." Tyr frowned when a new thought came to him. "Unless Sindr can change herself into a bird, as some giants can."

Lorelei thought upon the matter for a moment. "I think if that were possible, she'd have abandoned the two of you in the cell," she said, referring to what they'd told her of their escape from the dungeon. "Her power must be restricted, perhaps only to a mantle similar enough to her own. Dwarf, troll, even human, but not something like a vole or a sparrow. Be grateful she doesn't have the facility of your brother Loki when it comes to shifting her shape, or we might never catch her."

The hunters pressed on across the Plain of Ida, always straying northward. The only time their course wavered was when an arm of the sea stretched inland. Then the course veered westward for a time. "She keeps away from the water," Tyr observed. "One might expect that of the fire giant's daughter. The elements are ever in opposition."

"I think it more likely Sindr is trying to avoid places that are inhabited," Lorelei said. "If her boasts are to be believed, she has ventured to Niffleheim and fought Nidhogg. What has a creature that has endured the ice of Niffleheim to fear from the waters of Marmora? They will not be enough to quench her flame."

Lorelei's words were proven within the hour when Tyr came upon the smoking ruins of what had been a farm. The steading had been burned to the ground, its inhabitants annihilated down to the last hog and chicken. Sindr was leaving no survivors to tell of what they'd seen. It was easy enough to find her tracks where she'd chased down a bondsman trying to get away.

"Murdering monster!" Bjorn cursed the giant. He dropped his sword and took up an axe he found in the charred ruins. "I shall avenge you," he promised the dead Asgardians.

Tyr looked across the destruction with a cold fury. All of this was his fault. He'd let himself be tricked by Sindr and brought her through the barriers into Asgard. This carnage was his responsibility. As God of War, he'd seen such scenes played out many times across many lands, from Midgard to Jotunheim. This was the true face of war, not the glory and celebration of heroes, but the suffering of the innocents caught in the path of armies and battles. He fought down the anger that was kindled by the slaughter he saw around him. The first one who let emotion control them in a conflict was often the one who made the first mistake. He had to think of Sindr not as a marauding killer, but as the vanguard of an invading army. In that context it was easier to understand what she'd done and evaluate it from a tactical aspect.

Doing so made Tyr appreciate the advantage the giant-hunters had been given. "Sindr was delayed here some time by the bondsmen." He looked away from the ruins and considered the closeness of the smoking trail they'd been following. Perhaps it would be just beyond the next knoll or hillock that they'd get a glimpse not merely of her tracks, but find themselves near enough to see the giant herself. He tapped Bjorn with his arm. "No time to mourn the dead. If you would fulfill your vow of vengeance, then we must make haste." He turned to Lorelei, frowning when he saw her lingering over the bodies. "There's no time to give them proper rites," he apologized.

Lorelei pointed to the axe Bjorn had scavenged. "To fight Sindr, we need what weapons we can take. He has his, I have mine." Briefly she opened her hand and Tyr saw that the sorceress hadn't been tending the bodies for burial, but instead had been collecting their tongues.

"Necromancy." Tyr spat the word. Of all the arcane arts, there was none more repugnant. Even the feared Enchanters Three of Ringsfjord shunned the practice.

Lorelei paled when Tyr spoke, but she held her head high with defiance in her eyes. "Only in the practice of charms would I consider myself unsurpassed, but I've learned something about most sorts of magic." She stowed the morbid collection in her bag. "If we're to stop Sindr, we can't be too proud to use any weapon... no matter how distasteful. It might be that you'll be grateful I enticed a necromancer into teaching me a few of his secrets. The spirits of the dead can make for potent allies in a crisis."

"Please to the All-Father it doesn't come to that." Tyr turned from her and started off on the giant's trail again. "If we must resort to necromancy, it will be because there's no other weapon left in our arsenal."

They came upon two more steadings, each demolished in the same manner as the first. Then the trail led away towards a tall hill, its summit dotted with ancient barrows. From their approach, Tyr could see no evidence that the smoldering tracks left the vicinity. "Either Sindr's trail continues on the other side, or else she's lingered here," Bjorn said.

"Or she's changed her shape," Tyr advised. "It may be that these tombs suit her purpose and she's discarded the role of ravening monster to take on a more subtle strategy."

The slopes of the hills were veiled in tall grass. It was apparent that the farmers in the region didn't allow their flocks to graze near the old graves and the vegetation had been left unchecked. The result was a treacherous climb, where the contours of the terrain were hidden beneath the foliage. It was easier to walk in the tracks left by the giant, despite the unpleasant heat that continued to emanate from them. Tyr thought they must be very close to their quarry now, for some of these prints were so new that embers yet glowed around their edges.

"Stay on your guard," Tyr reminded his companions. "Don't underestimate Sindr's craftiness."

THIRTY-THREE

The top of the hill had been flattened long ago to make space for the half-dozen funeral mounds that now clustered together in a rough circle around its crest. The grass grew thick over the barrows, but the stone doors remained visible, crudely worked slabs covered in runes.

"I see no sign of smoke below," Bjorn said as he ascended the side of one mound and gazed across the terrain beyond.

"Either she's changed her shape or she's still here," Lorelei declared. At the last farm they'd passed through, she'd availed herself of a doeskin tunic and boots that had escaped the consuming flames, a costume more suited to the rigors of the hunt than the gown she'd been wearing. Her hand reached into the bag she carried, extracting what looked like a bit of horn. The object had a sinister appearance, reminding Tyr of the serpents that haunted the Sea of Fear.

Tyr focused on the smoldering tracks before him. He could see that they angled towards one of the barrows. Drawing nearer he saw that the door had been smashed in. It was here that the giant's trail ended. "Take a closer look at her tracks," he told Bjorn. He advanced to a few paces from the mound's yawning entrance, Tyrsfang clenched in his fist. "I'll keep watch."

Bjorn studied the tracks for a moment, peering closely at them. "There are footprints inside the footprints." He waved his axe at the marks, following them from track to track. "She did change her shape. No longer a giant, but something much closer to a human in size. She's had to jump to match her old stride." The wolfhunter turned from the smoldering trail and indicated another one. He followed for only a few steps, then turned back to Tyr, a smile on his face. "You were right to call her crafty. She both changed her shape *and* stayed here." He pointed at the tracks. "I don't know how far she laid a false trail for us to follow, but I can tell you she backtracked. She didn't quite manage to keep in her own footsteps, and they overlap here."

"If Sindr did come back, then she knew she was being followed," Lorelei said. She peered into the darkness of the open barrow. "She might be just inside watching us right now."

Tyr took a few steps forward. The musty, decayed smell of the tomb reached out to him, but there was no hint of Sindr's brimstone scent. That didn't reassure him overmuch. She'd been careful enough to mask the smell when she posed as Nilfli. "If she stayed, then it's because she knew she was already being trailed, otherwise she'd put as much distance between this place and herself as she could. There's no use laying a false path for your enemies if you linger behind at the end."

"She might have seen us when she reached the top of the

hill. Sindr would recognize you even at a distance," Lorelei told Tyr.

"And if she did, she'd lie here in wait for us," Tyr agreed. He frowned at the sea serpent horn in Lorelei's hand. "Right now, we need some sort of spell to light our way."

"We're going in?" Bjorn asked, uneasy at the prospect. "We know where she's gone. Let's just seal the tomb up again and leave her trapped until we can get help."

"She'd easily break out," Lorelei chided the huntsman. She grimaced as she added, "You saw what the monster did to my castle."

"Nor can we send someone to pass along a warning," Tyr sighed. "That would further diminish our strength and might be just the advantage Sindr is waiting for. After all she's done to get this far, she won't take any risk she doesn't have to."

Bjorn scratched his beard. "So we go in," he said, waving his axe at the desecrated barrow.

"We go in." Lorelei retained hold of the horn in her right hand, but there was now a polished stone in her left. She closed her eyes, and the stone began to shine with light.

"Keep close and watch for the least trace of her," Tyr said as he led the way into the sepulchral blackness. His boots crunched on old bones, and by Lorelei's light he could see that the floor within was littered with skeletal fragments. He noted the skulls of dogs and horses. Whoever the ancient thane had been, he must have been wealthy to have so many of his animals entombed with him when he died. Tyr dreaded to see human remains mixed among the bones. He knew in Midgard some of the people buried slaves with their dead kings. Fortunately, that tradition had never been widely practiced in even the most barbarous regions of Asgard.

The walls of the tomb were fashioned from unworked stone and a clumpy gray mortar. Tyr noted the urns and jars that rested against the walls. He smiled at drinking horns and the withered residue of what must have been a lavish meal. An old custom, to bury the royal dead with the viands to hold a mighty feast. The whole of this antechamber was made so that the entombed thane could fete ancestral ghosts and impress them with the luxury of his grave.

A flight of steps at the back of the antechamber descended deeper into the hill. By the magic light Tyr could see marks in the dust. Human footprints that trailed away down the stairs. He motioned his companions to keep silent and pointed at the marks. They both nodded their understanding. It was impossible to keep their advance hidden from Sindr, but there was no reason to tell her anything more than that. Let her guess what they knew and didn't know.

The decayed reek only became worse as Tyr went down the steps. Lorelei's light threw its rays about twenty feet ahead of him. For many minutes, the only thing to be seen was the rough slabs winding deeper into the hill. Then he saw that the stairs came to an end, an opening that led into some kind of chamber. He made a warning gesture with his arm.

Lorelei kept close behind Tyr as they entered the chamber. The light revealed rotten chests on the floor, coins and jewelry spilling from their ruptured sides. A stand of armor rested against the wall, and arrayed around it was an assortment of swords, axes, and shields. Everything was coated in a thick layer of dust.

In the middle of the tomb was a block of stone etched with runes. Resting upon its surface was a skeleton, its hands folded across the chest and holding a sword. The empty sockets of the skull seemed to stare at Tyr with the enmity of the dead towards the living. He saw threads of gold strewn about the body, all that had lingered from what must have been a robe of incredible richness. A massive ring cast into the semblance of a wolf circled one of the fingers. Tyr recognized that emblem as the mark of the Ulfhednar, the fierce warrior cult that had worshiped Fenris as a god when the Great Wolf roamed Asgard unfettered. This thane, then, was an enemy of old, for, after binding Fenris, the Ulfhednar had sought to avenge their chained god, battling Tyr until their cult was exterminated.

At the moment Tyr had to focus upon the enemies of today rather than those of yesterday. He peered about the chamber, searching for any sign of Sindr. He started when he caught a flash of motion from the corner of his eye. Something had moved near the thane's stone bed. For an instant he thought the ancient chieftain had risen from his grave, but then he saw that the figure was one of flesh and blood, not bones and dust.

Cringing against the side of the stone slab was a young bondswoman. Her face was grimy from soot, her clothes and hair were singed, the hands that clutched at the stone were cut and bleeding. She fixed eyes wild with terror on Tyr and at his least motion she recoiled from him like a whipped dog.

"She must have escaped from that last farm," Lorelei said, her voice filled with sympathy for the refugee. Bjorn shrugged off his wolfskin, intending to give the bondswoman something better than her scorched rags to cover her.

Tyr waved him back. He kept his eyes on the bondswoman. "A nice try, but we found only one trail leading to the hill." He wasn't as certain as he sounded, for it was barely possible that Sindr had carried this woman here for some reason.

The giant, however, was taken in by his feigned confidence. The fear vanished from the bondswoman's face in the blink of an eye, replaced by a look of amusement. "Of course, you would notice that." Her hand came out from behind her and revealed the sword that had been hidden between her and the side of the table. As her fingers tightened around it, a line of flame crackled down the length of Twilight.

"You noticed that, but you came here anyway," Sindr smiled. The bondswoman's eyes became pits of fire. "Like flies leaping into the spider's web."

THIRTY-FOUR

Tyr lunged at the transformed giant, thinking to strike her before she could defend herself. One slash from Tyrsfang could have been enough to bring Sindr down, end the fight before it truly began. It was their best chance to finish the menace that now threatened all Asgard.

It almost worked. By a hair's breadth was Sindr able to intercept Tyr's gleaming sword as it flashed at her. The white tooth of Fenris crashed against the dark blade of Surtur with an impact that echoed through the tomb. Sparks flashed from the weapons as the two enemies strove against each other's strength. At first Tyr was able to prevail and forced Twilight back towards the bondswoman's face. Then, with a swelling of might, Sindr forced his arm back. He brought his left arm up against Tyrsfang's guard, driving more of his own weight into his effort to hold her.

"Hai! Murdering beast!" Bjorn shouted. He charged at Sindr, swinging his axe at the woman's body. The giant caught him with a kick that sent him flying back into one of the decayed chests. Bjorn crashed through the rotten wood and sprawled in a pile of tarnished coins.

The wolfhunter's distraction allowed Tyr to press his advantage. He shoved Twilight back and brought the edge of his blade against Sindr's face. From brow to chin, his sword cut into the flesh and created a furrow of blood.

Sindr hissed, more from anger than pain. Her body expanded, growing in size as the appearance she wore cracked and crumbled into cinders, exposing the giant's true shape beneath. Horns sprouted from her head, fangs lengthened in her jaws. Her strength surged in keeping with her growth and Tyr was forced back. Even then he might have held her a little longer had the giant's tail not snaked around his leg and tripped him. Tyr pitched over, slamming onto his back.

"One less son of Odin," Sindr sneered as she loomed above him. Before she could strike with Twilight, her eyes were blotted out by a sheet of hoarfrost. She snarled in fury and whipped her sword against the floor. The instant of blindness was enough for Tyr to scramble away, and the blade slashed only earth instead of flesh.

Sindr turned, and steam billowed from her eyes as the fires within evaporated the frost. She glared straight at Lorelei. "You've played that trick on me before, witch. You'll not do so again!" The giant had now grown to a height of ten feet, Twilight still keeping apace. She pointed the sword at Lorelei as she retreated toward the steps. From the tip of the sword, a swirl of coruscating fire shot at the sorceress. Lorelei cried out and dove to one side as the flames whipped around her, scorching her clothes and blistering her skin.

Tyr's tactical mind at once saw the threat that could bring immediate doom to them all. Should Sindr continue to grow, she could bring the barrow crashing down on them all, as she had nearly done with Lorelei's castle. The only chance he saw for them was to keep the giant distracted, enrage her so much that she didn't pause to consider employing such a strategy.

"The son of Odin is still here!" Tyr sprang at Sindr, his move taking the giant by surprise. Had she been braced for his lunge, she might have defied the god's strength, but, as it was, she was carried back by his momentum. Both of them went crashing into the stone table. It disintegrated under the giant's weight, sending the thane's bones rattling across the tomb.

The giant took the worst of the impact, but Tyr wasn't left unphased. His head glanced off the rubble and his right arm was pinned under Sindr's bulk. He strove to bring his sword against her body, but found all he could do was slide it slightly back and forth in a sawing motion. It might take hours to saw through the tough hide and reach her spine.

Unable to visit a serious hurt against Sindr, the motion of Tyr's sword was enough to agitate her. She struck at him with Twilight, but as he twisted away she nearly slashed her own leg. She snarled in frustration and grabbed him with her other hand. Forcing him up, she held him in place while she made ready to strike again with her sword.

"Did you forget about me?" Bjorn howled as he charged the giant. His axe chopped down, biting deep into the hand that held Tyr and breaking Sindr's grip. She snarled in pain and rolled aside as the huntsman drove another blow at her chest.

Tyr whipped away from the giant, his arm free again. He slapped it with the metal cup on his left wrist, trying to knock feeling back into the numbed limb. He could be thankful he was Aesir – a less powerful being would have had their bones pulverized under the giant's weight.

While he tried to regain sensation in his sword arm, Tyr saw Bjorn press his attack on Sindr. His friend managed a deft blow to the giant's leg as she rolled across what was left of the shattered table. The stroke was expertly delivered, but the giant's hide was thicker about the leg than the hand. The axe rang off it as though he'd struck solid stone, and the cut it left behind was little more than a scratch.

Sindr's roll ended in a crouch, and from this pose she lashed out with Twilight. The flaming sword came so near to Bjorn that it caught his hair on fire when he ducked beneath its sweep. The wolfhunter cried out and threw himself to the floor, grabbing a fistful of charnel dust to smother his burning scalp.

Before Sindr could attack Bjorn again, Tyr intervened. His sword crashed once more against Twilight. He whipped his blade along the flaming edge and drove at the arm that gripped it. Fire flashed from the giant's mouth, scorching his hand. The flare of pain nearly made him lose his grip, but as he twisted away from the searing blast, he drove the metal cup on his arm against her jaw. Sindr lurched back at the impact, stunned just enough by the blow to spoil the pursuing thrust with Twilight.

"The cold air of Asgard doesn't agree with you," Tyr told

the giant. "You're getting clumsy here. You should have stayed in Muspelheim."

The mockery infuriated Sindr. Her body swelled in size, bigger than the confines of the barrow could comfortably contain. Dirt pattered down from the roof as her horns scraped the ceiling. "When I bring my father across the Rainbow Bridge, Asgard *will be* Muspelheim!"

Tyr smiled at her. It was a dangerous game to play, but he recognized that the weakest link in Sindr's armor was her caustic temper. If he could keep her angry rather than thinking, they might just have a chance. "Your father must think highly of you to send you off to die," he jeered, punctuating the slight by piercing her hand with Tyrsfang. He had to keep her reacting rather than thinking, focusing on fighting rather than using her size to take proper advantage.

Tyr didn't expect the unbridled rage his remark provoked. The flames that erupted from Sindr's body reached across the whole tomb, charring the walls. Her eyes were infernos now, her size such that she had to remain kneeling on the floor for there was no longer room for her to stand. Twilight was big enough to run a mastodon through from trunk to tail. In her fury, however, she didn't think to grow still larger and shatter the crypt. She was too fixated on cutting Tyr down with her blade.

"My father knows my worth!" Sindr snarled at Tyr. Her hand raked across the ground and sent a fistful of bones and rubble pelting the Aesir. While he tried to shield himself from the debris, she stabbed at him with Twilight. Only a hasty dive to one side kept him from being speared by the giant blade. "I am the First of the Flames, the first of Surtur's children to earn his respect!" She sent another fistful of rubble at Tyr, then stabbed again with Twilight. Tyr saw what she was doing. She was herding him into a corner, but there was nothing he could do to keep it from happening.

"Earn this!" Bjorn shouted as he rushed the giant from the side. He had his axe in one hand, in the other was the wolfskin he'd thought to offer Sindr when she seemed naught but a frightened Asgardian. He threw the cloak full into her face. The fires of her eyes ignited it almost instantly, but as the pelt erupted into flame, the smoke of its destruction billowed outward and obscured her vision. Bjorn seized that opportunity to clamp both hands on his axe and drive the edge into her shoulder.

The axe struck deep, and fiery ichor spurted from the wound. Sindr snarled in pain and snatched the wolfhunter away, flinging him across the tomb. This time he slammed into the rack of armor and sprawled in a heap beneath it on the floor.

Tyr darted in while the giant was distracted. He slashed at the hand that had thrown Bjorn, slicing open Sindr's palm. His real objective, however, was the axe still buried in her shoulder. Using his metal cup like the end of a hammer, he pounded the weapon's heft and drove it still deeper into her flesh. Sindr twisted her head around and slashed him with a downward jab of her horns. Now it was the Aesir who was sent tumbling across the barrow.

Sindr licked the cut across her palm and glowered down at Tyr. "I'm going to enjoy bringing your head to Surtur, Odinson." She started toward him, but the confines of the tomb made it difficult for the giant to move. Another moment and she might have calmed her temper enough to shrink back to a more advantageous size, but that moment was to be denied her.

After being scorched by Twilight's flame, Lorelei had kept away from the battle. Her choice was tactical, not timid. She'd been working her way around the barrow, putting herself in a position from which she could attack the giant from behind. While Tyr braced himself for Sindr's attack, he saw the sorceress spring from the shadows and strike.

The weird piece of horn, that weathered fragment from a sea serpent, was clenched in Lorelei's fist. She raked it across Sindr's back, in the very spot, Tyr estimated, where his own sword had sawed at the giant's hide. Where his effort had been a mere irritation, Lorelei's proved more efficacious. Sindr's entire body contorted in a pained spasm. The flames crackling about her body took on a green and sickly hue. Her face had a tortured expression Tyr would have thought impossible for such a diabolical visage to convey.

Pain ended the giant's attack, but what ensued was nearly as deadly. Sindr reared up, driving her head and shoulders against the roof, breaking through to the antechamber above. By blind accident, the giant provoked the catastrophe Tyr had hoped to avoid. Rubble crashed downwards into the tomb and, unlike in the castle, there was no tunnel to escape into. Tyr plunged across the chamber, diving past Sindr's legs to seize Lorelei and draw her back before the falling earth and stone could smash her.

THIRTY-FIVE

Maddened by anguish, Sindr crashed against the side of the barrow. The packed earth and rock spilled outwards, tumbling down the hillside. The giant smashed against it again and again until the fissure was no longer narrow enough to hold her back. With a ghastly howl she hurtled out the gap and down to the plain below.

Tyr caught up one of the old shields that now lay scattered on the floor and used it to brace himself as the ceiling above gave way. His legs set, both arms pressing against the shield, he formed a living arch under which Lorelei and the dazed Bjorn were able to shelter. The Aesir grunted under the strain of holding his position. It felt as though the whole of the hill were pushing down on him, trying to drive him into the ground.

"I don't know how long I can brace it," Tyr warned through clenched teeth. "Look for a way out." Tons of earth had already sealed the gap through which Sindr had fallen. He couldn't see if there was any way back to the stairs. It seemed to him that Lorelei's light showed only earth and rock all around them. Though he'd managed to keep them from being immediately crushed, loose earth was spilling down around the edges of the shield and quickly flooding into the pocket.

"This way," Lorelei gasped. She urged Bjorn onward, pushing him into an area just beyond Tyr. Here the roof had managed to hold, though part of the wall had been smashed through by Sindr's thrashing bulk. The glow from Lorelei's light revealed another tomb, albeit one that hadn't been devastated by a giant.

"Hurry," Tyr urged as he watched his companions duck into the neighboring crypt. As Lorelei hid inside, she drew the light away and he was left in utter darkness. The pressure pushing down on him seemed to be magnified by the blackness, grinding him down inch by inch. He felt his knees start to buckle.

A glimmer of light off to his left showed him the gap into which his friends had gone. The loose earth spilling into the pocket was now up to the level of Tyr's waist. When he shifted to face the opening into the other tomb it was as though he were wading through mud. The turn caused the weight above him to grow heavier. He knew he had only a moment to act or he would be lost. Drawing upon the last reserves of his superhuman stamina, Tyr let the shield fall and leaped for the opening.

Tyr hurtled through the broken wall just ahead of the collapse. He felt the tremor of the shifting hill shake everything around him. Then he felt loose earth rushing down over his legs, spreading across him like a smothering blanket. He dashed to his feet and waved his sword at Bjorn and Lorelei. "Up!" he shouted to them as they ran towards the steps at the front of the tomb. "Stay here and be buried!"

Loose earth rapidly poured through the hole in the wall, sweeping aside the funerary offerings in the tomb. Like a stormy sea, a wave of dirt crashed against the stone table on which the entombed chieftain was laid. As the tide surged onward, Tyr nearly lost his footing as he rushed for the stairs. Bjorn turned back to help him, but he waved at the huntsman to keep moving. The bottom-most step was already buried when he reached the stairs. The level continued to rise as he hurried up from the depths.

Only when they reached the antechamber above was Tyr certain of their safety. The displaced earth would level itself out and rise no higher. Since all of the barrows had been built at the same height, he knew the entry could only be a little lower, if at all, than the tomb they'd escaped from.

As in the other grave, the antechamber was littered with the bones of animals and the wretched remains of a meal laid out only for the dead. Bjorn leaned against one of the walls, trying to draw breath into his panting lungs. Tyr noted that he'd availed himself of another axe from one of the tombs.

"Getting to be a habit with you," Tyr said, pointing at the weapon.

"He's gotten all the use of it he could." Bjorn gestured with his thumb at the grave below them. "No sense leaving a good axe to go to waste." He struck it against the wall, knocking some of the dust and grit from it.

Tyr smiled at Bjorn's remark and turned to Lorelei. She

still had one hand around the horn she'd stabbed Sindr with, only now it had turned an ugly green and had a slimy texture. When she noticed that he was looking at it, she cast it aside hastily and wiped her hand in the dust.

"Whatever that was, it made Sindr howl," Tyr said, walking over to take a closer look at the discarded horn.

"Don't touch it!" Lorelei's voice was emphatic. "It's a creation of the dark elves, steeped in a dozen venoms of lethal potency." She gestured at the many cuts and bruises Tyr had suffered in the fight. "Let the horn brush against any open wound and the poison is drawn out to afflict the one who touched it. Let it enter the bloodstream..." Her voice trailed off. "Well, you saw how it hurt Sindr."

Tyr pointed at the bag. "Did you carry that with you into Muspelheim?"

"In case we ran afoul of Surtur," Lorelei explained. "To be truthful, I didn't want to use it against the fire giant. I wasn't certain it would work against him."

Lorelei's doubt made Tyr uneasy. "What about Sindr, then?"

"You saw how it hurt her," Lorelei said. She shook her head. "We haven't the time for me to explain the intricacies of magic, how and why a certain spell is potent or how it works. Sindr wasn't immune to the poison. That should tell you she's done for."

"I saw her hurt, not killed." Tyr marched toward the door of the tomb. "She might have survived." He drove his shoulder against the stone portal, forcing it outward. He pushed his way from the barrow and out onto the summit. The subsidence caused by the collapsed tomb had changed the ground considerably, altering it from a level plateau to a rolling, uneven crest. Several of the barrows had been broken in the turmoil, their roofs caved in or their sides caved out. It took Tyr a moment to orient himself. He listened for the giant's cries, but the only sound was the wind rippling across the plains.

"She's done for," Lorelei said as she scrambled after Tyr. "She has to be." Bjorn emerged from the tomb after her, his new axe resting across his shoulders.

"I'll believe that only when I see it," Tyr said. He strode past what remained of the first barrow and approached the side of the hill. He moved as close as he dared to the edge. Below him he could see the earth and rock that had been knocked loose by the giant. Any idea Sindr might be buried under there was banished when he saw a line of smoldering footprints leading away.

"So she did survive," Bjorn grumbled when he joined Tyr. "Figures that Surtur's daughter would be hard to stop."

Lorelei shook her head in disbelief. "There was enough poison in that horn to kill twenty frost giants," she claimed.

"Our problem is, she isn't a frost giant," Bjorn reminded the sorceress. He waved his hand at the trail of prints. "Doesn't look like her tracks go very far."

Tyr frowned at the optimism in his friend's tone. "That's because she changed her shape again. She won't make it easy to follow her now." He locked eyes with Lorelei. "For better or worse, she knows we can hurt her."

"So what will Sindr do? Hide?" Bjorn patted his axe. "It would take some doing, but I'm sure I can pick up her trail again. Wherever she tries to hide, we'll find her."

"We can't risk it," Tyr said. "If we don't catch up to her, if she gives us the slip, then she might get past us."

Lorelei ran her fingers through her singed hair. "She's been hurt. That means she'll either try to find someplace to recover or she'll try to rush ahead and accomplish the task Surtur has set her." She pulled a strand of burnt hair from her scalp and scowled at it before letting the wind pluck it from her hand. "From all I've seen, Sindr won't step aside if she thinks she has any chance at all of completing her mission."

Tyr considered the violent reaction he'd provoked from Sindr and what had caused it. "She wants to impress Surtur." He gave Lorelei a knowing look. "We each of us have felt that drive to prove ourselves a credit to our families, to show those with whom we share our blood that we are their equals. To show our parents the measure of our worth." He was silent for a moment, reflecting on his own desperation to earn Odin's esteem. "That same passion dominates Sindr. The quicker she opens the Rainbow Bridge to him, the more she'll impress him."

"Then she won't lie low. She'll head straight for Bifrost," Lorelei declared. Tyr could tell from the tension in her voice that she was thinking of Amora and how she'd struggled to emerge from her older sister's shadow.

"It'll be better if we catch her first," Tyr told his companions, "but if we can't, we know where she's going. What we have to do is be near enough to stop her but not so close that we scare her away."

THIRTY-SIX

Watching from the rocks heaped outside the city of Asgard's walls, Tyr and his companions kept vigil over the Himinbjörg. He wondered if Heimdall would appreciate the irony, that the guardian of the Rainbow Bridge was himself being guarded. Or at least as much as they could afford to from a half mile away.

Tyr's mind was tormented by the burden he bore. It would be so easy to pass a warning along, alert his father to all that had happened. But to do so would risk a response that would be certain to make Sindr go into hiding. How long could they maintain a strengthened guard over Bifrost? Worse, if she saw no chance to use the Rainbow Bridge to bring Surtur across, Sindr might seek another way to breach the barriers. Lorelei thought it might be possible, though Bifrost was the most certain route. King Geirrodur's rock trolls had drills that could punch holes from the Realm Below into Midgard. If they harnessed Twilight, they might be able to create a tunnel to Muspelheim that Surtur could use.

Alerting Heimdall was another course of action. The Vanir's extraordinary senses were continually searching for any invader who threatened Asgard, peering across the Nine Worlds from his post at the end of the Rainbow Bridge. The most dire enemies of Asgard knew of Heimdall's powers and employed powerful magic to balk his abilities. The mere fact that Sindr had been able to cross into the realm was argument enough that such spells had been woven about her. Perhaps it was the evil sorcery of Twilight itself that concealed the plot from the sight of the All-Seer. By whatever means, Heimdall was unaware that the giant had bypassed his post, just as he didn't know three Asgardians had slipped past him to reach Muspelheim.

No, Tyr was convinced Sindr and Twilight were hidden from Heimdall. If she saw one of them slip down to the Himinbjörg to warn him, she might change her strategy. That was something he simply couldn't chance. Not when the life of his father and the safety of all Asgard were in the balance.

"Another one headed towards Bifrost." Bjorn's remark dragged Tyr from his troubled thoughts. He peeked out from behind the rocks and watched as an Asgardian with the look of a scholar about him walked towards Heimdall's outpost.

"That makes four," Lorelei commented. "Three since we climbed into these rocks to watch the gate and not a one of them who we're looking for."

"As far as we know." Bjorn tapped the edge of his axe. "I still say we should have stopped that merchant Heimdall turned away. He could have been Sindr coming along to see if it was safe."

Lorelei laughed at the suggestion. "Sindr wouldn't have walked away. She'd have struck. She knows she'll have to face Heimdall at the very least. If she found him alone, she'd make her move." The sorceress shook her head. "If we'd moved against that merchant and Sindr was watching, it would have spoiled everything. Don't forget, she might have the semblance of anyone. We won't recognize her, but she'll recognize us."

Something in what Lorelei said spurred an idea. Tyr stared more intently at the scholar. The man had what looked like a long roll of parchment strapped across his back. The waxen seals and tassels hanging from it made it look like a bundle of maps, but something about its dimensions troubled the Aesir. "Lorelei, in your brief study of Twilight did you learn something of the sword's powers? We know it will change size to suit the one who carries it, but was there anything to suggest it can alter its shape as well?"

The sorceress gave him a puzzled look. "I found nothing that would lead me to suspect such a thing, but I'll be the first to admit I didn't have the opportunity to probe too deeply into its secrets."

A grim smile formed on Tyr's face. "Watch that man," he told the others. "Does it seem that bundle of maps he's carrying might be big enough to hide a sword?"

"You think that's Sindr?" Bjorn asked.

"We'll know soon enough," Tyr answered, drawing his sword. "Be ready to move if it is. Every second might count."

Tyr watched in tense silence as the scholar walked to the domed Himinbjörg. His fingers tightened about Tyrsfang's grip when he saw Heimdall step out to challenge the visitor.

He couldn't hear the conversation, but he knew the sentry was asking why the man wanted to cross the Rainbow Bridge and judging if his reason was worthy.

Without warning, it happened. One moment Heimdall and the scholar were talking, the next the man reached to his back and ripped the sword hidden inside the heavy parchment rolls free. Flame bristled about Twilight's dark blade as it swung towards the sentry's head!

Heimdall thwarted the strike with his own sword, the fearsome Hofund. The two weapons crashed together in an explosion of electricity and flame. The sentry was unaccustomed to being taken by surprise, and so reacted more by reflex than thought. He used both hands to wield Hofund. Sindr only employed one to swing Twilight. The other darted to Heimdall's chest and from her palm a wave of fire spilled across the Vanir, green flames that crackled across his armor.

"The poison you set into her has tainted her fire!" Tyr shouted as he ran from the rocks and started towards Himinbjörg.

"Wonderful," Bjorn snarled. "Instead of killing the giant, you made her stronger."

"Perhaps you'd have preferred I let her just crush you down in that barrow," Lorelei growled back at them.

Tyr saw Heimdall staggered by Sindr's flame. The green fire didn't scorch the sentry's beard or mar his armor, but what it did do was weaken him with pain. Had Sindr moved to strike him with Twilight in that moment she would have found him helpless. The giant, however, was already turning to a more important goal. While the semblance of an Asgardian scholar crackled and flaked away, she lunged past Heimdall and into his bastion.

Heimdall had regained his feet when Tyr reached him. A sickly pallor was upon his face, but the Vanir was strong enough to lift Hofund. He scowled at the sounds of destruction echoing from within his home. "I'd know how the giant took me unaware," he swore.

Tyr sprinted beside him as they entered the Himinbjörg. "That's a long story. You'll hear it when we've stopped her."

The inside of the fortress was a shambles. It seemed anything that could be smashed had been. This wasn't wanton destruction though. Tyr saw at once what Sindr's objective had been. Not among the debris was the Gjallarhorn, the enchanted instrument by which Heimdall could alert every Aesir in the Nine Worlds when Asgard was under attack. The giant had taken it with her.

Heimdall's eyes widened with alarm when he saw the empty spot where the Gjallarhorn should be. "Then she doesn't mean to simply escape," he said as they rushed past the wreckage. "This is an invasion."

"More than that," Tyr told him. "She means to free Surtur and loose him upon Asgard."

"Then she's either mad or a fool," Heimdall snarled as they passed through another ruined room. "Surtur will destroy everything if he's freed… including her."

Something in what Heimdall said nagged at Tyr's mind, but he dismissed it when they emerged from the Himinbjörg and stood before the Rainbow Bridge. Ahead of them was Sindr, all semblance of an Asgardian burned away. Twenty feet tall, she towered above them, the equally enormous

Twilight clenched in both hands. The flames that crackled around her still had a green tinge, and Tyr thought the fires in her eyes were less robust than they had been before.

The giant lifted the Gjallerhorn and cast it over the edge. She fixed her fiery gaze on her enemies. "The Leavings of the Wolf." Sindr scowled at Tyr. She laughed when she saw Lorelei and Bjorn. "And entourage. I've much to repay you." The flames around her briefly turned orange before collapsing back to a sickened green. "I'll ask my father to let me kill you so I can make sure you are a long time dying."

"Surrender and I promise you'll return to Muspelheim," Heimdall said. He brandished Hofund. "Fight and I promise you'll find me not so easy to surprise a second time."

Sindr's face split in a fanged grin. "And I promise you'll be the first victim of Asgard's conqueror. Grovel and I may ask Lord Surtur to kill you quickly, but of that I make no promises."

"This ends now!" Tyr charged toward Sindr. She swatted him aside with a flourish of Twilight, casting him back against the walls of Himinbjörg. He felt stone crack beneath his impact, and sparks flashed across his vision. The reckless attack had been meant as a distraction, but the opening he made availed Heimdall and Bjorn little. The sentry directed a ray of cosmic energy from Hofund at the giant, but Twilight drew the blast into itself, devouring it greedily. Bjorn's axe glanced off the giant's leg and he was forced to retreat before her lashing tail.

"End?" Sindr chortled. "This is only the beginning! Already Twilight calls out to its master!"

Tyr could see the hazy distortion that shimmered across

Bifrost, the heat haze he'd become so familiar with while trekking across Muspelheim. Through the distortion were dark figures. For a moment they were indistinct and unmoving. It was only a matter of moments before the scene beyond the haze came into sharper clarity. When it did, Tyr recognized the figures as fire demons... and no longer motionless. The warriors of Muspelheim surged forward through the haze. A great body of them emerged onto Bifrost. Their exultant cries rang out as they charged across the span toward the Himinbjörg.

Tyr shook his head and started towards the bridge. He'd only taken a few steps when he suddenly froze. There was another figure taking shape on the other side of the portal, behind the cohorts of fire demons. A monstrous being of gargantuan proportions, an aura of flame surrounding the horned head, the red skin cracking and splitting as geysers of fire erupted from the flesh. The face was inhuman in its fiendish malevolence, an infernal visage with a maw like the mouth of a volcano and eyes that burned with eternal hate.

Surtur! The fire giant himself, come to lead his hordes in the destruction of Asgard!

THIRTY-SEVEN

Tyr glared at Surtur, the devil prophesied to be the murderer of his father. "You'll not enter Asgard," he snarled. If he could get Twilight away from Sindr, He knew it would be the first step to closing the breach.

Heimdall again crossed swords with Sindr, Hofund cracking against Twilight in a struggle of light and darkness. The cosmic energies of the Vanir's blade rippled through Twilight, at times smothering the sword's fire, at others having its brilliance fade when the giant's sword absorbed its power. Back and again the two fought until at last the greed of Twilight took too much from Hofund. The moment of weakness was enough for Sindr to exploit. Exerting her strength to the full, the flames around her turning yellow, she swung the dark blade and shoved Heimdall back.

Had the stamina been left to her, Sindr might have finished her enemy, but if the tainted flames could sear her foes, the toll they wrought upon her was worse. After the exertion that drove Heimdall back, the yellow flames shifted to pallid green and with the shift came a slackening of Sindr's posture, as though all the strength had drained out of her. It took a moment for her to recover even a flicker of orange in the fire that billowed about her body.

In that moment, Tyr put himself between the giant and the Vanir. Tyrsfang slashed at her, raking down along one leg and sending a stream of fiery ichor to sizzle against the edge of Asgard. Without Heimdall, they wouldn't be able to close the breach. Whatever peril it invited against himself, he had to keep Sindr away from the Vanir. "Forgot about me already?" he jeered, trying to provoke the giant's ire.

Sindr scowled at him. "Your prattle will bring you a lingering death in the bellies of my hellhounds," she snarled.

Tyr struck at her again, twisting aside when she moved Twilight to block him. His blade instead cut across her already injured leg. "If I've a chance, I might tell Svafnir who helped me overcome him. I'm sure he'd like that. Dragons are very forgiving about such things."

From the corner of his eye, Tyr could see Heimdall and Bjorn start to flank Sindr. Before they could strike, however, the foremost of the fire demons were upon them. The Asgardians strove against the monstrous surge, trying to keep them from gaining a foothold on Asgard's soil. Bjorn's axe and the coruscating blade Hofund took a brutal toll on the warriors of Muspelheim. In their vicious rush to cross the bridge, the fire demons threw their own dead and wounded off the edge to clear room for those still able to fight.

Sindr would brook no interference in her conflict with Tyr. Infuriated by his verbal barbs, she slapped fire demons aside with her tail. "This one belongs to me," she hissed.

She brought Twilight down to parry Tyrsfang as the blade darted once more at her leg. Her eyes flared with a cold rage as she looked past Tyr. "Keep your witch out of this," she demanded.

Tyr angled away from Sindr to see Lorelei behind him. "No magic against her unless she lets the fire demons take a hand," he said. It wasn't a matter of honor. Not for him. It was merely the appreciation that he couldn't fight both the giant and the fire demons at the same time.

"I've other matters to focus upon," Lorelei told him. Tyr noted that she'd removed the collection of tongues from her bag. Whatever else she had to do to evoke the dark powers of necromancy, he didn't want to see. In a perverse way, he was grateful when Sindr resumed her attack.

"Few in the Nine Worlds have dared challenge me as often as you have, Odinson," Sindr seethed.

"Well, people get busy," Tyr said. Sindr's body swelled with anger, the flames changing to a vivid orange before quickly contracting into a diseased green again, constraining her growth. Tyr caught the edge of Twilight on his sword and twisted out from beneath its murderous sweep. He studied the way the green color waxed and waned in the giant's flames. When it was dominant, she was weak. The more she exerted herself and expended her strength, the quicker and more complete the fade back into exhaustion.

The best way to keep her exhausted was to keep provoking her. If Tyr could keep doing that, then they might have a chance of stopping Sindr and getting Twilight away from her before…

Tyr took the chance of looking past his foe to note

the portal that had taken shape on Bifrost. Fire demons continued to troop out onto the bridge, but more imposing was the infernal colossus behind them. Surtur seethed with impatience, waiting for the instant when the gate would be strong enough to allow his passage. He reached to the portal with a gigantic hand, probing it, testing to see if it would allow him to cross.

Abruptly the air around Tyr became cold. Not the clean frostiness that numbed flesh and crackled bone, but an unnatural chill that curdled the blood and filled the mind with unease. When he blocked one of Sindr's blows, he saw that the giant felt the sensation too. Though her body was still wreathed in flame, he could see her flesh shiver. Tyr guessed what could make even the fire giant's daughter feel cold: necromancy.

His suspicion became a certainty when a spectral curtain arose before the breach Sindr had opened. Tyr thought at first it was a wall of ice, then he saw the phantasmal forms that composed it struggling to manifest with ever greater distinction and independence. The spell Lorelei had invoked, however, bound the ghostly shades into a unified whole, a grotesque barrier across the gate to Muspelheim. A few fire demons tried to force their way through the wall, but these emerged as withered husks, their vitality drained away by the necromantic force.

Behind him, Tyr could hear Lorelei conjuring the spirits, but her voice was merged with a whispering chorus. He shuddered when he thought of what produced that chorus.

"You try to distract me while the witch works her spells!" Sindr's flames flared in keeping with her anger. Tyr dodged the cleaving edge of Twilight while the fires burned orange, then darted in and cut her across the waist when they turned green again.

"The agreement was she wouldn't interfere in *our* fight," Tyr taunted the giant. "Nothing was said about spoiling your plan."

No more fire demons emerged to cross into Asgard and those that already had were being driven back by Heimdall and Bjorn. Tyr was beginning to hope they could win when he noticed that if the fire demons had retreated from their side of the breach, the fire giant hadn't. Surtur continued to probe the gate with his hand, his face growing more enraged each time he was balked. Then a wicked smile formed on his monstrous visage. Tyr saw at once why.

Surtur drew back and clenched his hands together. Upon the bridge, beyond the gate, a dwarfish figure manifested. A minuscule image of the fire giant that copied his every motion. Tyr had heard of such fell sorcery, the dark art of translocation. Through the connection with Twilight, Surtur was casting an aspect of himself past the barriers. While his greater essence remained in Muspelheim, this fragment was being projected onto Bifrost. With each moment, the diminutive figure grew a little more, channeling the giant's wrath into itself.

The spectral curtain Lorelei had raised, a barrier that could shrivel fire demons, wasn't able to injure the projected shade of their master. Bit by bit, Surtur was feeding more of himself across the gate, swelling his image with his infernal might!

Thirty-Eight

Surtur's image grew in size, swelling from the stature of a dwarf to that of a troll as more of the fire giant's essence seeped onto Bifrost. The image began to move, aping the motions of the towering monster visible on the other side of the gate. Translocation, existing simultaneously in both worlds, yet governed by a single mind. A mind determined upon absolute destruction.

Tyr was forced back by Twilight as the blade was engulfed in writhing flames, their heat blistering his skin. It seemed to him that the sword was responding to the nearness of its true master, growing in power as its master's image expanded, as more of Surtur's essence was drawn onto Bifrost. A shudder swept through him at the thought, for already he was being taxed to the utmost by Twilight's might.

Sindr's face was lit by the heat of her rage. The shift between the yellow fires of her anger and the green flames of Lorelei's poison became ever more rapid, testing Tyr's ability to react to the changes that ravaged her. For truly the transition from strength to weakness was ravaging the giant, mauling her far worse than any of his attacks did. Sindr seemed oblivious to the toll being exacted upon her, her entire being filled with nothing but the urge to overcome her enemy.

Around them, Heimdall and Bjorn attacked the hordes of fire demons with an almost frantic disregard. Steadily they pushed themselves against the warriors of Muspelheim, cutting them down with sword and axe. They too were assisted in a strange way by the fury of their adversaries. The demons threw themselves at the Asgardians like berserkers, fighting with the savage abandon of rabid beasts. Each one that fell was trampled by those who followed behind. Any who faltered were thrown aside by warriors more eager to join the fray. The vicious frenzy only became more desperate the larger the image of Surtur grew. One and all, the fire demons knew they were under the merciless gaze of their overlord.

Yet, as much as it frayed and fractured, the barrier continued to resist. The chorus of ghostly whispers that accompanied Lorelei's incantation grew faster with each utterance, words – if such they were – blending together into a babbling stream. Unversed in the ways of magic, Tyr wondered how long the sorceress could coax more power from her spell. How long she could pit her arcane art against the ancient malevolence of Surtur.

"Asgard will burn!" Sindr howled as a blast of flame from Twilight crackled past Tyr's ear. "My father will avenge his long imprisonment upon the gods!"

Tyr sprang in beneath the huge blade's shadow to stab the giant while her fires burned green. Molten ichor spurted from the wound and singed his arm. Another hurt to add to the long list of his injuries. He darted back as Sindr tried to stomp him beneath her foot. "Remember who imprisoned him in the first place! Odin All-Father remains King of Asgard!" The yellow fire that crackled around her body told him not to attempt to block the vicious thrust of her sword, but to dodge it as she drove its point into the ground. Rock sizzled under the blade's heat. "Surtur's impatience will be his undoing! Had he waited for the final Ragnarok, he could have let strong allies do his fighting for him instead of trotting out the dregs of Muspelheim!"

Sindr's body seethed with the light of her fury. She slashed at him with Twilight again and again, but her attacks were too hurried for precision. Tyr spun away from each strike and raked her arms with his sword, sending more of her fiery blood streaming from her veins.

Then, abruptly, Sindr drew back. The flames in her eyes flickered. "You should be grateful my father didn't wait for prophecy," she sneered down at Tyr. "Now the Great Wolf needn't slip its bonds to finish the meal it started long ago. Tell me, Odinson, do you think Fenris still has your taste in its mouth?"

Tyr watched the giant with a heightened wariness. Through her rage, she'd realized the trick he'd been using against her, exploiting her anger, encouraging it to make her reckless. To make her stop thinking. Now she was trying to goad him with the same tactic. He smiled back at her. If she thought he'd take her bait, she would be disappointed.

"You must know little of the doom that has been foretold for me," Tyr shot back. He threw himself to one side as a sheet of fire billowed from Sindr's hand to boil the ground he'd held a moment before. "I'm not destined to face Fenris again." He held up his arm and let the light of Sindr's own flames reflect off the metal cup. "The Great Wolf must have disliked my taste, or else has wits enough to avoid me after what happened before. It has been foretold that I'm to die in the jaws of Garm, that Hela's hound will be set upon me in the final battle."

Sindr lashed at him with her sword, narrowly missing him as it whipped through the air. Tyr retaliated with a glancing slash that cut her from knuckle to wrist. "So you see, this is all for naught. I'm to be eaten by a dog. Do you think I'd succumb to a lesser fate?"

The giant had been striving to maintain some measure of control, but her pride was too great to ignore Tyr's insults. Flames surged all around Sindr, an aura of fire that blazed across Bifrost's edge and seared wounded fire demons with its fury. She rushed at him, each step leaving a molten furrow behind when she stepped from the Rainbow Bridge onto the edge of Asgard. The sight of her awesome rage was such to make Tyr appreciate the formidable foe with whom he was playing his dangerous game.

In her surge forward, Sindr expended the momentum of the anger that revitalized her poisoned frame. The green fire washed out the yellow flames, and her attack faltered as weakness assailed her body. Tyr charged in, slashing once again at the leg he'd been concentrating on. If he could render the giant immobile, he might yet prevail over her before it was too late.

If it wasn't too late already. Farther down Bifrost, Tyr

could see Surtur's image had grown to a height of twenty feet. Now the giant was starting to advance down the bridge, the aspect's motions copied by the far greater colossus still in Muspelheim. Lorelei's spectral barrier was burning away in the fire giant's heat. While he looked on, the fiend's horned head broke through the ghostly curtain. Surtur towered over the span now, twice the size of his daughter and surrounded by billowing flames. He imagined that the fiery light cast by the monster could be seen from the city of Asgard's mighty walls.

The thought gave Tyr an idea, a ploy by which he should whip Sindr into such a fury that she'd exhaust her formidable stamina and collapse under the blight of Lorelei's poison. "A foolish notion, to throw away the Gjallarhorn," he mocked the giant, dodging the angry slash of her sword. "Did you think we have no other way to alert our people that Asgard is under attack? Already the alarm has been given in the city and Odin is marching with his forces to clear away your army and thwart this feeble invasion."

Sindr's eyes flared. "You lie, Odinson! Your people will be trapped like rats in their city and there will be no escape for them when Surtur puts it to the torch!"

Tyr struck again at her weakened leg, but only managed a shallow slice below the knee before he had to avoid her whipping tail. He had to stoke the fires of her temper still further, make her abandon all restraint. The thoughts running through his mind were manipulative and unsavory. He wondered if he'd spent too much time in Loki's company and something of the trickster had infected him that he should conceive such a tactic. Yet not for one moment did he doubt the necessity of the lies he shot at Sindr.

"You still believe you can win?" Tyr mocked her. "The moment you revealed yourself, Odin knew your plan." He swung at her arm when she made a grab for him, gashing one of her fingers. Twilight gouged the side of the Himinbjörg as he threw himself from its deadly path. "You've been allowed to get this far only because the All-Father intends to trap Surtur in a prison still more inescapable than Muspelheim. Perhaps he thinks to make a gift of the fire giant to Ymir."

The flames that blazed around Sindr were nearly blinding in their intensity. She took a few steps toward him, then slumped as the green fire drained her strength. "I will still your lying tongue," she panted through the pain ravaging her.

Tyr darted in and managed a stab at her foot before she rallied and forced him back. "Be quick about it, First of the Flames. Every moment you dawdle brings Odin's army closer." He saw the determination in the giant's face when he spoke of imminent failure. Like the fire demons, Sindr would not relent while the eyes of her father were upon her.

No, Tyr corrected himself, it was more than that. More than the fearful obedience of a slave or the honor-bound duty of a warrior. Sindr was striving for something else, something he'd recognized in her before. He felt disgusted to use it against her, but it was the only way to overcome her.

"Surtur's plan almost worked," Tyr called to Sindr as he avoided the blast of fire she unleashed from Twilight. "Now he's caught in the trap he thought to set for others."

He drove the crux of his provocation home like the tip of a spear. "All because he entrusted his daughter with a task she was unequal to."

A roar of unmatched fury echoed across the battlefield. A conflagration of white-fire exploded from Sindr's skin, searing earth and stone, even discoloring the prismatic bands of Bifrost. She swung at Tyr, sinking Twilight so deep into the ground that he thought it would hew through to the underside of the realm.

Smoke rose from Tyr's garments, and he slapped the fires that smoldered in his braided hair with his arm. His skin felt as though he'd been plunged into boiling water, even the slightest motion filling him with pain.

The ploy had worked, though. After unleashing her full fury, Sindr was spent. The noxious green fires crackled about her, and she sagged to her knees. Her eyes were the merest flicker, hollow and empty. Tyr knew that gaze. He'd seen it many times in Midgard after battering down the gates of a city following a long siege. It was the stare of abject exhaustion.

The frenzied assault by the fire demons intensified, pushing Heimdall and Bjorn back. The two had wrought a terrible toll upon the creatures, but there were still dozens of Muspelheim's warriors trying to strike them down. Beyond, Surtur's gigantic image continued to expand, copying the horned tyrant visible through the hazy portal to his fiery realm. Surtur's merciless gaze was locked upon the city's walls, his mouth curled with murderous anticipation. Lorelei's ghostly barrier was in tatters, but still she strove to maintain the spell and delay the fire giant's advance. Tyr didn't want to consider what would happen when the strain was too much for her magic.

Tyr started toward the drained Sindr. "It's over," he told her, brandishing Tyrsfang. She made an effort to lift her horned head, but even that much appeared to be beyond her. Tyr approached more boldly, ready to subdue the giant and capture Twilight. Then Surtur would have no choice but to withdraw.

His confidence was nearly his undoing. The flaming sword erupted up from where it was buried in the ground. Tyr was swatted aside by a glancing blow, almost pitching over the edge of Bifrost. He raised himself from where he fell, looking aghast as he saw Sindr lurch forward again. Green fire still swathed her, and her eyes were no more vibrant than they'd been before. Twilight, however, rippled with deadly purpose.

Tyr realized that Sindr no longer controlled the sword, but had instead become its puppet. Twilight was using her, forcing her into motion, dredging up not strength but the giant's vitality itself. He could actually see the life being sucked out of her with each step she took. How long she could last, he didn't know, but he feared long enough to achieve the sword's purpose. Directly in the giant's path sat Lorelei, surrounded by the macabre materials of her necromancy. The sorceress was aware of the doom that stalked toward her, but she was unwilling to break off her conjuring and remove the last barrier to Surtur.

Hand clenched around the grip of his sword, Tyr charged at Sindr. "Odin!" he invoked his father's name in a mighty war cry. Dominated by Twilight, the giant paid no notice to him. Her huge arm raised the dark sword. Energy crackled down its length and a gout of fire swept over Lorelei and her morbid tools. The dead tongues flashed and were reduced to ashes instantly. The sorceress was thrown back to crumple against the Himinbjörg's doorway.

"Lorelei!" Tyr was stunned by the emotion he still felt for the sorceress despite all her plotting and intrigues. Ultimately, she'd been an Asgardian and when the realm was threatened she'd stepped forward to do her utmost to defend it. That was something to be lauded. And avenged.

Tyr came at Sindr from behind and struck at her already weakened leg. The giant slumped as he sliced his blade across the back of her knee. A swat from her tail knocked him flat, but with far less impact than he'd expected. He rolled away as the tail tried to smash him again and sprang to his feet.

Twilight continued to blaze with savage energies. Despite the damage done to her, its influence compelled Sindr to stand again. She teetered unsteadily, a prisoner to her own flesh.

Tyr lunged at the giant, hoping that there was some limit to how much Twilight could command Sindr. If the sword had to focus its energies to make her stand, it might be lax in other respects while doing so. His leap bore him towards her arm and with another war cry he slashed his blade across her fingers.

Sindr howled in pain as Tyr's blow knocked Twilight from her grip. The monstrous sword slammed to the ground, its impact reverberating through the rocks. Devoid of a wielder, it retained its imposing size. The giant, however, didn't. She rapidly diminished, shrinking before Tyr's gaze from dozens of feet tall, to a form only slightly bigger than himself. The green fire lessened and some animation returned to her fiery eyes. She glared at him and turned her horned head. When she saw Twilight, she started to crawl towards it.

"That sword has worked enough evil," Tyr told her. He stood above the fallen giant and once again the point of his sword was at her throat. "Leave it where it lies."

"Twilight has done its work," Sindr gloated. She pointed her gashed hand across the Rainbow Bridge.

With the disruption of Lorelei's spell, the last restraint upon Surtur's aspect was gone. Tyr saw the fire giant stride boldly down the bridge, the titan on the other side of the portal still matching the motions, but now beginning to grow smaller as more of the fiend's essence spilled onto Bifrost. Surtur was a colossal figure wreathed in flickering flames, his skin glowing from the inferno that blazed inside him. With each step he took, Surtur's stature grew. Fifty feet, then sixty, then seventy. Tyr wondered if the tyrant of Muspelheim would even need to break the city walls or if he would merely step over them.

THIRTY-NINE

It was Heimdall now who gave way to rage. Charged with guarding Bifrost and protecting Asgard, now the Vanir saw the realm's deadliest enemy on the verge of triumph and the ultimate failure of his duty. A wave of celestial force emanated from Hofund, sending the last fire demons tumbling away in every direction. He stepped past his vanquished foes and pointed the massive sword at Surtur's avatar. "The way is closed to you," the sentry declared.

Surtur's aspect crackled with laughter. His humor faltered when Heimdall unleashed a beam of cosmic force at him, the energy of the heavens blasting into the fire giant. The hazy breach behind him collapsed in upon itself, unable to withstand both Hofund's power. The vision of the colossal fiend that yet remained in Muspelheim vanished. But even the fury of Hofund couldn't consume that which had already manifested upon Bifrost, the image of a titan who had emerged from the Eternal Flame at the dawn of time. Surtur raised his hand, appearing to catch Hofund's beam in his palm. With the other hand, he unleashed his own fire, a searing storm that Heimdall struggled to resist. Tyr dared hope for a moment that the sentry would withstand the firestorm, but at last the might of Surtur overwhelmed him and the Vanir was hurled back. Bjorn rushed over to help the fallen guardian. The fire giant grinned and marched forward, eager to claim his first victims.

Tyr's mind raced. He looked down at Sindr and back at that portion of her monstrous father which had emerged onto Bifrost. There was, perhaps, a way to make Surtur desist without the need of vanquishing him.

"Surtur!" Tyr shouted at the fire giant, raising his arm so the metal cup might draw the monster's notice and leave him in no doubt with whom he treated. "My blade is poised at your daughter's throat! Your scheme has failed! Already the All-Father's armies are moving to secure Asgard against you!" This time he was certain it was no idle boast. Gjallarhorn or no, someone had to have seen Surtur's fire from the city walls. "Return to Muspelheim and I guarantee I will spare Sindr!"

A demonic leer spread across Surtur's visage as he looked across the Rainbow Bridge to where Tyr stood over his daughter. Though the avatar had ceased to grow, enough of the giant had been drawn into it to bristle with infernal might. "All will burn," the fire giant snarled. "You, your army, and the All-fool who leads them. Nothing will escape." His eyes narrowed, focusing not on Sindr, but on where Twilight lay on the ground. He stretched out his hand and the enormous sword rose, lifted into the air by Surtur's command. Crackling with flames, it sped across Bifrost and returned to its master. Surtur's fingers tightened around the sword as it grew to match his tremendous size.

Tyr glared back at the colossal fire giant. "I mean what I say!" He knew even as he made the threat that his words were hollow. However villainous she might be, he couldn't slaughter Sindr while she was helpless beneath his blade.

Surtur shifted his gaze and this time he did train his focus upon Sindr. Tyr was stunned when he learned just how evil the fire giant was. "She'll burn too," Surtur declared. Whether he knew Tyr's threat was empty, he didn't care.

"Father!" Sindr cried out, and for the first time Tyr saw an expression he never expected to see on her face: despair.

Surtur was deaf to his daughter's pleas. He raised Twilight in his fist and pointed it at the city walls. "Doom is upon you, Odin All-fool! The Lord of the Eternal Flame has come to melt your throne and blacken your bones! Watch, you one-eyed worm, as all you've built, all you've loved, is consumed by the fires of Surtur!"

The fire giant lumbered onward, each stride bearing him nearer the Himinbjörg and the edge of Asgard. Tyr could hear now the war-horns and battle cries of Asgardians rushing from the city to defend the realm from the fire giant, but he knew they would arrive too late.

Tyr left Sindr where she lay and charged across the Rainbow Bridge. There was only one strategy he could think of that might delay Surtur if even Heimdall was unable to defy the fire giant's power. He had to provoke the monster's fury, just as he'd goaded Sindr's temper. Enrage the tyrant of Muspelheim so that he became fixated on annihilating Tyr before moving against the rest of Asgard. Whether envy of Thor or concern for Odin had motivated him more, it was his actions that had caused this crisis. If it meant his life, he had to do whatever he could to prevent the disaster that now threatened the realm.

"I'd raise a flagon to you in Valhalla," Bjorn told Tyr when the Aesir joined his friend, helping him get Heimdall back on his feet. The wolfhunter grimaced as Surtur approached. "Only I don't think there'll be a Valhalla left much longer."

"Know that any warrior who would stand his ground before Surtur himself would be certain of entering the halls of Valhalla," Tyr assured his friend.

Heimdall removed his horned helm and glanced at the Asgardians who stood to either side of him. "Hold me steady," he told them. "Don't allow me to falter." He clenched his eyes tight. "May Odin forgive me for failing my duty, I see no other way to protect the realm."

Tyr laid his arm on Heimdall's shoulder. "What are you going to do?"

"Break the Rainbow Bridge," the Vanir replied. Taking Hofund in both hands, he brought the sword stabbing down into Bifrost. The cosmic energy bound into the blade rippled through the prismatic span.

What effect the blow might have had, Tyr would never know, for there was a power that opposed Hofund's. Surtur swung Twilight in a sweeping arc across the bridge. The force unleashed by Heimdall was drawn out from the span, steaming away into the void. The fire giant repeated the motion, banishing the cosmic power as though he were brushing away a cloud of flies.

"All will burn," Surtur growled, glaring down at Heimdall. "But you will be the first."

Tyr left Bjorn to support Heimdall as the Vanir strained to channel Hofund's power into Bifrost. Holding his own sword high, he returned to his original plan and marched to meet Surtur's advance.

"Heimdall will not be the first," Tyr shouted at the enormous tyrant. "I will be, if you think yourself capable."

Surtur glowered down at him, his eyes reflecting the temper he'd passed along to his daughter.

"Audacity and pretension," Surtur hissed. "You dare presume, whelp of Odin? You think you can dictate terms to *me*?" The fire giant reached down with his hand. Tyr wouldn't have believed something so enormous could muster such speed. Before he could react, Surtur caught him in his fist. He screamed in agony as the flames licked across his flesh. The giant squeezed, and even the armor Lorelei had given him was incapable of resisting the tremendous force that was brought to bear.

"No," Surtur seethed, relaxing his hold. "You'd prefer it this way." He brought his hand up and stared directly at Tyr. The fires in the giant's eyes felt as though they pierced the Aesir's spirit. "No heroic finish for you, Odinson." His cruel smile twisted with amusement as he swept Twilight across the bridge and continued to banish Hofund's energies. "You'll not distract me from my destiny! Asgard will burn, and you will watch as it does! Broken and helpless, you'll see everything destroyed!"

"I see the whole family must be braggarts," Tyr spat at the giant. With the pressure around him relaxed, he was able to tilt forward and reach Surtur's face. Arrogant and proud, Surtur had dismissed Tyrsfang as a weapon too feeble to vanquish him. Perhaps it was, but if it couldn't kill Surtur, that didn't mean it was powerless to hurt an aspect with only a portion of the giant's terrible essence. Tyr raked the sword down Surtur's cheek, slashing a deep furrow along it that soon filled with molten ichor.

The fire giant snarled in surprise. His arm arched back, and he hurled Tyr to the ground. Tyr was grateful the surface he struck was the vaporous Rainbow Bridge rather than solid earth, otherwise the force with which he was thrown should have shattered every bone in his body.

"All. Will. Burn!" the giant roared. Both hands clenched about Twilight, Surtur brought the sword swinging down. Flame exploded across the Rainbow Bridge, blasting everything and everyone before it. The bodies of fire demons were flung against the Himinbjörg. Heimdall and Bjorn were blown back, slamming into the fortress walls.

Tyr hurtled through the air to crash against the edge of Bifrost. For a hideous instant he felt himself slipping, but a firm grip drew him back. Lorelei helped him onto the bridge. The sorceress was bruised and burned from Twilight's attack. The bag with her arcane devices was gone, but Tyr saw that she had one last instrument clenched in her hands. The Wayfarer's Mirror.

Lorelei saw him looking at the mirror. "It's the only thing left now," she said. She gave him an anxious smile. "I didn't mislead you when I said its power is capricious, but it does have power."

"Don't," Tyr told her, a sense of foreboding coming upon him. "Hofund couldn't prevail against Surtur..."

"I have to try," Lorelei said, glancing down at the mirror.

"If it will send him back, I have to try, whatever the danger." She shook her head. "Whatever happens, remember me to your brother."

Tyr started after Lorelei, keeping pace as she ran towards Surtur. The giant grinned down at her, so certain of his unstoppable power that it was impossible for him to believe she could pose any threat to him. Briefly it looked as though he would use Twilight to strike her down, then the fire giant reconsidered the idea. He leaned down to take her in his hand.

"We haven't finished our fight!" Tyr shouted at the giant. His blade raked across Surtur's hand, gashing the aspect's fingers. The monster reared back, snarling in pain. His blazing eyes fixed upon Tyr and he brought Twilight sweeping down for the Aesir, determined to cut him in two.

That was when the eerie light from the Wayfarer's Mirror appeared at Surtur's feet. The giant scowled at the strange luminescence, but too late did he associate it with the woman who so boldly defied him. By then the light had spread to surround him and was beginning to climb up the monster's legs. Surtur roared his wrath to the stars as the light climbed higher, steadily ascending to engulf him. Already the legs had faded, washed away by the reflection from the mirror.

It was a more gradual process than Tyr had seen in the forge, when Lorelei and Bjorn had transitioned from Muspelheim to Asgard, but he knew he was seeing the same process in reverse. Surtur rebelled against the magic that was casting his essence back to rejoin the rest of his being in Muspelheim. He exerted Twilight's flame again, trying to break the enchantment. For a dreadful moment, it seemed the sword would accomplish just that. The light of the mirror began to retreat, sinking down to his waist after climbing as high as his chest.

Lorelei trembled as she compelled the mirror's sorcery. Tyr noted the arcane gestures she made with her hand, as if to catch strands of magic and weave them into the mirror. He saw something else as well. Something he was certain the sorceress was unaware of. The same light that was climbing up Surtur was now gathering around her own feet. By the sneer that formed on the giant's face, Tyr knew it must be some devilry of his, reflecting the light back upon her.

"If I return to Muspelheim, I don't return alone," Surtur hissed. He wore a look of triumph, but his expression changed when the light continued to rise. A bestial howl of fury rang out and he struggled even more fiercely against the spell that was sending him back.

"You have to stop!" Tyr shouted to Lorelei. The reflected light was now above her knees. She didn't say anything, only shook her head. Tyr started forward, but hesitated. He was no enchanter. He didn't know what would happen if he disrupted the spell. For all he knew, Lorelei would be torn in two, part of her remaining in Asgard, the other part cast into Muspelheim.

"Don't do this," Tyr implored Lorelei, yet he knew she was doing what had to be done. Maybe there was another way to turn back Surtur, but this was the only way to do it before the fire giant could really begin his assault on Asgard.

Surtur fought to the end to resist the spell laid upon him. He raised Twilight over his head and sent pulse after pulse of infernal flame searing down into the light. Each time the fire would drive the light back, but each time the retreat was less than before. Tyr thought that the giant was merely trying to outlast Lorelei, aware that she was likewise being transported by the light. Maybe if the sorceress were to vanish before he did, all her work would be undone.

"Tyr! You must hold the light upon him!" Lorelei called out to him. Sheathing his sword, he took the Wayfarer's Mirror from her grasp as the light swept up past her neck. As she directed, he kept the reflection focused on Surtur. It became a hideous race to see which would disappear first, Twilight or Lorelei. The pulsations from Surtur's sword put the outcome in doubt to the very last. A ten-foot length of the blade remained untouched when only the very top of her head remained. Tyr didn't dare to breathe in that last moment when a final jump of the light took the last part of Twilight, and the faint outline of Surtur's gigantic form vanished utterly. At the same moment, the last vestige of Lorelei vanished.

The moment the fire giant was gone, the Wayfarer's Mirror burned with all the fires of Muspelheim. Tyr tried to retain his grip, but the pain was too much for him. There was a loud crash as the mirror fell onto the Rainbow Bridge. Although the nebulous fabric of Bifrost had been too ethereal to hurt Tyr when he was thrown by Surtur, it possessed enough solidity to shatter the Wayfarer's Mirror.

"Was that Lorelei?" The question was asked by Bjorn. Unnoticed by Tyr, the wolfhunter had joined him on Bifrost, limping from his many injuries.

Tyr bowed his head. "She felt as responsible as any of

us for allowing Surtur to come here," he said in a low, grim voice. "Her magic brought Twilight here, it was her magic that sent the sword and its master back. She knew what it would cost her, but she refused to surrender."

"A warrior of Asgard," Bjorn said.

Tyr's eyes remained fixed on the spot from which Lorelei had vanished. "A warrior of Asgard," he agreed. He slammed Tyrsfang back into its sheath. "What she did here will not be forgotten."

Heimdall was standing guard over Sindr when Tyr and Bjorn made their way back to the head of the bridge. In the distance they could hear the sound of the mustered army marching to the Himinbjörg. Tyr was surprised that his father hadn't ridden ahead on eight-legged Sleipnir, but then he realized no army would let its leader go before it into battle. Odin would be with his people to give them heart as they entered the fight. The city walls were high and thick, but no gate opened to face the Rainbow Bridge, a measure to force any invader to march around the battlements to force their way in. There was time yet before the host of Asgard arrived.

Sindr glared at him when Tyr approached. Though there was still a green hue to her flames, it wasn't as vivid as it had been before. Her exertions in the battle and the cruel use Twilight had made of her had weakened her, but she'd survived. Tyr expected the poison would be completely burned away before it could overcome her.

"I would speak with our prisoner," Tyr told Heimdall.

"She seems little inclined to speak," the Vanir advised

him. He shrugged his shoulders. "But see what you can do."
Heimdall took a few steps back, but kept Hofund ready.

"I say we have her head and be done with it," Bjorn
said, fingers tapping the edge of his axe. "Recompense for
Lorelei."

Tyr shot his friend a stern look. "It is of Lorelei that I'm
thinking." He turned back to Sindr and crouched down
beside the fallen giant.

She gave him a defiant smile. "The witch was caught in
her own trap," Sindr laughed. She cocked her horned head
to the side. "Tell me, Odinson, how do you think she'll fare
in the dungeons of Muspelheim?"

"Better than you will here," Bjorn snarled at her. Tyr
waved him back.

"Surtur has her," Tyr said. "But we have you."

A simple statement, but it quenched the arrogance in
Sindr's pose. Steam boiled off her face. Tyr was stunned to
see that a molten tear was sliding down the giant's cheek.
"What you're thinking is useless. You can't exchange me for
her." She looked down at the ground. "Surtur won't bargain
for me."

Tyr was well aware of how callous the fire giant had been
of his daughter when the chance of destroying Asgard was
before him, but he hadn't imagined Surtur would forsake
her utterly. He could read the terrible truth in Sindr's
posture. The proud, boastful warrior was tortured not
simply by defeat but by a failure that went beyond the attack
against Odin's realm. Even when he was jealous of Thor and
felt that his father's favor was always fixed upon his brother,
he still knew he had his father's love. That was something

Sindr had never known, something she'd fought fiercely to earn. He felt a strange pity for her, because what she wanted was something that simply wasn't there. There was only one thing Surtur cared about, and that was the destruction of Asgard.

"It is an awful thing when a father cares nothing for his child," Tyr said.

Sindr raised her head at his words. Defiance shone in her eyes. "Surtur will know my worth," she snarled. "If it means I must wrest the crown of Muspelheim from him and hold it before his dying eyes, he will know who I am."

"Who you are is a prisoner," Bjorn growled.

Sindr scowled at the wolfhunter, then looked back at Tyr. "My father won't bargain with you. I will. Let me go and I vow that your friend will escape Surtur's dungeons."

"How can I trust your word?" Tyr asked her.

"My father used me as a mere pawn in his schemes," Sindr said, her voice crackling with bitterness. She waved her hand at the dead fire demons heaped against the Himinbjörg. "No different from these. I believed that when he came here and saw victory in his grasp he would come not as a destroyer, but as a conqueror." Her hand clenched into a fist. "And that I would rule by his side. Do you think I will allow my father to profit by his misuse of me?"

Tyr shook his head. He reached down and helped the giant rise. "It isn't for me to say," he told her. The sounds of Asgard's forces were louder now. Soon they would reach the Himinbjörg. "Odin will judge."

"And will he trade the daughter of Surtur for your friend?" Sindr challenged him. She suddenly wrested free of his grip and jumped onto the Rainbow Bridge.

Weary from the fight, it still would have been easy for Tyr to catch Sindr, but as he turned to give chase, he stumbled against Bjorn and kept the huntsman from pursuing her. Bjorn struggled for a moment to break free of Tyr's hold then gave him a stunned look when he realized the obstruction was deliberate.

"You're going to let her get away?" Bjorn stared in astonishment. "You trust her promise that much?"

Tyr shook his head and turned to watch Sindr. "No, I trust her pride. She made a vow to us, but it isn't her honor that will bind her to it. It will be her ego that does. She spoke the truth when she said she wouldn't let Surtur profit by his exploitation of her devotion."

Heimdall stepped down to the edge of Bifrost. He raised Hofund and brought its tip against the crimson bands of the Rainbow Bridge. "Let's speed her on her way then." Energy crackled from the sword into Bifrost. This time not to disperse its power, but to harness it. A few yards from Sindr, a portal took shape. The giant moved towards it. In a few moments she stepped through and the gate closed behind her.

It was Tyr's turn to be amazed. Heimdall smiled at his surprise. "I owe Lorelei a debt too," he said. "Her magic kept me from failing my duty to Asgard."

Tyr shared a knowing look with Bjorn. They wondered how the Vanir would feel if he knew that it was also Lorelei's magic that had frustrated his role as guardian of Bifrost and allowed them passage to Muspelheim in the first place.

There was little time to ponder the question. The sound

of galloping hooves charging through the ruins of the Himinbjörg told that the vanguard of Asgard's army was upon them. A troop of mounted Valkyries emerged from the ruined fortress and spread out, spears at the ready. Through their cordon, eight-legged Sleipnir tromped toward Bifrost. Odin peered over the battlefield with his single eye, his gaze seeming to read every aspect of the fight from a single glance. Behind the All-Father, the other gods of Asgard rode forth, each ready to join the fray.

Thor frowned and let Mjolnir fall from his hand to dangle against his side by the cord that bound the hammer to his wrist. "It looks like the fight is won already." He nodded to Tyr. "You might have saved the rest of us a bit of the glory, brother," he said with a laugh.

Odin's piercing gaze latched onto Tyr. "Yes, there's a story to be told here."

Unlike Thor, there was no amusement in the All-Father's voice.

EPILOGUE

Odin sat upon his throne, hands drawn across the arms of his chair, the three-pronged spear Gungnir leaned against the side of his seat while the scepter Thrudstok rested across his lap. The ravens perched upon the back of the throne, their eyes gleaming and their heads bobbing as they listened to Tyr's tale. The wolves crouched at the All-Father's feet, sometimes curling their lips and displaying their fangs at the sound of Tyr's voice, for they were always illdisposed towards him.

The King of Asgard's gaze never left Tyr, but it was impossible for him to read the thoughts behind that stare. While he related the tale of his trek into Muspelheim to steal the sword of Surtur, Tyr had no way to gauge his father's reaction to his account. No emotion cracked the stern attentiveness he kept fixed upon his eldest son.

The hall was cleared of all others save one. The hero who had so recently returned from Niffleheim had been permitted by Odin to listen to their father's judgment and act as witness to the justice of his decision. Thor, at least, was easier to gauge than the All-Father. The God of Thunder leaned against one of the tables in the grand hall, a smile on his face as he listened to Tyr relate his deeds in Muspelheim and the battles fought against its monstrous inhabitants. He drank mead and picked morsels of meat from the platter that rested beside him, savoring the story as he would a saga related by the skalds during any feast. When he'd frowned at some particular incident, Tyr realized that Thor was comparing the feats to his own during his venture against Ymir.

When he finished the tale, Tyr bowed his head and waited for their father to speak. Odin peered at him for a moment, then lifted Thrudstok from his lap and pointed it at him. "So that is your account," he said, his voice severe. Tyr paled at the grave tone, but it wasn't unexpected.

"I know my choices were ill-advised–"

Odin cut him off with a flourish of the scepter. "Ill-advised? Rather say reckless. Rather say idiotic. For a prince of my realm to conduct himself in such manner is outrageous! You've put the whole of Asgard at risk! Perhaps the whole of the Nine Worlds, for don't think the fire of Surtur would be satisfied with anything less than complete destruction of all that is, was, or ever shall be!" His hand shook with anger. "And to what is this recklessness owed? You speak of the hubris of Sindr, but you don't credit your own nearly as much as you should! Headstrong pride and audacity, to take it upon yourself to venture against the stronghold of our mightiest enemy and seek to steal from him his greatest weapon!" Odin shook his head. "You, the

God of War, supposedly the greatest general in Asgard and yet you contrive to pursue such a foolish course."

Tyr accepted the anger of his father, for he knew it was deserved. He'd focused too much on what was to be gained by stealing Twilight and given scant thought to what stood to be lost. Whatever punishment Odin decreed, he would have earned it for putting the realm in danger.

There was one in the hall, however, who didn't agree. "Is this the same Odin Borson who sat in this same hall and celebrated my victory over Ymir?" Thor stepped away from the table and approached the throne. "You had no scolding words for me when I journeyed to Niffleheim and fought the King of the Ice Giants in his frozen lair."

Odin scowled at Thor. "Yours was a venture that threatened disaster to none but yourself. *That* is heroism." He turned his attention back to Tyr. "There's nothing courageous when the innocent are put in danger, even if you yourself share in that danger. Subjects of Asgard have died because of Sindr's trespass into the realm. Far more would have perished had Surtur won his way across Bifrost."

"Brother, I don't ask you to defend what I've done," Tyr told Thor, surprised by his sibling's support.

"You don't have to," Thor replied. "What you sought to accomplish, the great battles you fought to achieve your goal cry out to me already. Your deeds ask – nay, demand – that I not keep silent!"

"What deeds might these be?" Odin prodded Thor. "To bring Surtur's image to the very threshold of Asgard from sheer hubris?"

Thor shook his head. "You can be wise, father, but you

can also be stubborn. Did you hear Tyr's story or merely listen?" He clapped his brother on the back. "Maybe you were jealous of me that night at the feast," he said to Tyr, "but it wasn't such an unworthy thing that set you on the path to Surtur's castle." He turned back to Odin. "It was concern for you that made Tyr embark on his quest. To wrest Twilight from the fire giant and thwart the doom foretold for you."

"Neither god nor mortal can easily balk the dictates of fate," Odin declared.

Tyr bristled at the fatalism he heard in his father's voice. "I thought it was worth whatever price I had to pay to try," he said. "To save you, no sacrifice asked of me would be too great." As he spoke, his hand closed about the metal cup at the end of his left arm. "When I learned the peril I'd brought into Asgard, I did everything in my power to thwart it. My only regret is that others suffered because of my mistake." His voice had an edge of guilt when he thought of the farmsteads Sindr had destroyed and Lorelei's fate when she was caught by the same spell that banished Surtur back to Muspelheim.

"You're the King of Asgard, as well as our father," Tyr said. "By both counts I am sworn to defend you no matter where the danger arises."

Odin leaned back in his chair. He waved his hand at Tyr. "Do you think any of that absolves you of responsibility? Your actions have imperiled the realm! An example must be made." He sighed and shook his head. "Tell me, Tyr, what example should I make of you? What should I do?"

Thor slapped his arm over Tyr's shoulder. "Let me

answer him, brother. Our king asks what to do with you, so I will tell him." He gestured with his other arm at the empty hall. "This place should be filled with revelry! Mead should flow in a mighty torrent and the songs of the skalds should linger long into the night. Let a high table be set before your throne so that all might pay honor to Tyr Odinson!"

Odin rose from the throne and glared down at Thor. "You'd have me celebrate deeds that I should punish?" The growl in his voice made his ravens take flight and brought low whines from his wolves.

"Yes, lest people think the King of Asgard is unjust," Thor answered. "In this hall you held a feast for a son who stood and boldly fought a giant of ice. Justice would dictate that you can host no less a feast for a son who fought a giant of fire!" He looked over at Tyr and smiled. "There was no malice in anything you did and once you saw how you'd been tricked your efforts were valiant to undo the wrong." Thor winked at his brother. "Even when the least of your worries was that I might be forced to a loveless wedding."

Tyr returned Thor's smile and clasped his hand. "It comes hard for the elder to be eclipsed by the younger," he said.

Thor laughed at the remark. "That is more foolish than anything our father blames you of! Are we not each a conqueror of giants?" He nodded to Odin. "That is what all Asgard will think," he said, just a hint of warning in his tone.

Odin slapped the scepter against his palm. "You aren't the only one who plots strategy," he told Tyr. "Today your brother has maneuvered me into a position where I can do nothing except what he proposes. Though you've been reckless, there will be no punishment."

"If that is your decision, father," Tyr said.

"It is your king's decree," Odin replied, making a dismissive gesture with his scepter.

Thor swung Tyr around and led him from the hall. "Let's not tarry here. We must leave father to prepare the feast. While we wait, we'll find us a brewhouse where the ale is strong. Once we're deep in our cups, I'll tell you lies about my fight with Ymir."

Tyr laughed and nodded. "And I'll swap you lies about my fight with Surtur."

"Lie for lie then!" Thor exclaimed. "The one whose boasts don't outdo the other's, has to sit next to Loki at the feast!"

"With that as the wager," Tyr said, "I'll give Surtur four heads and twelve arms before I stop stretching the truth!"

There was a sparkle in Odin's eye as he watched his sons march from the hall. When he was sure they weren't looking, he let a smile pull at his beard. For some time he'd noted the resentment growing between the brothers. Tyr feeling insignificant beside Thor's exploits, turning bitter from the idea that heroic deeds were something relegated to his past. Thor becoming haughty and overconfident, not as mindful of how his actions made those around him feel.

For now, they were amiable. Tyr's adventures in Muspelheim and his efforts against Surtur had drawn from Thor something the younger had almost forgotten to show the elder: respect. Thor's defense of Tyr against Odin's anger had drawn from the elder something his envy refused to bestow on the younger: admiration. Odin had always known the quality of his sons but now, at least for a time, they could see that in each other. He regretted his treating Tyr so harshly, but the quickest way to unite the brothers was to give them a common foe.

A tear shone in Odin's eye as he was reminded of the truth of that wisdom. He thought of his own brothers, Villi and Ve. They'd all had their petty grudges against each other, but in the end they'd been willing to give up their lives that he might live. As he'd listened to Tyr's story, Odin was reminded of his own journey into Muspelheim and his struggle against Surtur. Well could he recall the blistering heat and the unforgiving land, the cinders falling from the skies and the noxious fumes rising from the earth. It was impossible to forget a land where he'd left the bodies of two brothers.

Tyr was too fixated on what he'd tried to accomplish and his failure to accomplish it. He didn't understand that the very thing he considered a catastrophe might be of even greater benefit to Asgard. Until she'd passed through the Eternal Flame with him and broken through the barrier, Sindr had been Surtur's devoted child, eager – even desperate – to prove her worth to the fire giant. Now, because of Tyr, Sindr had been forced to see how little her father valued her. Odin could foresee conflict brewing in Muspelheim, and Surtur might yet come to regret his indifference to his daughter. Should Sindr manage to prevail, the threat from Muspelheim would be much different. Her ambition was that of the conqueror, and so she would seek to dominate Asgard, not destroy it. Surtur's only goal was annihilation. He'd been there at the start of time and was obsessed with bringing about the end of everything. If all there was to fear from the fire giant was his own death, Odin would be content to meet his doom on Twilight's blade, but it was the knowledge that all else would be consumed in Surtur's fire that haunted him when he slipped into the Odinsleep.

Like Tyr, Odin felt guilt over those who'd been lost in the ordeal, but he had a greater share in the responsibility. He'd foreseen the path the future might take when he stirred Tyr's jealousy at the feast. He'd weighed what was to be lost against what might be saved. However onerous, it was a choice he felt had to be taken, and so he'd set things into motion.

Odin fixed his gaze on the door by which his sons had departed. What he hadn't foreseen was how long their rediscovered camaraderie would last. He hoped it would be a long time, because the threat remained. Even if the fire giant was one day overthrown by his daughter, Asgard was certain to again know the menace that was the sword of Surtur.

About the Author

C L WERNER is a voracious reader and prolific author from Phoenix, Arizona. His many novels and short stories span the genres of fantasy and horror, and he has written for *Warhammer's Age of Sigmar* and *Old World, Warhammer 40,000*, Warmachine's *Iron Kingdoms*, and Mantic's *Kings of War*.

RETURN TO THE REALM ETERNAL

The young Heimdall must undertake a mighty quest to save Odin – and all of Asgard – in the time before he became guardian of the Rainbow Bridge.

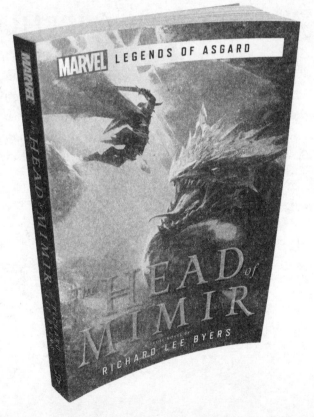

MARVEL UNTOLD

Our thrilling new line bringing new tales of
Marvel's Super Heroes and villains begins with
the infamous Doctor Doom risking all to steal
his heart's desire from the very depths of Hell.

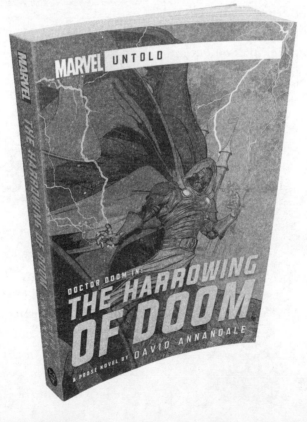

MARVEL HEROINES

Superhuman powers can be both a gift and a curse. A lucky few are taught to control their abilities while others master their uniquely dangerous powers alone. Explore the stories of Marvel's iconic heroines.

Sharp-witted, luck-wrangling super mercenary Domino takes on both a dangerous cult and her own dark past, in this explosive high-octane action novel.

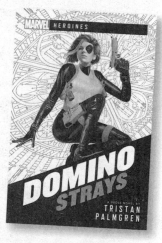

Rogue's frightening new mutant powers keep her at arms-length from the world, but two strangers offer a chance to change her life forever, in this exhilarating Super Hero adventure

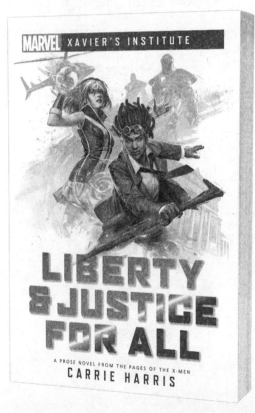